The Squire's Daughter

Archibald Marshall

THE SQUIRE'S DAUGHTER

Being the First Book in the Chronicles of the Clintons

BY ARCHIBALD MARSHALL

1912

TO
ANSTEY GUTHRIE

Archibald Marshak.

CONTENTS

CHAPTER I   A COURT BALL

CHAPTER II   IN THE BAY OF BISCAY

CHAPTER III   THE CLINTONS OF KENCOTE

CHAPTER IV   CLINTONS YOUNG AND OLD

CHAPTER V   MELBURY PARK

CHAPTER VI   A GOOD LONG TALK

CHAPTER VII   THE RECTOR

CHAPTER VIII   BY THE LAKE

CHAPTER IX   THE QUESTION OF MARRIAGE

CHAPTER X   TOWN VERSUS COUNTRY

CHAPTER XI   A WEDDING

CHAPTER XII   FOOD AND RAIMENT

CHAPTER XIII   RONALD MACKENZIE

CHAPTER XIV   THE PLUNGE

CHAPTER XV   BLOOMSBURY

CHAPTER XVI   THE PURSUIT

CHAPTER XVII   THE CONTEST

CHAPTER XVIII   AFTER THE STORM

CHAPTER XIX   THE WHOLE HOUSE UPSET

CHAPTER XX   MRS. CLINTON

CHAPTER XXI   CICELY'S RETURN

CHAPTER XXII   THE LIFE

CHRONICLES OF THE CLINTONS

CHAPTER I

A COURT BALL

"I recollect the time," said the Squire, "when two women going to a ball were a big enough load for any carriage. You may say what you like about crinolines, but I've seen some very pretty women in them in my time."

There were three people in the carriage passing slowly up the Mall in the string, with little jerks and progressions. They were the Squire himself, Mrs. Clinton, and Cicely, and they were on their way to a Court Ball.

The Squire, big, florid, his reddish beard touched with grey falling over the red and gold of his Deputy-Lieutenant's uniform, sat back comfortably beside his wife, who was dressed in pale lavender silk, with diamonds in her smooth, grey-yellow hair. She was short and rather plump. Her grey eyes, looking out on the violet of the night sky, the trees, and the crowd of hilarious onlookers who had not been invited to Buckingham Palace, had a patient and slightly wistful expression. She had not spoken since the carriage had left the quiet hotel in which they were staying for their fortnight in London.

Cicely sat on the back seat of the carriage. On such an occasion as this she might have been expected to be accorded the feminine privilege of sitting at the side of her mother, but it had not occurred to the Squire to offer it to her. She was a pretty girl, twenty-two years of age, with a fair skin and abundant brown hair. She was dressed in costly white satin, her gown simply cut. As she had stood before her glass, while her mother's maid had held for her her light evening cloak, her beautiful neck and shoulders had seemed warmly flushed by contrast with the dead pallor of the satin. She also had hardly spoken since they had driven off from their hotel, which was so quiet and private that it was hardly like an hotel, and where some of the servants had stood in the hall to see them get into their carriage, just as they might have done at home at Kencote.

It was a great occasion for Cicely. Her brothers—Dick, who was in the Grenadier Guards, and Humphrey, who was in the Foreign Office—were well enough used to the scenes of splendour offered by a London season, but Cicely had hardly ever been in London at all. She had been brought up four years before to be presented, and had been taken home again immediately. She had seen nothing of London gaieties, either then or since. Now she was to enjoy such opportunities of social intercourse as might be open to the daughter of a rich squire who had had all he wanted of town life thirty years before, and had lived in his country house ever since. A fortnight was as long as the Squire cared to be away from Kencote, even in the month of June; and a fortnight was to be the extent of Cicely's London season. This was to be the crowning night of it.

The Squire chattered on affably. He had had a good dinner and had not been hurried over it, or afterwards. That was the worst of those theatres, he would say; they didn't give you time even to drink your glass of wine; and he had not been affable with his wife and daughter the evening before, when driving to the play. But now he was rather pleased with himself. He did not care for all this sort of thing, of course; he had had quite enough of it as a subaltern, dancing about London all night, and going everywhere—all very well for a young fellow, but you got tired of it. Still, there was a certain flavour about a Court Ball, even for a one-time subaltern in the Blues, who had taken part in everything that was going on. Other people scrambled for such things—they had to if they wanted them, and why they should want them if they didn't come to them naturally, the Squire couldn't tell. To a man of the importance of Edward Clinton of Kencote, they came as a matter of course, and he accepted them as his due, but was pleased, too, at having his social importance recognised in such a way, without his stirring a finger. As a matter of cold fact, a finger had been stirred to procure this particular honour, although it had not been his. But of that he was not aware.

The carriage drove slowly with the rest into the big court-yard, where a military band was playing bright music. Cicely suddenly felt exhilarated and expectant. They drove up before the great entrance, red-carpeted, brightly lit, and went through the hall up the stairs into the cloak-room. Cicely had a flush on her cheeks now as she waited for her mother, who seemed to be taking an interminable time to settle her lace and her jewels. Mrs. Clinton looked her over and her eyes brightened a little. "Are you nervous, darling?" she asked; and Cicely said, "No, mother, not a bit." The scent of flowers was in her nostrils, the strains of the music expectantly in her ears. She was going to dance in a royal palace, and she was such a country mouse that she was excited at the prospect of seeing royalty at close quarters. She had been far too nervous to take in anything when she had been presented, and that had been four years ago.

They went out and found the Squire waiting for them. He did not ask them, as he generally did, why they had been so long.

They seemed to go through interminable wide corridors, decorated in red and gold, with settees against the walls and beautiful pictures hanging above them, but came at last to the great ball-room.

Cicely drew her breath as she entered. This was better than the Meadshire County Ball, or the South Meadshire Hunt Ball. The women were mostly in white, or pale colours, but their jewels were beyond anything she had ever imagined. The lights from the great lustre chandeliers seemed to be reflected in those wonderful clusters and strings and devices of sparkling gems. Cold white and cold fire for the women, colour for the men. Scarlet and gold pre-dominated, but there were foreign attaches in uniforms of pale blue and silver, and other unfamiliar colours, eastern robes and dresses encrusted with jewels or richly embroidered in silks. It was gorgeous, a scene from fairyland.

There was a sudden ebbing of the tide of chatter. The band in the gallery began to play "God save the King." Doors were thrown open at the end of the great room, and the royal party came in slowly, passed down the open space on the red carpet between the lines of bowing and curtseying guests, and took their places on the dais. Cicely gazed her fill at them. They were just as she had seen them a hundred times in pictures in the illustrated papers, but more royal, and yet, more human.

They danced their opening quadrille, and after that every one could dance. But of all the people there Cicely knew no one who would be likely to dance with her. She sat by her mother on one of the raised settees that ran in four rows the length of the room. The Squire had found friends and was talking to them elsewhere. Her brother Dick, who she knew was to have been there, she had not yet seen. Everything depended upon him. Surely, people did not come casually late to a Court Ball! If something had prevented his coming at all, it seemed to her that she would have to sit there all the evening.

Her eyes brightened. There was Dick making his way towards them. He looked very smart in his guardsman's uniform, and very much at home with himself, as if the King's ball-room was no more to him than any other ball-room. He was always provokingly leisurely in his movements, and even now he stopped twice to talk to people whom he knew, and stood with them each time as if he would stay there for ever. Really, Dick could be almost as provoking as the Squire, where their womenfolk were concerned.

But at last he came, smiling very pleasantly. "Hullo, mother!" he said. "Hullo, Siskin! Now you've seen the Queen in her parlour, eh? Well, how do you like yourself?"

He was a good-looking fellow, Dick, with his well-shaped, closely cropped head, his well-trained moustache, his broad, straight shoulders and lean waist and hips. He was over thirty, but showed few signs as yet of the passing of youth. It was quite plain by the way he looked at her that he was fond of his sister. She was nearly ten years younger than he and still a child to him, to be patronised and petted, if she was taken notice of at all. He didn't take much notice of his mother, contenting himself with telling her that she "looked as smart as any of 'em." But he stood and talked to Cicely, and his eyes rested on her as if he were proud of her.

In the meantime the delicious strains of a valse were swinging through the great room, and the smooth floor was full of dancers, except in the space reserved for the royalties, where only a few couples were circling. Cicely's feet were moving. "Can't we dance, Dick?" she said.

"Come on," said Dick, "let's have a scurry," and he led her down on to the floor and floated her out into a paradise of music and movement. Dick was the best partner she had ever danced with. He had often snubbed her about her own dancing, but he had danced with her all the same, more than most brothers dance with their sisters, at country balls, which were the only balls she had ever been to. He was a kind brother, according to his lights, and Cicely would have liked to dance with him all the evening.

That, of course, was out of the question. Dick knew plenty of people to dance with to-night, if she didn't. In fact, he seemed to know half the people in the room, although he gave her the impression that he thought Court Balls rather mixed affairs. "Can't be certain of meeting your friends here," he said, and added, "of course," as admitting handsomely that people might be quite entitled to be asked who did not happen to be his friends. "You're not the only country cousins, Siskin," he said, which gave Cicely somehow a higher opinion of herself, his dissociation of himself in this matter of country cousinhood from his family striking her as nothing unreasonable. Indeed, it was not unreasonable with regard to the Clintons, the men taking their part, as a matter of course, in everything to which their birth and wealth entitled them, so long as they cared to do so, the women living, for the most part, at home, in a wide and airy seclusion.

"Want to dance, eh?" said Dick, in answer to her little plea. "All right, I'll bring up some young fellows."

And he did. He brought up a succession of them and delivered them off-hand to his mother and sister with a slight air of authority, doing his duty very thoroughly, as a kind brother should.

Most of them were quite young—as young, or younger than Cicely herself. Some of them wore the uniform of Dick's own regiment, and were presumably under his orders, professionally if not in private life. Some of them were amazingly patronising and self-possessed, and these did not ask Cicely to dance again. She felt, when they returned her to her mother, that she had not been a success with them. Others were boyish and diffident, and with them she got on pretty well. With one, a modest child of nineteen or so with a high-sounding title, she was almost maternally friendly, and he seemed to cling to her as a refuge from a new and bewildering world. They ate ices together—he told her that he had been brought up at home in Ireland under a priest, and had never eaten enough ices at a sitting until he had joined his regiment a fortnight before. He could not dance well, indeed hardly at all, although he confessed to having taken lessons, and his gratitude when Cicely suggested that they should go and look at some of the rooms instead, warmed her heart to him and put their temporary friendship on the best possible footing.

They stayed together during three dances, went out on to the terrace, explored wherever they were permitted to explore, paid two visits to the buffet, and enjoyed themselves much in the same way as if they had been school-children surreptitiously breaking loose from an assembly of grown-ups. The boy became volubly friendly and bubbling over with unexpected humour and high spirits. He tried to persuade Cicely to stay away from the ball-room for a fourth dance. Nobody would miss them, he explained. But she said she must go back, and when they joined the crowd again her partner was haled off with a frightened look to the royal circle, and she found her mother standing up before the seat on which she had sat all the evening searching anxiously for her with her eyes, and her father by her side.

An old man, looking small and shrunken in his heavy uniform, but otherwise full of life and kindliness, with twinkling eyes and a short white beard, was with them, and she breathed a sigh of relief, for if she was not frightened of what her mother might say about her long absence, she rather dreaded the comments her father might be pleased to pass on it. But her kinsman, Lord Meadshire, Lord-Lieutenant of the county, a great magnate in the eyes of the world, was to her just a very kind and playful old man, whose jokes only, because of their inherent feebleness, caused her any discomfort. Cousin Humphrey would preserve her from the results of her fault if she had committed one.

"Well, my dear," he said in an affectionate, rather asthmatical voice, "you've brought us some of the Meadshire roses, eh, what? Hope you're enjoying yourself. If you had come a little earlier, I would have asked you to dance with me."

"Where have you been so long, Cicely?" asked her mother, but the twinkle in Lord Meadshire's eyes showed that a joke was in progress, and he broke in hurriedly, "Forty or fifty years earlier, I mean, my dear," and he chuckled himself into a fit of coughing.

The Squire was not looking quite pleased, but whatever the cause of his displeasure it was not, apparently, Cicely's prolonged absence, for he also asked if she was enjoying herself, and looked at her with some pride and fondness. Going home in the carriage, she learned later that Lord Meadshire, who would have done a great deal more to provide her with social gaiety if he had not been living, now, mostly in retirement with an invalid wife, had procured those commands which had brought them up to London, and are not generally bestowed unasked on the belongings of a country squire, however important he may be in the midst of his own possessions.

Lord Meadshire stayed with them for some little time and pointed out to her some of the notabilities and the less familiar royalties. Then Dick came up and took her away to dance again. After that she sat by her mother's side until the end. She saw the boy with whom she had made friends eying her rather wistfully. He had danced a quadrille with a princess, and the experience seemed so to have shattered his nerve that he was not equal to making his way to her to ask her to bear him company again, and she could not very well beckon him, as she felt inclined to do. The ball became rather dull, although she looked a good deal at the King and Queen and thought how extraordinary it was that she should be in the same room with them.

Before she had quite realised that it had begun, the ball was over. The band played "God save the King" again. Everybody stood up and the royal procession was formed and went away to supper. With the light of royalty eclipsed, her own supper seemed an ordinary affair. At country dances she had shirked it whenever she could, taking advantage of a clearer floor to dance with some willing partner right through a valse or a two-step from beginning to end. After supper she danced once or twice, but as she drove back to the very private hotel at about half-past one, she only felt as if she had not danced nearly enough, and as she undressed she hardly knew whether she had enjoyed herself or not.

CHAPTER II

IN THE BAY OF BISCAY

On the night on which Cicely Clinton was enjoying herself at the Court Ball, the *Punjaub* homeward bound from Australia *via* Colombo and the Suez Canal was steaming through the Bay of Biscay, which, on this night of June had prepared a pleasant surprise for the *Punjaub's* numerous passengers by lying calm and still under a bright moon.

Two men were leaning over the side of the upper deck, watching the phosphorescent gleam of the water as it slid past beneath them, and talking as intimate friends. They were Ronald Mackenzie, the explorer, returning home after his adventurous two years' expedition into the wilds of Tibet, and Jim Graham, whose home was at Mountfield, three miles away from Kencote, where the Clintons lived. They were not intimate friends, in spite of appearances. They had joined the ship together at Colombo, and found themselves occupying the same cabin. But acquaintanceship ripens so fast on board ship that the most dissimilar characters may adhere to one another for as long as a voyage lasts, although they may never meet again afterwards, nor particularly wish to.

Mackenzie was a tall, ruggedly fashioned man, with greying hair and a keen, bold face. Jim Graham was more slightly built. He had an open, honest look; he was rather deliberate in speech, and apparently in thought, for in conversation he would often pause before speaking, and he sometimes ignored a question altogether, as if he had not heard it, or had not understood it. There were those who called him stupid; but it was usually said of him that he was slow and sure. He had a rather ugly face, but it was that pleasant ugliness which, with a well-knit athletic body, clear eyes and a tanned skin, is hardly distinguishable, in a man, from good looks.

They were talking about London. "I can smell it and see it," said Mackenzie. "I hope it will be raining when I get home. I like the wet pavements, and the lights, and the jostling crowds. Lord! it will be

9

good to see it again. How I've pined for it, back there! But I'll be out of it again in a month. It's no place for a man like me, except to get back to every now and then."

"That's how most of us take it," said Jim, "unless we have to work there. I'm glad I haven't to, though I enjoy it well enough for a week or two, occasionally."

"Do you live in the country all the year round?"

"Yes."

Mackenzie threw him a glance which seemed to take him in from top to toe. "What do you do?" he asked.

Jim Graham paused for a moment before replying. "I have a good deal to do," he said. "I've got my place to look after."

"That doesn't take you all your time, does it?"

"It takes a good deal of it. And I'm on the bench."

"That means sending poor devils to prison for poaching your game, I suppose."

"Not quite that," said Jim, without a smile.

"I suppose what it all does mean is that you live in a big country house and shoot and hunt and fish to your heart's content, with just enough work to keep you contented with yourself. By Jove, some men are lucky! Do you know what my life has been?"

"I know you have been through many adventures and done big things," said Jim courteously.

"Well, I'm obliged to you for putting it like that. Seems to me I didn't put my idea of your life quite so nicely, eh?" He stood up and stretched his tall figure, and laughed. "I'm a rough diamond," he said. "I don't mind saying so, because it's plain enough for any one to see. I sometimes envy people like you their easy manners; but I've got to be content with my own; and after all, they have served my turn well enough. Look at us two. I suppose I'm about ten years older than you, but I had made my name when I was your age. You were born in a fine country house."

"Not so very fine," said Jim.

"Well, pretty fine compared to the house I was born in, which was the workhouse. You were educated at Eton and Christchurch, and all that sort of thing — —"

"I don't want to spoil any comparison you are going to make," said Jim, "but I was at Winchester and New College."

"That will do," said Mackenzie. "I was dragged up at the workhouse school till I was twelve. Then I ran away and sold papers in the streets, and anything else that I could pick up a few coppers by — except steal. I never did that. I always made up my mind I'd be a big man some day, and — I'm glad I didn't steal."

"I didn't either, you know," said Jim, "although I'm not a big man, and never shall be."

"Ah, that's where the likes of me scores. You've no call to ambition. You have everything you can want provided for you."

"There have been one or two big men born as I was," said Jim. "But please go on with your story. When did you go on your first journey?"

"When I was sixteen. I looked much older. I shipped before the mast and went out to Australia, and home round Cape Horn. By Jove, I shan't forget that. The devil was in the wind. We were five months coming home, and nearly starved to death, and worked till we were as thin as hungry cats. Then I shipped with the Boyle-Geering expedition — you know — North Pole, and three years trying to get there. Then I tried a change of climate and went to Central Africa with Freke. I was his servant, got his bath, shaved him, brushed his clothes — he was always a bit of a dandy, Freke, and lived like a gentleman, though I don't believe he was any better than I was when he started; but he could fight too, and there wasn't his equal with niggers. We had trouble that trip, and the men who went out with him were a rotten lot. They'd found the money, or he wouldn't have taken them. He knew a man when he saw one. When we came home I was second in command.

"It was easy after that. I led that expedition through Uganda when I was only twenty-five; and the rest—well, the rest I dare say you know."

"Yes, I know," said Jim. "You've done a lot."

"Not so bad, eh, for a workhouse brat?"

"Not so bad for anybody."

"I'm up top now. I used to envy lots of people. Now most people envy me."

Jim was silent.

Mackenzie turned to him. "I suppose you've had a pretty easy time travelling," he said. There was a suspicion of a sneer on his long thin lips.

"Pretty easy," said Jim.

"Ah! Your sort of travelling is rather different from mine. If you had been roughing it in Tibet for the last two years you would be pretty glad to be getting back."

"I'm glad to be getting back as it is."

Mackenzie turned and leaned over the rail again. "Well, I don't know that I don't envy you a bit after all," he said. "I've got no friends in England. I'm not a man to make friends. The big-wigs will take me up this time. I know that from what I've seen. I shall be a lion. I suppose I shall be able to go anywhere I like. But there's nowhere I want to go to particularly, when I've had enough of London. You've got your country home. Lord, how I've thought of the English country, in summer time! Thirsted for it. But it has to belong to you, in a way. I've a good mind to buy a little place—I shall be able to afford it when my book comes out. But I should want a wife to keep it warm for me. You're not married, I suppose?"

"No."

"Going to be?"

Jim made no reply.

Mackenzie laughed. "Mustn't ask questions, I suppose," he said. "I'm a rough diamond, Graham. Got no manners, you see. Never had any one to teach 'em to me. I apologise."

"No need to," said Jim.

There was silence for a space. The great round moon shone down and silvered the long ripples on the water.

"I don't mind answering your question," said Jim, looking out over the sea. "There are some country neighbours of mine. One of the sons is my chief pal. We were brought up together, more or less. He's going to marry my sister. And—well, I hope I'm going to marry his."

His face changed a little, but Mackenzie, looking straight before him did not notice it. "Sounds a capital arrangement," he said drily.

Jim flushed, and drew himself up. "Well, I think I'll be turning in," he said.

Mackenzie faced him quickly. "Tell me all about it," he said. "How old is she? You have known her all your life. When did you first find out you wanted to marry her? When are you going to be married?"

Jim looked at him squarely. "You are taking liberties," he said.

Mackenzie laughed again—his harsh, unamused laugh. "All right," he said. "One has to be as delicate as a fine lady talking to fellows like you. It's not worth it. When you live like a savage half your life, you sort of hunger after hearing about things like that—people living in the country, falling in love and getting married, and going to church every Sunday—all the simple, homely things. A man without all the nonsense about good form and all that sort of thing—a man who'd done things—he would know why you asked him, and he would know he couldn't find anybody better to tell his little happy secrets to."

"Oh, well," said Jim, slightly mollified.

"I dare say you're right, though," said Mackenzie. "One doesn't blab to every stranger. Even I don't, and I'm a rough diamond, as I've told you."

"Yes, you've told me that."

"Is the fellow who is going to marry your sister a country gentleman, too?"

"No. His father is. He's a younger son. He's a doctor."

"A doctor! Isn't that a funny thing for a country gentleman's son to be?"

"I don't know that it is. He's a clever fellow. He went in for science at Oxford, and got keen."

"That's good hearing. I like to hear of men getting keen about a real job. You might tell me about him, if I'm not taking another liberty in asking."

"Oh, look here, Mackenzie, I'm sorry I said that. I didn't understand why you asked what you did."

"I've told you. I like to hear about everything that goes on in the world. It isn't curiosity, and yet in a way it is. I'm curious about everything that goes on—everywhere. It isn't impertinent curiosity, anyway."

"I see that. I'll tell you about Walter Clinton. He's a good chap. His father has a fine place next to mine. He's a rich man. His family has been there since the beginning of all things. Walter is just my age. We've always been a lot together."

"Is there a large family? What do his brothers do?"

"There's Dick, the eldest son. He's in the Guards. There's Humphrey in the Foreign Office, and a younger son, a sailor. And—and there are three girls—two of them are children—twins."

"Well, now, aren't I right in saying it's odd for a son in a family like that to become a doctor?"

"Oh, well, I suppose in a way you are, though I can't see why he shouldn't be. The fact is that they wanted to make a parson of him— there's a rather good family living. But he wasn't taking any."

"Ah! I thought I knew something about your country gentry. Well, I admire the doctor. Was there a row?"

"His father was rather annoyed. Perhaps it's not to be wondered at. His half-brother is Rector at Kencote now, and when he dies they'll have to give the living to a stranger. Of course they would rather have one of the family."

"It's like a chapter in a book—one of the long, easy ones, all about country life and the squire and the parson. I love 'em. And the doctor is going to marry your sister. Can I give 'em a skin for a wedding present?"

"I'm sure they would be gratified. You'd better come down and make their acquaintance."

"I'll do that. I'd like to come and see you, Graham; and you mustn't mind my roughness peeping out occasionally. I haven't had many chances in life."

There was a pause, and then Jim said, "Walter Clinton's sister comes next to him in the family. She's six or seven years younger. Of course, I've known her ever since she was a baby. When I came back from Oxford one summer vac., I found her almost grown up. She seemed quite different somehow. I was always over there all the summer, or she was with my sister. We fixed it up we would get married some day. They laughed at us, and said we had better wait a few years; but of course they were pleased, really, both my people and hers, though they thought it a bit premature; she was only seventeen. When I went back to Oxford and thought it over I said to myself it wasn't quite fair to tie her down at that age. I would wait and see. So we fell back to what we had been before."

He stopped suddenly. "Is that all?" asked Mackenzie in some surprise.

"It's all at present."

There was a long pause. "It's disappointing, somehow," said Mackenzie. "I suppose I mustn't ask questions, but there are a lot I'd like to ask."

"Oh, ask away. When the ice is once broken one can talk. It does one good to talk sometimes."

"Women talk to each other about their love affairs. Men don't—not the real ones—except on occasions."

"Well, we'll let this be an occasion, as you have started the subject." He laughed lightly. "You've got a sort of power, Mackenzie. If any one had told me yesterday that I should be talking to you to-night about a thing I haven't mentioned to a soul for five years—except once or twice to Walter Clinton—I should have stared at them. I'm not generally supposed to be communicative."

"It's impersonal," said Mackenzie, "like telling things to a priest. I'm not in the same world as you. Five years, is it? Well, now, what on earth have you been doing ever since? She's not too young to marry now."

"No. I was at Oxford a year after what I told you of. Then I went for a year to learn estate management on my uncle's property. When I came home I thought I would fix it up with my father—he was alive then. He said, wait a year longer. He was beginning to get ill, and I suppose he didn't want to face the worry of making arrangements till he got better. But he never got better, and within a year he died."

"And then you were your own master. That's two years ago, isn't it? And here you are coming back from a year's trip round the world. You seem to be pretty slow about things."

16

"One doesn't become one's own master immediately one succeeds to the ownership of land. These death duties have altered all that. I shan't be free for another year. Then I hope you will come to my wedding, Mackenzie."

"Thanks. Didn't the young lady object to keeping it all hanging on for so long?"

Jim did not reply for a moment. Then he said a little stiffly, "I wrote to her from Oxford when I had thought things over. I thought it wasn't fair to tie her up before I was ready to marry, and she so young."

"And that means that you have never allowed yourself to make love to her since."

"Yes, it means that."

"And yet you have been in love with her all the time?"

"Yes."

"Well, it shows a greater amount of self-control than most people possess—certainly a good deal more than I possess, I suppose you are sure of her."

Jim did not reply to this, but he said presently, "If it wasn't for the death duties I should have hoped to be married before this."

"I'll tell you what I don't understand," said Mackenzie. "I suppose you live in much the same way as your father did before you."

"Yes. My mother lives with me, and my sister."

"Well, surely you *could* get married if you wanted to. You've got your house and everything, even if there isn't quite so much money to spend for a bit. And as for ready money—it doesn't cost nothing to travel for a year as you're doing."

"Oh, an uncle of mine paid for that," said Jim. "I got seedy after my father's death. There was a lot of worry, and—and I was fond of the old man. The doctors told me to go off. I'm all right now. As for the rest—well, there are such things as jointures and dowries. No, I couldn't marry, giving my wife and my mother and sister everything they ought to have, before another year. Even then it will be a close thing; I shall have to be careful."

They fell silent. The dark mass of the ship's hull beneath them slipped on through the water, drawing ever nearer towards home. The moon climbed still higher into the sky. "Well, we've had an interesting talk," said Mackenzie, drawing himself up. "What you have told me is all so entirely different from anything that would ever happen in my life. If I wanted to marry a girl I should marry her, and let the money go hang. She'd have to share and share. But I dare say when I want a thing I want it for the moment a good deal more than you do; and, generally, I see that I get it. Now I think I shall turn in. Give me ten minutes."

He went down to the cabin they both occupied. As he undressed he said to himself, "Rather a triumph, drawing a story like that from a fellow like that. And Lord, *what* a story! He deserves to lose her. I should like to hear her side of it."

Jim Graham smoked another cigarette, walking round the deck. He felt vaguely dissatisfied with himself for having made a confidant of Mackenzie, and at the same time relieved at having given vent to what he had shut up for so long in the secret recesses of his mind.

A day or two later the two men parted at Tilbury. They had not again mentioned the subject of their long conversation in the Bay of Biscay.

CHAPTER III

THE CLINTONS OF KENCOTE

Cicely was returning home with her father and mother after her short taste of the season's gaieties. It was pleasant to lean back in a corner of the railway carriage and look at the rich Meadshire country, so familiar to her, running past the window. She had not wanted to go home particularly, but she was rather glad to be going home all the same.

The country in South Meadshire is worth looking at. There are deep-grassed water-meadows, kept green by winding rivers; woods of beech and oak; stretches of gorse and bracken; no hills to speak of, but gentle rises, crowned sometimes by an old church, or a pleasant-looking house, neither very old nor very new, very large nor very small. The big houses, and there are a good many of them, lie for the most part in what may be called by courtesy the valleys. You catch a glimpse of them sometimes at a little distance from the line, which seems to have shown some ingenuity in avoiding them, standing in wide, well-timbered parks, or peeping from amongst thicker trees, with their court of farm and church and clustered village, in dignified seclusion. For the rest, there are picturesque hamlets; cottages with bright gardens; children, and fluttering clothes-lines; pigs and donkeys and geese on the cropped commons; a network of roads and country lanes; and everywhere a look of smiling and contented well-being, which many an English county of higher reputation for picturesque scenery might envy.

The inhabitants of South Meadshire will tell you that it is one of the best counties for all-round sport. Game is preserved, but not over-preserved, and the mixture of pasture and arable land and frequent covert, while it does not tempt the fox-hunting Londoner, breeds stout foxes for the pleasure of those who know every inch of it; and there is enough grass, enough water, and stiff enough fences to try the skill of the boldest, and to provide occasionally such a run as from its comparative rarity accords a gratification unknown to the frequenter of the shires. Big fish are sometimes caught in the clear streams of South Meadshire, and they are caught by the people who own them, or by their friends. For in this quiet corner of England the life of the hall and the village still goes on unchanged. At the meets—on lawn, at cross-road, or by covert-side—everybody knows everybody else, at least by sight; neighbours shoot with one another and not with strangers; and the small fry of the countryside get their share of whatever fun is going on.

In the middle of this pleasant land lies the manor of Kencote, and a good many fat acres around it, which have come to the Clintons from time to time, either by lucky marriages or careful purchase, during the close upon six hundred years they have been settled there. For they are an old family and in their way an important one, although their actual achievements through all the centuries in which they have enjoyed wealth and local consideration fill but a small page in their family history.

The Squire had, in the strong room of the Bathgate and Medchester Bank, in deed-boxes at his lawyers, and in drawers and chests and cupboards in his house, papers worthy of the attention of the antiquary. From time to time they did engage the antiquary's attention, and, scattered about in bound volumes of antiquarian and genealogical magazines, in the proceedings of learned societies, and in county histories, you may find the fruits of much careful and rewarding research through these various documents. When the Squire was approached by some one who wished to write a paper or read a paper, or compile a genealogy, or carry out any project for the purposes of which it was necessary to gain access to the Clinton archives, he would express his annoyance to his family. He would say that he wished these people would let him alone. The fact was that there were so few really old families left in England, that people like himself who had lived quietly on their property for eight or nine hundred years, or whatever it might be, had to bear all the brunt of these investigations, and it was really becoming an infernal nuisance. But he would always invite the antiquary to Kencote, give him a bottle of fine claret and his share of a bottle of fine port, and every facility for the pursuit of his inquiries.

A History of the Ancient and Knightly Family of Clinton of Kencote in the County of Meadshire, was compiled about a hundred years ago by the Reverend John Clinton Smith, M.A., Rector of Kencote, and published by Messrs. Dow and Runagate of Paternoster Row. It is not very accurate, but any one interested in such matters can, with due precaution taken, gain from it valuable information concerning the twenty-two generations of Clintons who have lived and ruled at Kencote since Sir Giles de Clinton acquired the manor in the reign of Edward I.

The learned Rector devoted a considerable part of his folio volume to tracing a connection between the Clintons of Kencote and other families of Clintons who have mounted higher in the world. It is the opinion of later genealogists that he might have employed his energies to better purpose, but, in any case, the family needs no further shelter than is supplied by its own well-rooted family tree. You will find too, in his book, the result of his investigations into his own pedigree, in which the weakest links have to bear the greatest strain, as is often the case with pedigrees.

It remains only to be said that the Squire, Edward Clinton, had succeeded his grandfather, Colonel Thomas, of whom you may read in sporting magazines and memoirs, at the age of eighteen, and had always been a rich man, and an honest one.

Kencote lies about six miles to the south-west of the old town of Bathgate. The whole parish, and it is an exceptionally large one, belongs to the Squire, with a good deal more land besides in neighbouring parishes. Kencote House is a big, rather ugly structure, and was built early in the eighteenth century after the disastrous fire which destroyed the beautiful old Tudor hall and nearly all its hoarded treasures. This catastrophe is worth a brief notice, for nowadays an untitled family often enjoys some consideration from the possession of an old and beautiful house, and the Clintons of Kencote would be better known to the world at large if they did not live in a comparatively new one.

It happened at the dead of a winter night. Young William Clinton had brought home his bride, Lady Anne, only daughter and heiress of the Earl of Beechmont, that afternoon, and there had been torches and bonfires and a rousing welcome. Nobody knew exactly how it happened, but they awoke to find the house in flames, and most of the household too overcome by the results of their merry-making to be of any use in saving it. The house itself was burnt to a shell, but it was long enough in the burning to have enabled its more valuable contents to have been saved, if the work had been set about with some method. The young squire, in night-cap, shirt, and breeches, whether mindful of his pedigree at that time of excitement, or led by the fantastic spirit that moves men in such crises, threw as much of the contents of his muniment room out of the window as he had time for, and the antiquarians bless him to this day. Then he went off to the stables, and helped to get out his horses. My Lady Anne, who was only sixteen, saved her jewels and one or two of her more elaborate gowns, and then sat down by the sun-dial and cried. The servants worked furiously as long as the devouring flames allowed them, but when there was nothing left of Kencote Hall but smouldering, unsafe walls, under a black, winter sky, and the piled-up heap of things that had been got out into the garden came to be examined, it was found to be made up chiefly of the lighter and less valuable pieces of furniture, a few pictures and hangings, many tumbled folios from the library, kitchen and house utensils, and just a few pieces of plate and other valuables to salt the whole worthless mass.

So perished in a night the chief pride of the Clintons of Kencote, and the noble house, with its great raftered hall, its carved and panelled chambers, its spoil of tapestries and furniture, carpets, china, silver, pictures, books, all the possessions that had been gathered from many lands through many years, was only a memory that must fade more and more rapidly as time went on.

The young couple went back to her ladyship's father, not many miles away, and Kencote was left in its ruins for ten years or so. Then my Lord Beechmont died, sadly impoverished by unfortunate dealings with the stock of the South Sea Company, the house and land that remained to him were sold, and Kencote was rebuilt with the proceeds, much as it stands to-day, except that Merchant Jack, the father of Colonel Thomas, bitten with the ideas of his time, covered the mellow red brick with a coating of stucco and was responsible for the Corinthian porch, and the ornamental parapet surmounted by Grecian urns.

Merchant Jack had been a younger son and had made his fortune in the city. He was modern in his ideas, and a rich man, and wanted a house as good as his neighbours. Georgian brick, and tall, narrow, small-paned windows had gone out of fashion. So had the old formal gardens. Those at Kencote had survived the destruction of the house, but they did not survive the devastating zeal of Merchant Jack. They were swept away by a pupil of Capability Brown's, who allowed the old walls of the kitchen garden to stand because they were useful for growing fruit, but destroyed walls and terraces and old yew hedges everywhere else, brought the well-treed park into relation, as he thought, with the garden, by means of sunk fences, planted shrubberies, laid down vast lawns, and retired very well pleased with himself at having done away with one more old-fashioned, out-of-date garden, and substituted for it a few more acres of artificial ugliness.

He did just one thing that turned out well; he made a large lake in a hollow of the park and ringed it with rhododendrons, which have since grown to enormous size. At the end of it he caused to be built a stucco temple overhung with weeping ashes, designed "to invite Melancholy." There is no showing that Merchant Jack had any desire to respond to such an invitation, but it was the fashion of the time, and no doubt he was pleased with the idea.

Merchant Jack also refurnished the house when his architect had had his way with it and the workmen had departed. A few good pieces he kept, but most of the furniture, which had been brought into the house when it was rebuilt after the fire, disappeared, to make way for heavy mahogany and rosewood. Some of it went down to the dower house, a little Jacobean hall in a dark corner of the park, and there is reason to fear that the rest was sold for what it would fetch.

In all these lamentable activities, good, rich, up-to-date Merchant Jack was only improving his property according to the ideas of his time, and had no more idea of committing artistic improprieties than those people nowadays who buy a dresser from a farm-house kitchen to put in their drawing-room, and plaster the adjacent walls with soup plates. His memorial tablet in Kencote church speaks well of him and his memory must be respected.

But we have left Edward Clinton with his wife and daughter sitting for so long in the train between Ganton and Kencote, that we must now return to them without any further delay.

Having got into the railway carriage at the London terminus as a private gentleman, of no more account than any other first-class passenger, and weighed only by his potential willingness to pay handsomely for attentions received, as the successive stages of his journey were accomplished, he seemed to develop in importance. At Ganton, where a change had to be made, although it was twenty miles and more from his own parcel of earth, peaked caps were touched to him, and the station-master himself, braided coat and all, opened his carriage door, expressing, as he did so, a hope that the present fair weather would continue. One might almost, until one had thought it over, have imagined him to be appealing to the Squire as one who might take a hand in its continuance if he were so minded, at any rate in the neighbourhood of Kencote.

At Kencote itself, so busy was the entire station staff in helping him and his belongings out of the train, that the signal for starting was delayed a full minute, and then given almost as an after-thought, as if it were a thing of small importance. Heads were poked out of carriage windows, and an impertinent stranger, marking the delay and its cause, asked the station-master, as he was carried past him, where was the red carpet. The answer might have been that it was duly spread in the thoughts of all who conducted the Squire from the train to his carriage, and was as well brushed as if it had been laid on the platform.

The Squire had a loud and affable word for station-master and porters alike, and another for the groom who stood at the heads of the two fine greys harnessed to his phaeton. He walked out into the road and looked them over, remarking that they were the handsomest pair he had seen since he had left home. Then he took the reins and swung himself up on to his seat, actively, for a man of his age and weight. Mrs. Clinton climbed up more slowly to her place by his side, Cicely sat behind, and with a jingle and clatter the equipage rolled down the road, while the groom touched his hat and went back to the station omnibus in which Mrs. Clinton's maid was establishing herself in the midst of a collection of wraps and little bags. For, unless it was unavoidable, no servant of the Clintons sat on the same seat of a carriage as a member of the family.

It was in the drowsiest time in the afternoon. The sun shone on the hay-fields, from which the sound of sharpened scythes and the voices of the hay-makers came most musically. Great trees bordered the half-mile of road from the station to the village, and gave a grateful shade. The gardens of the cottages were bright with June flowers, and the broad village street, lined with low, irregular buildings, picturesque, but not at all from neglected age, seemed to be dozing in the still, hot air. A curtsy at the lodge gates, a turn of the Squire's wrist, and they were bowling along the well kept road through the park.

A minute more, and they had clattered on to the stones under the big porch.

"Well, here we are again, Probin," said the Squire to his head coachman, who himself took the reins from his hands. "And here, please God, we'll stay for the present."

CHAPTER IV

CLINTONS YOUNG AND OLD

The family tradition of the Clintons, whereby the interests and occupations of the women were strictly subordinated to those of the men, had not yet availed to damp the spirits or curb the activities of Joan and Nancy, of whom Mrs. Clinton had made a simultaneous and somewhat belated present to the Squire thirteen years before. Frank, the sailor, the youngest son, had been seven at the time the twins were born, and Dick a young man at Cambridge. Joan and Nancy were still the pets of the household, strong and healthy pets, and unruly within the limits permitted them. Released from their schoolroom, they now came rushing into the hall, and threw themselves on to their parents and their sister with loud cries of welcome.

The Squire kissed them in turn—they approached him first as in duty bound. It had taken him three or four years to get used to their presence, and during that time he had treated them as the sort of unaccountable plaything a woman brings into a house and a male indulgently winks his eye at, a thing beneath his own notice, like a new gown or a new poodle, or a new curate, but one in which she must be permitted, in the foolish weakness of her sex, to interest herself. Then he had gradually begun to "take notice" of them, to laugh at their childish antics and speeches, to quote them—he had actually done this in the hunting-field—and finally to like to have them pottering about with him when duties of investigation took him no further than the stables or the buildings of the home farm. He had always kept them in order while they were with him; he had never lost sight of the fact that they were, after all, feminine; and he had never allowed them to interfere with his more serious pursuits. But he had fully accepted them as agreeable playthings for his own lighter hours of leisure, just as he might have taken to the poodle or the curate, and so treated them still, although their healthy figures were beginning to fill out, and if they had been born Clintons of a generation or two before they would have been considered to be approaching womanhood.

He now greeted them with hearty affection, and told them that if they were good girls they might come and look at the pheasants with him when he had read his letters and they had had their tea, and then took himself off to his library.

Mrs. Clinton's greeting was less hearty, but not less affectionate. She lingered just that second longer over each of them which gives an embrace a meaning beyond mere convention, but she only said, "I must go and see Miss Bird. I suppose she is in the schoolroom." She gathered up her skirts and went upstairs, but when the twins had given Cicely a boisterous hug, they went back to their mother, and walked on either side of her. She was still the chief personage in their little world, although their father and even their brothers were of so much more importance in the general scheme of things. And not even in the presence of their father and brothers did they "behave themselves" as they did with their mother.

The schoolroom was at the end of a long corridor, down two steps and round a corner. It was a large room, looking on to the park from two windows and on to the stableyard from a third. There were shelves containing the twins' schoolbooks and storybooks, a terrestrial and a celestial globe, purchased many years ago for the instruction of their great-aunts, and besides other paraphernalia of learning, signs of more congenial occupations, such as bird-cages and a small aquarium, boxes of games, a big doll's house still in tenantable repair though seldom occupied, implements and materials for wood-carving, and in a corner of the room a toy fort and a surprising variety of lead soldiers on foot or on horseback. Such things as these might undergo variation from time to time. The doll's house might disappear any day, as the rocking-horse had disappeared, for instance, a year before. But the furniture and other contents of the room were more stable. It was impossible to think of their being changed; they were so much a part of it. The Squire never visited the room, but if he had done so he would have recognised it as the same room in which he had been taught his own letters, with difficulty, fifty years before, and if any unauthorised changes had been made, he would certainly have expressed surprise and displeasure, as he had done when Walter had carried off to Oxford the old print of Colonel Thomas on his black horse, Satan, with a view of Kencote House, on a slight eminence imagined by the artist, in the background. Walter had had to send the picture back, and it was hanging in its proper place now, and not likely to be removed again.

Miss Bird, commonly known as "the old starling," to whom Mrs. Clinton had come to pay an immediate visit upon entering the house, as in duty bound, was putting things away. She was accustomed to say that she spent her life in putting things away after the twins had done with them, and that they were more trouble to her than all the rest of the family had been. For Miss Bird had lived in the house for nearly thirty years, and had acted as educational starter to the whole race of young Clintons, to Dick, Humphrey, Walter, Cicely, and Frank, and had taken a new lease of life when the twins had appeared on the scene with the expectation of a prolonged period of service. She was a thin, voluble lady, as old as the Squire, to whom she looked up as a god amongst mankind; her educational methods were of an older generation and included the use of the globes and the blackboard, but she was most conscientious in her duties, her religious principles were unexceptionable, and she filled a niche at Kencote which would have seemed empty without her.

"O Mrs. Clinton I am so glad to see you back," she said, almost ecstatically, "and you too Cicely dear—oh my a new hat and such a pretty one! You look quite the town lady, upon my word and how did you enjoy the ball? you must tell me all about it every word now Joan and Nancy I will not put away your things for you once more and that I declare and you hear me say it you are the most shockingly untidy children and if I have told you that once I have told you a hundred times O Mrs. Clinton a new bonnet too and I declare it makes you look five years younger *at* least."

Mrs. Clinton took this compliment equably, and asked if the twins had been good girls.

"Well, good!" echoed the old starling, "they know best whether they have been good, of their lessons I say nothing and marks will show, but to get up as you might say in the dead of the night and let themselves down from a window with sheets twisted into a rope and not fit to be seen since, all creased, *most* dangerous, besides the

28

impropriety for great girls of thirteen if any one had been passing as I have told them and should be *obliged* to report this behaviour to you Mrs. Clinton on the first opportunity."

Joan and Nancy both glanced at their mother tentatively. "We were only playing Jacobites and Roundheads," said Joan. "It makes it more real."

"And it wasn't in the middle of the night," added Nancy. "It was four o'clock, and quite light."

"Why, you might have killed yourselves!" exclaimed Cicely.

"*Exactly* what I said the very words," corroborated the old starling.

"We tied the sheets very tight," said Joan.

"And tested them thoroughly," added Nancy.

"And we won't do it again, mother," said Joan coaxingly.

"Really, we won't," said Nancy impressively.

"But what else will you do?" asked Mrs. Clinton. "You are getting too big for these pranks. If your father were to hear of it, I am sure I don't know what he would say."

She knew pretty well that he would have laughed boisterously, and told her that he didn't want the children molly-coddled. Time enough for that by and by when they grew up. And the twins probably knew this too, and were not unduly alarmed at the implied threat. But there was a quality in their mother's displeasure, rare as it was, which made them apprehensive when one of their periodical outbursts had come to light. They were not old enough to perceive that it was not aroused by such feats as the one under discussion, which showed no moral delinquency, but only a certain danger to life and limb, now past. But their experience did tell them that misbehaviour which caused her displeasure was not thus referred to their father, and with many embraces and promises of amendment they procured future oblivion of their escapade.

"Well, I have done my duty," said the old starling, "and very unpleasant it was to have to welcome you home with such a story, Mrs. Clinton, and now it is all over and done with I will say and am glad to say that it is the only *blot*. And that is what I said to both Joan and Nancy that it was *such* a pity to have spoilt everything at the last moment, for otherwise two better behaved children it would have been impossible to find anywhere."

At which Joan and Nancy both kissed the old starling warmly, and she strained them to her flat but tender bosom and called them her precious pets.

They went with Cicely into her bedroom while she "took off her things." They betrayed an immense curiosity for every detail of her recent experiences, particularly that crowning one of the Court Ball. She was exalted in their eyes; she had long been grown up, but now she seemed more grown up than ever, a whole cycle in advance of their active, sexless juvenility.

"I don't know," said Joan doubtfully, fingering the new hat which Cicely had taken off, "but I almost think it must be rather fun to wear pretty things sometimes."

But Nancy, the younger by some minutes, rebuked that unwholesome weakness. "What rot, Joan," she said indignantly. "Sis, we have made up our minds to ask mother if we may wear serge knickerbockers. Then we shall be able to do what we like."

When this sartorial revolution had been discussed, Cicely asked, "Has Muriel been over while I have been away?"

"Yes," replied Joan. "Walter was at Mountfield on Sunday, and they came over in the afternoon. They prowled about together. Of course they didn't want us."

"But they had us all the same," said Nancy, with a grin. "We stalked them. They kissed in the Temple, and again in the peach-house."

"But there were lucid intervals," said Joan. "They have made up their minds about something or other; we couldn't quite hear what it was. They were in the kitchen garden, and we were on the other side of the wall."

"You weren't listening, darling?" hazarded Cicely.

"Oh, rather not! We wouldn't do such a thing. But Nancy and I like to pace up and down the yew walk in contemplation, and of course if they liked to pace up and down by the asparagus beds at the same time, we couldn't help hearing the murmur of their voices."

"It is something very serious," said Nancy. "Walter is going to tackle Edward about it at once. And Muriel is quite at one with him in the matter. She said so."

"How they do go on together, those two!" said Joan. "You would think they had never met in their lives until they got engaged six months ago. When they came out of the peach-house Nancy said, 'And this is love!' Then she ran away."

"Only because Walter ran after me," said Nancy.

"And Muriel put her arm round my neck," continued Joan, "and said, 'O Joan, *darling*! I am so happy that I don't care *who* sees me.' Positively nauseating, I call it. You and Jim don't behave like that, Sis."

"I should think not," said Cicely primly.

"Well, you're engaged—or as good as," said Nancy. "But I do rather wonder what Walter is going to tackle Edward about. It can't be to hurry on the wedding, for it's only a month off now."

"We shall know pretty soon," said Joan. "Father doesn't keep things to himself."

"No, I expect Edward will make a deuce of a row," said Nancy.

"Nancy!" said Cicely sharply, "you are not to talk like that."

"Darling!" said Nancy in a voice of grieved expostulation. "It is what Walter said to Muriel. I thought there *couldn't* be any harm in it."

The twins—they were called "the twankies" by their brothers—went off after tea in the schoolroom to see the young pheasants with their father. They were lively and talkative, and the Squire laughed at them several times, as good-humoured men do laugh at the prattle of innocent childhood. Arrived at the pens he entered into a long and earnest conversation with his head keeper, and the twins knew better than to interrupt him with artless prattle at such a time as that. But going home again through the dewy park, he unbent once more and egged Nancy on to imitate the old starling, at which he roared melodiously. He was a happy man that evening. He had come back to his kingdom, to the serious business of life, which had a good deal to do with keepers and broods of pheasants, and to his simple, domestic recreations, much enhanced by the playful ways of his "pair of kittens."

The mellow light of the summer evening lay over the park, upon the thick grass of which the shadows of the trees were lengthening. Sheep were feeding on it, and it was flat round the house and rather uninteresting. But it was the Squire's own; he had known every large tree since the earliest days of his childhood, and the others he had planted, seeing some of them grow to a respectable height and girth. He would have been quite incapable of criticising it from the point of view of beauty. The irregular roofs of the stables and other buildings, the innumerable chimneys of the big house beyond them, seen through a gap in the trees which hemmed it in for the most part on three sides, were also his own, and objects so familiar that he saw them with eyes different from any others that could have been turned upon them. The sight of them gave him a sensation of pleasure quite unrelated to their æsthetic or even their actual value. They meant home to him, and everything that he loved in the world, or out of it. The pleasure was always there subconsciously—not so much a pleasure as an attitude of mind—but this evening it warmed into something concrete. "There's plenty of little dicky-birds haven't got such a nest as my two," he said to the twins, who failed to see that this speech, which they wriggled over, but privately thought fatuous, had the elements of both poetry and religion.

In the meantime Cicely had made her way over the park in another direction to visit her aunts in the dower-house, for she knew they would be itching for an account of her adventures, and she had not had time to write to them from London.

Aunt Ellen and Aunt Laura were the only surviving representatives of the six spinster daughters of Colonel Thomas Clinton, the Squire's grandfather. One after the other Aunt Mary, Aunt Elizabeth, Aunt Anna and Aunt Caroline had been carried out of the dark house in which they had ended their blameless days to a still darker and very narrow house within the precincts of Kencote church, and the eldest sister, now an amazingly aged woman, but still in the possession of all her faculties, and the youngest, who although many years her junior, was well over seventy, were all that were left of the bevy of spinster ladies.

On their father's death, now nearly forty years ago, they had removed in a body from the big house in which they had lived in a state of subdued self-repression to the small one in which, for the first time, they were to taste independence. For their father had been a terrible martinet where women were concerned, and would as readily have ordered Aunt Ellen to bed, at the age of fifty, if he had been displeased with her, as if she had been a child of ten. And if he had ordered her she would have gone.

Some of the rooms in the dower-house had been occupied by the agent to the Kencote estate who at that time was a bachelor, and the rest had been shut up. The six sisters spent the happiest hours they had hitherto known in the arrangement of their future lives and of the beautiful old furniture with which the house was stocked. The lives were to be active, regular, and charitable. Colonel Thomas, who had allowed them each twenty pounds a year for dress allowance and pocket-money during his lifetime, had astonished everybody by leaving them six thousand pounds apiece in his will, which had been made afresh a year before his death. He had just then inherited the large fortune of his younger brother, who had succeeded to the paternal business in Cheapside, lived and died a bachelor, and saved a great deal of money every year. By his previous will they would have had a hundred a year each from the estate, and the use of the dower-house. But even that would have seemed wealth to these simple ladies as long as they remained together, and all of them alive. For Colonel Thomas had forgotten, in that first will, to make provision for the probability of one of them outliving the rest and being reduced to a solitary existence on a hundred pounds a year. However, with fifteen hundred a year or so between them, and no rent to pay, they were exceedingly well off, kept their modest carriage, employed two men in their garden, and found such pleasures in dividing their surplus wealth amongst innumerable and deserving charities that the arrival by post of a nurseryman's catalogue excited them no more than that of an appeal to subscribe to a new mission.

The beautiful old furniture, huddled in the disused rooms and in the great range of attics that ran under the high-pitched roof, gave them immense happiness in the arrangement. They were not in the least alive to its value at that time, though they had become so in some degree since, but kept rather quiet about it for fear that their nephew might wish to carry some of it off to the great house. They thought it very old-fashioned and rather absurd, and they also held this view of the beautifully carved and panelled rooms of their old house, which were certainly too dark for perfect comfort. But they disposed everything to the best advantage, and produced without knowing it an effect which no diligent collector could have equalled, and which became still more delightful and satisfying as the years went on.

Cicely walked across the level park and went through a deep wood, entering by an iron gate the garden of the dower-house, which seemed to have been built in a clearing, although it was older than the oldest of the trees that hemmed it round. On this hot summer afternoon it stood shaded and cool, and the very fragrance of its old-fashioned garden seeming to be confined and concentrated by the heavy foliage. There was not a leaf too many. But in the autumn it was damp and close and in the winter very dark. A narrow drive of about a hundred yards led straight from the main road to the porch and showed a blue telescopic glimpse of distant country. If all the trees had been cut down in front to the width of the house it would have stood out as a thing of beauty against its green background, air and light would have been let into the best rooms and the pleasant view of hill and vale opened up to them. But the Squire, tentatively approached years before by his affectionate and submissive aunts, had decisively refused to cut down any trees at all, and four out of the six of them had taken their last look of this world out of one or other of those small-paned windows and seen only a great bank of laurels—even those they were not allowed to cut down—across a narrow space of gravel, and the branches of oaks not quite ripe for felling, above them.

Cicely went through a garden door opening on to a stone-floored passage which ran right through the house, and opened the door of her aunts' parlour. They were sitting on either side of the fireless grate with their tea-table not yet cleared between them. Aunt Ellen, ninety-three years of age, with a lace cap on her head and a white silk shawl over her shoulders, was sitting upright in her low chair, knitting. She wore no glasses, and her old hands, meagre, almost transparent, with large knuckles, and skin that looked as if it had been polished, fumbled a little with her needles and the thick wool. Her eyesight was failing, though in the pride of her great age she would not acknowledge it; but her hearing was almost perfect. Aunt Laura, who was seventy-five, looked, except for her hair, which was not quite white, the older of the two. She was bent and frail, and she had taken to spectacles some years before, to which Aunt Ellen alluded every day of her life with contempt. They said the same things to each other, on that and on other subjects, time after time. Every day for years Aunt Ellen had said that if dear Edward had only been able to cut down the trees in front of the house it would give them more light and open up the view, and she had said it as if it had only just occurred to her. And Aunt Laura had replied that she had thought the same thing herself, and did Ellen remember how dear Anne, who was always one to say out what she wanted, had asked him if he thought it might be done, but he had said—quite kindly—that the trees had always been there, and there they would stay.

The two old ladies welcomed Cicely as if she had been a princess with whom it was their privilege to be on terms of affectionate intimacy. She was, in fact, a princess in their little world, the daughter of the reigning monarch, to whom they owed, and gave, loyal allegiance. Aunt Laura had been up to the house that morning and heard that they were to return by the half-past four o'clock train.

They had been quite sure that Cicely would come to see them at once and tell them all her news, and they had debated whether they would wait for their own tea or not. They had, in fact, waited for a quarter of an hour. They told her all this in minute detail, and only by painstaking insistence was Aunt Ellen herself prevented from rising to ring the bell for a fresh supply to be brought in. "Well, my dear, if you are quite sure you won't," she said at last, "I will ring for Rose to take the things away."

Cicely rang the bell, and Rose, who five-and-thirty years before had come to the dower-house as an apple-cheeked girl from the village school, answered the summons. She wore a cap with coloured ribbons—the two sisters still shook their heads together over her tendency to dressiness—and dropped a child's curtsey to Cicely as she came in. She had been far too well-trained to speak until she was spoken to, but Aunt Ellen said, "Here is Miss Clinton returned from London, Rose, where she has seen the King and Queen." And Rose said, "Well, there, miss!" with a smile at Cicely, and before she removed the tea-tray settled the white shawl more closely round Aunt Ellen's shoulders.

"Rose is a good girl," said Aunt Ellen, when she had left the room, "but I am afraid more fond of admiration than she should be. Well, dear, now tell us all about what you have seen and done. But, first of all, how is your dear father?"

"Oh, quite well, thank you, Aunt Ellen," replied Cicely, "and very pleased to get home, I think."

"Ah!" said Aunt Ellen. "We have all missed him sorely. I am sure it is wonderful how he denies himself all kinds of pleasure to remain here and do his duty. It is an example we should all do well to follow."

"When he was quite a young man," said Aunt Laura, "there was no one who was gayer—of course in a *nice* way—and took his part in everything that was going on in the higher circles of the metropolis. Your dear Aunt Elizabeth used to cut out the allusions to him in the *Morning Post*, and there was scarcely a great occasion on which his name was not mentioned."

"But after two years in his regiment he gave it all up to settle down amongst his own people," said Aunt Ellen. "All his life has been summed up in the word 'duty.' I wish there were more like him, but there are not."

"It seems like yesterday," said Aunt Laura, "that he joined the Horse Guards Blue. We all wished very much to see him in his beautiful uniform, which so became him, and your dear Aunt Anne, who was always the one to make requests if she saw fit, asked him to bring it down to Kencote and put it on. Dear Edward laughed at her, and refused—quite kindly, of course—so we all took a little trip to London—it was the occasion of the opening of the International Reformatory Exhibition at Islington by the Prince of Wales, as he was then—and your dear father was in the escort. How noble he looked on his black horse! I assure you we were all very proud of him."

Cicely sat patiently silent while these reminiscences, which she had heard a hundred times before, were entered upon. She looked at Aunt Ellen, fumbling with her knitting-needles, and wondered what it must be like to be so very old, and at Aunt Laura, who was also knitting, with quick and expert fingers, and wondered if she had ever been young.

"Did the King show your dear father any special mark of esteem?" asked Aunt Ellen. "It did occur to your Aunt Laura and myself that, not knowing how heavy are the duties which keep him at Kencote, His Majesty might have been—I will not say annoyed, because he would not be that—but perhaps disappointed at not seeing him more often about his Court. For in the days gone by he was an ornament of it, and I have always understood, though not from him, that he enjoyed special consideration, which would only be his due."

"The King didn't take any notice of father," said Cicely, with the brusque directness of youth, and Aunt Ellen seemed to be somewhat bewildered at the statement, not liking to impute blame to her sovereign, but unable for the moment to find any valid excuse for him.

"I thought," she said hesitatingly, "that sending specially—the invitation for all of you—but I suppose there were a great many people there."

Cicely took her opportunity, and described what she had seen and done, brightly and in detail. She answered all her aunts' questions, and interested them deeply. Her visits, and those of her mother, or the twins with Miss Bird, were the daily enlivenment of the two old ladies, and were never omitted. The Squire seldom went to the dower-house, but when he did look in for a minute or two, happening to pass that way, they were thrown into a flutter of pleasure and excitement which lasted them for days.

When Cicely took her leave an hour later, Aunt Ellen said: "The consideration with which dear Edward's family treats us, sister, is something we may well be thankful for. I felt quite sure, and I told you, that some one would come to see us immediately upon their return. Cicely is always so bright and interesting—a dear girl, and quite takes after her father."

"Dear Anne used to say that she took after her mother," said Aunt Laura; to which Aunt Ellen replied: "I have not a word to say against Nina; she has been a good wife to dear Edward, though we all thought at the time of their marriage that he might have looked higher. But compared with our nephew, quiet and unassuming as she is, she has very little character, while Cicely *has* character. No, sister, Cicely is a Clinton—a Clinton through and through."

CHAPTER V

MELBURY PARK

Family prayers at Kencote took place at nine o'clock, breakfast nominally at a quarter past, though there was no greater interval between the satisfaction of the needs of the soul and those of the body than was necessary to enable the long string of servants to file out from their seats under the wall, and the footmen to return immediately with the hot dishes. The men sat nearest to the door and frequently pushed back to the dining-room against the last of the outflowing tide; for the Squire was ready for his breakfast the moment he had closed the book from which he had read the petition appointed for the day. If there was any undue delay he never failed to speak about it at once. This promptness and certainty in rebuke, when rebuke was necessary, made him a well-served man, both indoors and out.

Punctuality was rigidly observed by the Clinton family. It had to be; especially where the women were concerned. If Dick or Humphrey, when they were at home, missed prayers, the omission was alluded to. If Cicely, or even Mrs. Clinton was late, the Squire spoke about it. This was more serious. In the case of the boys the rebuke hardly amounted to speaking about it. As for the twins, they were never late. For one thing their abounding physical energy made them anything but lie-abeds, and for another, they were so harried during the ten minutes before the gong sounded by Miss Bird that there would have been no chance of their overlooking the hour. If they had been late, Miss Bird would have been spoken to, and on the distressing occasions when that had happened, it had put her, as she said, all in a twitter.

When it still wanted a few minutes to the hour on the morning after the return from London, Cicely was standing by one of the big open windows talking to Miss Bird, the twins were on the broad gravel path immediately outside, and two footmen were putting the finishing touches to the appointments of the table.

It was a big table, although now reduced to the smallest dimensions of which it was capable, for the use of the six people who were to occupy it. But in that great room it was like an island in the midst of a waste of Turkey carpet. The sideboards, dinner-wagon, and carving-table, and the long row of chairs against the wall opposite to the three windows were as if they lined a distant shore. The wallpaper of red flock had been an expensive one, but it was ugly, and faded in places where the sun caught it. It had been good enough for the Squire's grandfather forty years before, and it was good enough for him. It was hung with portraits of men and women and portraits of horses, some of the latter by animal painters of note. The furniture was all of massive mahogany, furniture that would last for ever, but had been made after the date at which furniture left off being beautiful as well as lasting. The mantelpiece was of brown marble, very heavy and very ugly.

At one minute to nine Mrs. Clinton came in. She carried a little old-fashioned basket of keys which she put down on the dinner-wagon, exactly in the centre of the top shelf. Cicely came forward to kiss her, followed by Miss Bird, with comma-less inquiries as to how she had spent the night after her journey, and the twins came in through the long window to wish her good morning. She replied composedly to the old starling's twittering, and cast her eye over the attire of the twins, which was sometimes known to require adjustment. Then she took her seat in one of the big easy-chairs which stood on either side of the fireplace, while Porter, the butler, placed a Bible and a volume of devotions, both bound in brown leather, before the Squire's seat at the foot of the table, and retired to sound the gong.

It was exactly at this moment that the Squire, who opened his letters in the library before breakfast, was accustomed to enter the room, and, with a word of greeting to his assembled family, perch his gold-rimmed glasses on his fine straight nose, and with the help of two book-markers find the places in the Bible and book of prayers to which the year in its diurnal course had brought him. The gong would sound, either immediately before or immediately after he had entered the room, the maids and the men who had been assembling in the hall would file in, he would throw a glance towards them over his glasses to see that they were all settled, and then begin to read in a fast, country gentleman's voice the portion of Scripture that was to hallow the day now officially beginning.

The gong rolled forth its sounding reverberation, Miss Bird and the three girls took their seats, and then there was a pause. In a house of less rigid habits of punctuality it would have been filled by small talk, but here it was so unusual that when it had lasted for no more than ten seconds the twins looked at one another in alert curiosity and Cicely's eyes met those of her mother, which showed a momentary apprehension before they fixed themselves again upon the shining steel of the fire bars. Another ten seconds went by and then the library door was heard to open and the Squire's tread, heavy on the paved hall.

Four pairs of eyes were fixed upon him as he entered the room, followed at a short but respectful interval by the servants. Mrs. Clinton still looked inscrutably at the grate. The Squire's high colour was higher than its wont, his thick grizzled eyebrows were bent into a frown, and his face was set in lines of anger which he evidently had difficulty in controlling. He fumbled impatiently with the broad markers as he opened the books, and omitted the customary glance towards the servants as he began to read in a voice deeper and more hurried than usual. When he laid down the Bible and took up the book of prayers he remained standing, as he sometimes did if he had a touch of rheumatism; but he had none now, and his abstention from a kneeling position amounted to a declaration that he was willing to go through the form of family prayers for routine's sake but must really be excused from giving a mind to it which was otherwise occupied.

It was plain that he had received a letter which had upset his equanimity. This had happened before, and the disturbance created made manifest in much the same way. But it had happened seldom, because a man who is in possession of an income in excess of his needs is immune from about half the worries that come with the morning's post, and any annoyance arising from the administration of his estate was not usually made known to him by letter. The Squire's letter-bag was normally as free of offence as that of any man in the country.

The twins, eying one another with surreptitious and fearful pleasure, conveyed in their glances a knowledge of what had happened. The thing that Walter and Muriel had made up their minds about, whatever it was—that was what had caused the Squire to remain behind a closed door until he had gained some slight control over his temper, and led him now to prefer the petitions appointed in the book bound in brown leather in a voice between a rumble and a bark. Perhaps everything would come out when Porter and the footman had brought in the tea and coffee service and the breakfast dishes, and left the room. If it did not, they would hear all about it later. Their father's anger held no terrors for them, unless it was directed against themselves, and even then considerably less than might have been supposed. He was often angry, or appeared to be, but he never did anything. Even in the memorable upheaval of seven years before—when Walter had finally refused to become a clergyman and announced his determination of becoming a doctor—which had been so unlike anything that had ever happened within their knowledge that it had impressed itself even upon their infant minds, and of which they had long since worried all the details out of Cicely, he had made a great deal of noise but had given way in the end. He would give way now, however completely he might lose his temper in the process. The twins had no fear of a catastrophe, and therefore looked forward with interest, as they knelt side by side, with their plump chins propped on their plump hands, to the coming storm.

The storm broke, as anticipated, when the servants had finally left the room, and the Squire had ranged over the silver dishes on the side-table for one to his liking, a search in which he was unsuccessful.

"I wish you would tell Barnes that if she can't think of anything for breakfast but bacon, and scrambled eggs, and whiting, and mushrooms, she had better go, and the sooner the better," he said, bending a terrifying frown on his wife. "Same thing day after day!" But he piled a plate with bacon and eggs and mushrooms and carried it off to his seat, while his daughters and Miss Bird waited round him until he had helped himself.

"I have just had a letter from Walter," he began directly he had taken his seat, "which makes me so angry that, 'pon my word, I scarcely know what to do. Nina, this milk is burnt. Barnes shall go. She sends up food fit for the pig-tub. Why can't you see that the women servants do their duty? I can't take *everything* on my shoulders. God knows I've got enough to put up with as it is."

"Joan, ring the bell," said Mrs. Clinton.

"Oh—God's sake—no, no," fussed the Squire. "I don't want the servants in. Give me some tea. Miss Bird, here's my cup, please. Take it, please, *take* it, Miss Bird. I don't know when I've felt so annoyed. You do all you can and put yourself to an infinity of trouble and expense for the sake of your children, and then they behave like this. Really, Walter wants a good thrashing to bring him to his senses. If I had nipped all this folly of doctoring in the bud, as I ought to have done, I might have been able to live my life in peace. It's too bad; 'pon my word, it's too bad."

The twins, sustaining their frames diligently with bacon and eggs and mushrooms—the whiting was at a discount—waited with almost too obvious expectation for the full disclosure of Walter's depravity. Cicely, alarmed for the sake of Muriel, ate nothing and looked at her father anxiously. Miss Bird was in a state of painful confusion because she had not realised effectively that the Squire had wanted his cup of coffee exchanged for a cup of tea, and might almost be said to have been "spoken to" about her stupidity. Only with Mrs. Clinton did it rest to draw the fire which, if she did it unskilfully, might very well be turned upon herself. A direct question would certainly have so turned it.

"I am sorry that Walter has given you any further cause of complaint, Edward," she said.

This was not skilful enough. "Cause of complaint!" echoed the Squire irritably. "Am I accustomed to complain about anything without good reason? You talk as if I am the last man in the world to have the right to expect my wishes to be consulted. Every one knows that I gave way to Walter against my better judgment. I allowed him to take up this doctoring because he had set his mind on it, and I have never said a word against it since. And how now does he reward me when he has got to the point at which he might begin to do himself and his family some credit? Coolly writes to me for money—*to me—for money*—to enable him to buy a practice at Melbury Park, if you please. Melbury *Park*! Pah!!"

The Squire pushed his half-emptied plate away from him in uncontrollable disgust. He was really too upset to eat his breakfast. The utterance of the two words which summed up Walter's blind, infatuated stampede from respectability brought back all the poignant feelings with which he had first read his letter. For the moment he was quite beside himself with anger and disgust, and unless relief had been brought to him he would have left his breakfast unfinished and stalked out of the room.

Nancy brought the relief with the artless question, "Where is Melbury Park, father?"

"Hold your tongue," said the Squire promptly, and then drew a lurid picture of a place delivered over entirely to the hovels of nameless people of the lower middle classes, and worse, a place in which you would be as effectually cut off from your fellows as if you went to live in Kamschatka. Indeed, you would not be so cut off if you went to Kamschatka, for you might be acknowledged to be living there, but to have it said that you lived at Melbury Park would *stamp* you. It would be as easy to say you were living in Halloway Goal. It was a place they stopped you at when you came into London on the North Central Railway, to take your tickets. The Squire mentioned this as if a place where they took your tickets was of necessity a dreadful kind of a place. "Little have I ever thought," he said, "when I have been pulled up there, and looked at those streets and streets of mean little houses, that a son of mine would one day want to go and *live* there. 'Pon my word, I think Walter's brain must be giving way."

It was Cicely who asked why Walter wanted to live at Melbury Park, and what Muriel said about it.

"He doesn't say a word about Muriel," snapped the Squire. "I suppose Muriel is backing him up. I shall certainly speak to Jim and

Mrs. Graham about it. It is disgraceful—positively disgraceful—to think of taking a girl like Muriel to live in such a place. She wouldn't have a soul to speak to, and she would have to mix with all sorts of people. A doctor's wife can't keep to herself like other women. Oh, I don't know why he wants to go there. Don't ask me such questions. I was ready to start him amongst nice people, whatever it had cost, and he might have been in a first-class position while other men of his age were only thinking about it. But no, he must have his own silly way. He shan't have his way. I'll put my foot down. I won't have the name of Clinton disgraced. It has been respected for hundreds of years, and I don't know that I've ever done anything to bring it down. It's a little too much that one of my own sons should go out of his way to throw mud at it. I've stood enough. I won't stand any more. Melbury Park! A pretty sort of *park*!"

Having thus relieved his feelings the Squire was enabled to eat a fairly good breakfast, with a plateful of ham to follow his bacon and eggs and mushrooms, a spoonful or two of marmalade, and some strawberries to finish up with. It came out further that Walter was coming down by the afternoon train to dine and sleep, and presumably to discuss the proposal of which he had given warning, and that the Squire proposed to ask Tom and his wife to luncheon, or rather that Mrs. Clinton should drop in at the Rectory in the course of the morning and ask them, as he would be too busy.

Then Cicely asked if she might have Kitty, the pony, for the morning, and the Squire at once said, "No, she'll be wanted to take up food for the pheasants," after which he retired to his room, but immediately returned to ask Cicely what she wanted the pony for.

"I want to go over to Mountfield," said Cicely.

"Very well, you can have her," said the Squire, and retired again.

Mrs. Clinton made no comment on the disclosures that had been made, but took up her basket of keys and left the room.

"Now, Joan and Nancy, do not linger but get ready for your lessons at a quarter to ten punctually," Miss Bird broke forth volubly. "Every morning I have to hunt you from the breakfast table and my life is spent in trying to make you punctual. I am sure if your father knew the trouble I have with you he would speak to you about it and then you would see."

"Melbury Park!" exclaimed Nancy in a voice of the deepest disgust, as she rose slowly from the table. "'Pon my word, Joan, it's too bad. I spend my life in trying to make you punctual and then you want to go to Melbury Park! Pah! A nice sort of a *park*!"

"Are you going to see Muriel, Cicely?" asked Joan, also rising deliberately. "Starling, *darling*! Don't hustle me, I'm coming. I only want to ask my sister Cicely a question."

"Yes," said Cicely. "If I couldn't have had Kitty I should have walked."

"How unreasonable you are, Cicely," said Nancy. "The pony is wanted to take chickweed to the canaries at Melbury Park."

"Find out all about it, Cis," said Joan in process of being pushed out of the room. "Oh, take it, Miss Bird, *please*, TAKE IT."

Cicely drove off through the park at half-past ten. Until she had passed through the lodge gates and got between the banks of a deep country lane, Kitty went her own pace, quite aware that she was being driven by one whose unreasonable inclinations for speed must subordinate themselves to the comfort of pony-flesh as long as she was in sight of house or stables. Then, with a shake of her head, she suddenly quickened her trot, but did not escape the cut of a whip which was always administered to her at this point. With that rather vicious little cut Cicely expressed her feelings at a state of things in which, with fourteen or fifteen horses in the stable and half a dozen at the home farm, the only animal at the disposal of herself and her sisters was always wanted for something else whenever they asked for it.

The Squire had four hunters—sometimes more—which nobody but himself ever used, and the price of a horse that would carry a man of his weight comfortably ran into treble figures more often than not. Dick kept a couple always at Kencote, even Walter had one, and Humphrey and Frank could always be mounted whenever they wanted a day with the South Meadshire. There were nine or ten horses, standing in stalls or loose boxes or at grass, kept entirely for the amusement of her father and brothers, besides half a dozen more for the carriages, the station omnibus, the luggage cart, and all the dynamic demands of a large household. The boys had all had their ponies as soon as their legs could grip a saddle. This very pony that she was driving was really Frank's, having been rescued for him from a butcher's cart in Bathgate fourteen years before, and nobody knew how old she was. She was used for the mowing machine and for every sort of little odd job about the garden, and seemed as if she might go on for ever. It was only when Cicely or the twins drove her that the reminder was given that she was not as young as she had been, and must not be hustled.

And she was all they were ever allowed to drive, and then only when she was not wanted for something else. It was a Clinton tradition, deriving probably from Colonel Thomas and his six stay-at-home daughters, that the women of the family did not hunt. They were encouraged to drive and allowed to ride to the meets of hounds if there was anything to carry them, and in Cicely's childhood there had been other ponies besides Kitty, left-offs of her elder brothers, which she had used. But she had never been given a horse of her own, and the hunters were far too precious to be galled by a side-saddle. What did she want to ride for? The Squire hated to see women flying about the country like men, and he wasn't going to have any more horses in the stable. The men had more than enough to do as it was. It was part of the whole unfair scheme on which life at Kencote was based. Everything was done for the men and boys of the family, and the women and girls must content themselves with what was left over.

Pondering these and other things, Cicely drove along the country lanes, between banks and hedges bright with the growth of early summer, through woods in which pheasants, reared at great expense that her father and brothers and their friends might kill them, called one another hoarsely, as if in a continual state of gratulation at having for a year at least escaped their destined end; between fields in which broods of partridges ran in and out of the roots of the green corn; across a bridge near which was a deep pool terrifically guarded by a notice-board against those who might have disturbed the fat trout lying in its shadows; across a gorse-grown common, sacred home of an old dog-fox that had defied the South Meadshire hounds for five seasons; and so, out of her father's property on to that of Jim Graham, in which blood relations of the Kencote game and vermin were protected with equal care, in order that the Grahams might fulfil the destiny appointed for them and the Clintons and the whole race of squirearchy alike.

The immediate surroundings of Mountfield were prettier than those of Kencote. The house stood at the foot of a wooded rise, and its long white front showed up against a dark background of trees. It was older in date than Georgian Kencote, and although its walls had been stuccoed out of all resemblance to those of an old house, its high-pitched roof and twisted chimney stacks had been left as they were. The effect was so incongruous that even unæsthetic Alexander Graham, Jim's father, had thought of uncovering the red brick again. But the front had been altered to allow for bigger windows and a portico resembling that at Kencote, and the architect whom he had consulted, had pressed him to spend more money on it than he felt inclined to. So he had left it alone and spent none; and Jim, who was not so well off as his father by the amount of Muriel's portion and the never-to-be-forgiven Harcourt duties, was not likely to have a thousand pounds to spare for making his rooms darker for some years to come.

The old stable buildings, untouched by the restorer, flanked the house on one side and the high red brick wall of the gardens on the other. The drive sloped gently up from the gates through an undulating park more closely planted than that of Kencote. There were some very old trees at Mountfield and stretches of bracken here and there beneath them. It was a pity that the house had been spoilt in appearance, but its amenities were not wholly destroyed. Cicely knew it almost as well as she knew Kencote, but she acknowledged its charm now as she drove up between the oak and the young fern. Under the blue June sky strewn with light clouds, it stood for a peaceful, pleasant life, if rather a dull one, and she could not help wondering whether her friend would really be happier in a house of her own in Melbury Park, which, if painted in somewhat exaggeratedly dark colours by Cicely's father, had not struck her, when she had seen it from the railway, as a place in which any one could possibly live of choice. Perhaps Walter had over-persuaded her. She would know very soon now, for Muriel told her everything.

CHAPTER VI

A GOOD LONG TALK

Mrs. Graham—she was the Honourable Mrs. Graham, a daughter of the breeder of Jove II. and other famous shorthorns—came out of the door leading to the stableyard as Cicely drove up. She had been feeding young turkeys, and wore a shortish skirt of brown tweed, thick boots and a green Tyrolean hat, and was followed by three dogs—a retriever, a dachshund, and one that might have been anything. She was tall and spare, with a firm-set, healthy face, and people sometimes said that she ought to have been a man. But she was quite happy as a woman, looking after her poultry and her garden out of doors, and her dogs and her household within. She had hardly moved from Mountfield since her marriage thirty years before, and the only fly in the ointment of content in which she had embalmed herself was that she would have to leave it when Jim married. But she greeted Cicely, who was expected to supplant her, with bright cordiality, and lifted up a loud voice to summon a groom to lead off Kitty to the stable.

"My dear," she said; "such a nuisance as this wedding is you never knew. It's as much as I can do to keep the birds and the animals fed, and how *I* shall look in heliotrope and an aigrette the Lord only knows. But I suppose nobody will look at me, and Muriel will be a picture. Have you heard that Walter is going to take her to live at Melbury Park? It seems a funny place to go to live in, doesn't it? But I suppose they won't mind as long as they are together. I never saw such a pair of love-birds."

"Walter wrote to father about it this morning," said Cicely, "and he is coming down this afternoon. Father is furious with him."

"Well, I'm sure I don't know why," said Mrs. Graham equably. "I shouldn't care to live in Melbury Park myself, and I don't suppose Mr. Clinton would. But nobody asks him to. If *they* want to, it's their own affair. I'm all for letting people go their own way—always have been. I go mine."

"Why does Walter choose such a place as that to take Muriel to?" asked Cicely, who had not remained quite unimpressed by the Squire's diatribe against the unfortunate suburb.

"Oh, it's convenient for his hospital and gives him the sort of practice he wants for a year or two. *I* don't know. They won't live there for ever. I don't suppose it will kill them to know a few people you wouldn't ask to dinner. It hasn't killed me. I get on with farmers' wives better than anybody—ought to have been one."

"Father is going to ask you to put your foot down and say Muriel shan't go there," said Cicely.

"Well then, I won't," replied Mrs. Graham decisively. "I'm not a snob." Then she added hurriedly, "I don't say that your father is one either; but he does make a terrible fuss about all that sort of thing. I should have thought a Clinton was good enough to be able to know anybody without doing himself any harm. But you had better go and talk to Muriel about it, my dear. You will find her upstairs, with her clothes. Oh, those clothes! I must go and look after the gardeners. They are putting liquid manure on the roses, and I'm afraid they will mix it too strong."

Mrs. Graham went off to attend to her unsavoury but congenial task, and Cicely went indoors and up to Muriel's room, where she found her friend with a maid, busy over some detail of her trousseau. They greeted one another with coolness but affection, the maid was sent out of the room, and they settled down in chintz-covered easy-chairs by the window for the usual good long talk.

Muriel was a pretty girl, less graceful than Cicely, but with her big brown eyes and masses of dark hair, a foil to her friend's fair beauty. She had her mother's sensible face, but was better-looking than her mother had ever been.

"Now you must tell me every word from the beginning," she said. "You said nothing in your letters. You didn't make me see the room, or any one in it."

Cicely had a good deal to say about her late experiences, but her friend's own affairs were of more recent interest. "But I want to hear about Walter and Melbury Park first," she said. "There is a rare to-do about it at Kencote, I can tell you, Muriel."

"Is there?" said Muriel, after a short pause, as if she were adjusting her thoughts. "That was what Walter was afraid of."

"Don't you mind going to live in a place like that?" asked Cicely. "Father thinks it is a shame that Walter should take you there."

"O my dear," said Muriel, with a trifle of impatience, "you know quite well what I think about all that sort of thing. We have talked it over hundreds of times. Here we are, stuck down in the middle of all this, with nothing in the world to do but amuse ourselves, if we can, and never any chance of pushing along. We have *got* it all; there is nothing to go for. That's what I first admired about my darling old Walter. He struck out a line of his own. If he had been content just to lop over the fence into Kencote Rectory, I don't think I should ever have fallen in love with him. I don't know, though. He *is* the sweetest old dear."

"Oh, don't begin about Walter," urged Cicely.

"Yes, I will begin about Walter," replied Muriel, "and I'll go on with Walter. He says now that the only thing he is really keen about — except me — is his work. He always liked it, in a way, but when he made up his mind to be a doctor it was only because he knew he must have some profession, and he thought he might as well have one that interested him. But now it takes up all his thoughts, except when he comes down here for a holiday, and you know how the old pet enjoys his holidays. Well, I'm going to do all I can to help him to get on. He says this practice at Melbury Park is just what he wants, to get his hand in; he won't be worried with a lot of people who aren't really ill at all, but have to be kept in a good humour in case they should go off to another doctor. It will be hard, sound work, and he will be in touch with the hospital all the time. He is immensely keen about it. I don't want to say anything against Mr. Clinton, but why *can't* he see that Walter is worth all the rest of your brothers put together, because he has set out to do something and they are just having a good time?"

"Oh, well, Muriel, I can't allow that," said Cicely. "Dick is quite a good soldier. He got his D.S.O. in the war. And besides, his real work is to look after the property, and he knows as much about that as father. And Humphrey *has* to go about a lot. You must, in the Foreign Office. And Frank—he is doing all right. He was made doggy to his Admiral only the other day."

"Well, at any rate," replied Muriel, "they start from what they are. And you can't say that their chief aim isn't to have a good time. Walter has gone in against men who *have* to work, whether they want to or not, and he has done as well as any of them. He owes nothing to being the son of a rich man. It has been against him, if anything."

"Father hoped he was going to set up as a consulting physician," said Cicely.

"Yes, and why?" asked Muriel. "Only because he wants him to live amongst the right sort of people. He doesn't care a bit whether he would make a good consultant or not. Walter says he isn't ready for it. He wants more experience. It will all come in time. He is not even quite sure what he wants to specialise on, or if he wants to specialise at all. At present he only wants to be a G.P., with plenty of work and time for the hospital."

"What is a G.P.?" asked Cicely.

"Oh, a general practitioner. It's what Walter calls it."

"Then why can't he be a G.P. in a nicer place than Melbury Park? It is rather hard on you, Muriel, to take you to a place where you can't know anybody."

"O my dear, what *do* I care for all that nonsense about knowing people? Surely there's enough of that here! Is this person to be called on, who has come to live in a house which nobody ever called at before, or that person, because nobody has ever heard of her people? I'm sick of it. Even mother won't call on Bathgate people, however nice they may be, and she's not nearly so stuck up as most of the county women."

"Yes, I know all that, and of course it's nonsense. But you must admit that it is different with people who aren't gentle-people at all."

"I'm not a fool, and I don't pretend that I'm going to make bosom friends of all Walter's patients, though I *am* going to do what I can to make things pleasant all round. We shall see our friends in London, of course. Jim is going to give us a jolly good motor-car, and we shall be able to dine out and go to the play and all that if we want to, and people ask us. But it is all so unimportant, Cicely, that side of it. Walter wants to get out of it. He'll be very busy, and the best times we shall have will be in our own little house alone, or going right away when we get a holiday."

"I dare say you are quite right," said Cicely. "Of course it will be jolly to have your own house and do what you like with it. Has Walter got a house yet?"

"There is quite a decent one we can have where the man who wants to sell the practice lives. It is really bigger than we want, although it's only a semi-detached villa. I should be able to have my friends to stay with me. Cicely, you *must* come directly we move in, and help to get things straight, if we go there."

"Oh, you'll go there all right, if Walter has made up his mind about it," said Cicely. "Father thinks he will hold out, but he knows, really, that he won't. That's what makes him so wild."

Both the girls laughed. "He is a funny old thing," said Muriel apologetically, "but he has been very nice to me."

"Only because you have got ten thousand pounds, my dear, and are the right sort of match for Walter. He wouldn't be very nice to you if Walter had found you at Melbury Park; not even if you had your ten thousand pounds. Oh dear, I wish I had ten thousand pounds."

"What would you do with it?"

"I should travel. At any rate I should go away from Kencote. Muriel, I am sick to death of it."

"Ah, that is because it seems dull after London. You haven't told me a word about all that you have been doing, and I have been talking about myself all the time."

"I didn't care a bit about London. I didn't enjoy it at all—except the opera."

"Don't try to be *blasée*, my dear girl. Of course you enjoyed it."

"I tell you I didn't. Look here, Muriel, really it *is* unfair the way the boys have everything in our family and the girls have nothing."

"I do think it is a shame you are not allowed to hunt."

"It isn't only that. It is the same with everything. I have seen it much more plainly since I went to London."

"Well, my dear, you went to a Court Ball, and to all the best houses. The boys don't do more than that. I shouldn't do as much if I went to London in the season."

"Yes, I went. And I went because Cousin Humphrey took the trouble to get cards for us. He is an old darling. Do you suppose father would have taken the smallest trouble about it—for me and mother?"

"He knows all the great people. I suppose a Clinton is as good as anybody."

"Yes, a *man* Clinton. That is just it. Dick and Humphrey go everywhere as a matter of course. I saw enough of it to know what society in London means. It is like a big family; you meet the same people night after night, and everybody knows everybody else—that is in the houses that Cousin Humphrey got us invited to. Dick and Humphrey know everybody like that; they were part of the family; and mother and I were just country cousins who knew nobody."

"Well, of course, they are there all the time and you were only up for a fortnight. Didn't they introduce you to people?"

"O yes. Dick and Humphrey are kind enough. They wanted me to have a good time. But you are not supposed to want introductions in

London. You are supposed to know enough men to dance with, or you wouldn't be there. And the men don't like it. I often heard Dick and Humphrey apologising to their friends for asking them to dance with me. You know the sort of thing, Muriel: 'You might take a turn with my little sister, old man, if you've nobody better. She's up here on the spree and she don't know anybody.'"

"O Cicely, they wouldn't give you away like that."

"Perhaps not quite as bad as that. Dick and Humphrey are nice enough as brothers, and I believe they're proud of me too, in a way. They always danced with me themselves, and they always noticed what I was wearing, and said I looked a topper. I know I looked all right, but directly I opened my mouth I gave myself away, just like a maid in her mistress's clothes."

"O Cicely!"

"Well, it was like that. I had nothing to talk about. I don't know London; I can't talk scandal about people I don't know. Of course I had to tell them I had always lived in the country, and then they began to talk about hunting at once. Then I had to say that I didn't hunt, and then they used to look at me through their eyeglasses, and wonder what the deuce I did do with myself. The fact is, that I can't do anything. Even the ones with brains—there *were* a few of them— who tried me with things besides hunting, couldn't get anything out of me, because there is nothing to get. I've never been anywhere or seen anything. I don't know anything—nothing about books or pictures or music or plays. Why on earth *should* they want to talk to me? Hardly any of them did twice, unless it was those who thought I was pretty and wanted to flirt with me. I felt such a *fool*!"

She was almost in tears. Her pretty face under its white motor-cap was flushed; she twisted her gloves in her slender hands.

"O Cicely, darling!" said Muriel sympathetically, "you are awfully bright and clever, really. You've many more brains than I have."

"I'm not clever, but I've got as many brains as other girls. And what chance have I ever had of learning anything? Dick and Humphrey and Walter were all sent to Eton and Oxford or Cambridge. They have all had the most expensive education that any boys could have, and as long as they behaved themselves pretty well, nobody cared in the least whether they took advantage of it or not. What education have *I* had? Miss Bird! I don't suppose she knows enough to get a place as teacher in a village school. I suppose I know just about as much as the girls who do go to a village school. I haven't even had lessons in drawing or music, or anything that I might perhaps have been good at. I'm an ignorant *fool*, and it's all father's fault, and it isn't fair."

She had talked herself into actual tears now. Muriel said, in a dry voice which did not accord with her expression of face, "This sudden rage for learning is a new thing, my dear."

Cicely dabbed her eyes impatiently and sat up in her chair. "I dare say I am talking a lot of nonsense," she said, "but I have been wondering what I *do* get for being the daughter of a rich country gentleman; because father *is* rich, as well as being the head of an important family, as he is always reminding us, though he pretends to think nothing of it. He has never gone without anything he wanted in the whole of his life, and the boys have everything they want too, that can be got for money."

"Your allowance was just twice as much as mine, when father was alive," Muriel reminded her.

"Oh, I know I can have plenty of nice clothes and all that," said Cicely, "and I have nice food too, and plenty of it, and a nice room, and a big house to live in. But I don't call it living, that's all. Father and the boys can live. We can't. Outside Kencote, we're nobody at all—I've found that out—and mother is of no more importance than I am. We're just the women of the family. Anything is good enough for us."

"I don't think you are quite fair, Cicely. Mrs. Clinton doesn't care for going about, does she? It would depend more upon her than your father and brothers."

"What would depend on her?"

"Well, I mean you grumble at Dick and Humphrey knowing more people than you do."

"I suppose what you do mean is that the Birkets aren't as good as the Clintons."

There was the slightest pause. Then Muriel said, a little defiantly, "Well, the Grahams aren't as good as the Conroys."

"I know that mother isn't only as good as father; she is a great deal better."

Cicely spoke with some heat, and Muriel made a little gesture with her hands. "Oh, all right, my dear," she said, "if you don't want to talk straight." It was a formula they used.

Cicely hesitated. "If you mean," she began, but Muriel interrupted her. "You know quite well what I mean, and you know what I don't mean. You know I would never say that Mrs. Clinton wasn't as good as anybody in the world, in the sense you pretended to take my words. We were talking of something quite different."

"Sorry, Muriel," replied Cicely. This was another formula. "We did go to a dance at Aunt Emmeline's, you know. If I hadn't been to all those other houses I should have enjoyed it immensely. Well, I did enjoy it—better, really. Aunt Emmeline saw that I had heaps of partners and I got on well with them. They were mostly barristers and people like that. They took the trouble to talk, and some of them even made me talk. It is a lovely house—of course not like one of the great London houses, but with two big drawing-rooms, and Iff's band, and everything done very well. If I had gone straight up from here to that ball, it would have been one of the best I had ever gone to."

"Well, Mr. Birket is a famous barrister, and I suppose is very well off too. I should think he knows as many interesting people as anybody."

"Interesting people, yes; but there wasn't a soul there that I had seen at the other houses, except Dick and Humphrey."

"Were they there?"

"There!" cried Cicely triumphantly. "You see you are quite surprised at that."

"Well," said Muriel firmly, "they *were* there. And how did they behave?"

"Oh, they behaved all right. Humphrey went away early, but Dick stayed quite a long time. Dick can be very sweet if he likes, and he doesn't give himself airs, really—he only takes it for granted that he is a great personage. And so he is; you would say so if you saw him in London. Do you know, Muriel, I was next to the Duchess of Pevensey at Dunster House, and I heard her whisper to her daughter, quite sharply, 'Evelyn, keep a valse for Captain Clinton, in case he asks you.' Of course she hadn't an idea that I was Captain Clinton's sister. She had looked down her nose at me just before, and wondered what I was doing there."

"I suppose she didn't say so."

"Her nose did. You should have seen her face when Dick came up the moment after and said, 'Here you are, Siskin; come and have a spin'; and didn't take any notice of dear Evelyn, who must have been at least thirty."

"Well, go on about Mrs. Birket's."

"Yes, well, Dick said, 'Now, Siskin, I don't know any of the pretty ladies here, and I'm going to dance with you.' But when Aunt Emmeline came up and insisted upon introducing him to a lot of girls, he went off as nicely as possible and danced with the whole lot of them. And, you know, a man like Dick isn't supposed to have to do that sort of thing."

Muriel laughed; and Cicely, who had recovered her good humour, laughed too. "Of course, it wasn't anything to fuss about, really," she said, "but you see what I mean, Muriel, don't you?"

"No, I don't," said Muriel, "unless you mean exactly what I said just now, and you bit my head off for. Mr. Clinton is what some people call a swell, and Dick is a swell too. The Grahams aren't swells, and the Birkets aren't either. And if you want it quite straight, my dear, neither you nor I are swells; we're only what they call county."

"You're so sensible, Muriel darling!" said Cicely.

"And you've had your head turned, Cicely darling!" retorted Muriel. "You have been taken up by your great relations, and you have come back to your simple home discontented."

"It's all very well, though," said Cicely, becoming serious again, "but I'm a Clinton just as much as the boys are, and just as much as you are a Graham. You say the Grahams are not swells—you do use horrible language, Muriel dear—but I suppose Lord Conroy is, and so, according to your argument, you ought to be."

"Uncle Blobs isn't a swell—he's only a farmer with a title."

"Oh! then I don't know what you mean by a swell."

"Well, of course the Conroys *are* swells in a way, but they don't care about swelling. If mother had liked—and father had let her—she could have been a fashionable lady, and dear Muriel could have been a fashionable girl, with her picture in the illustrated papers, sitting in front of a lattice window with a sweet white frock and a bunch of lilies. 'We give this week a charming photograph of Miss Muriel Graham, the only daughter of the Honourable Mrs. Graham. Mrs. Graham is a daughter of' and so on. As it is, dear Muriel is just the daughter of a country squire."

"That is all dear Cicely is, though you said just now that father was a swell. I don't see, really, that he is much more of a swell than Mr. Graham was—here."

"No—he isn't—here. That's just it. That is what you are running your head against, my dear. Perhaps he isn't really a swell at all, now. But he could be if he liked, and he was when he was young. It is because he likes being a country squire best that you have got to put up with being a country squire's daughter. I'm sorry for you, as you seem to feel it so much, but I'm afraid there's no help for it. I don't think, really, you have much to grumble at, but I suppose if you live for a fortnight exclusively amongst dukes and duchesses, you *are* apt to get a little above yourself. Now tell me all about the Court Ball."

Cicely told her all about the Court Ball; then they talked about other things, and Muriel said, "You have never asked about Jim. His ship is due in London next Wednesday and he will be home the day after."

"Dear old Jim," said Cicely—she was at work on some embroidery for Muriel. "It will be jolly to see him back again. But it doesn't seem like a year since he went away."

"*You* don't seem to have missed him much."

"O yes, I have. But it was like when the boys went back to school or to Cambridge—frightfully dull at first, and then you got used to it, and they were back before you knew where you were."

"Yes, I know. But I don't feel like that about Walter now. I don't know what I should do if he were to go off for a year."

"Oh, that's quite different. You are deeply in love, my dear."

"So were you once."

"Never in the world, Muriel, and you know that quite well. I was a little donkey. I had only just put my hair up and I thought it a fine thing to be engaged. Not that that lasted long. Dear old Jim soon repented, and I don't blame him."

"Jim is pretty close about things, but I sometimes doubt whether he has repented."

"You mean that he still cherishes a tender passion for sweet Cicely Clinton."

"I shouldn't wonder."

"Well, I should. Anyway, it isn't returned. I love Jim, but if I heard that he had come home engaged, as I dare say he will, I shouldn't mind in the very least. I should be the first to congratulate him."

"No, you wouldn't. He would tell mother and me first. And you needn't give yourself airs, you know. Jim would be a very good match for you. You would be mistress of Mountfield. I'm not making half such a brilliant alliance."

"Brilliant! I'm quite sure you would rather be going to marry somebody who had his way to make, like Walter, than trickle off from one big, dull country house to another. Wouldn't you, now?"

"Well, yes, I would. But it wouldn't make any difference to me, really, if I had Walter. If Dick were to die, which I'm sure I hope he won't, and Walter were to succeed to Kencote, I should like it just as much."

"Well, I dare say it would be all right when one got older. At present I think it would be burying yourself alive when you ought to have the chance of doing something and seeing something. No, Muriel, dear. I have been a squire's daughter all my life, and there's no money in it, as Humphrey says. The last thing I want to be at present is a squire's wife. I believe Jim has forgotten all that silliness as much as I have. If I thought he hadn't, I shouldn't be so glad as I am at the prospect of seeing him back."

"I dare say he has. You're not good enough for him."

"And he isn't good enough for me. I must be going home, or father will accuse me of over-driving Kitty. I always do over-drive her, but he doesn't notice unless I am late. Good-bye, Muriel. It has done me good to talk to you."

CHAPTER VII

THE RECTOR

The Rector was shown into the library where the Squire was reading the *Times*, for which a groom rode over to Bathgate every morning at eleven o'clock, and woe betide him if he ever came back later than half-past twelve. It was a big room lined with books behind a brass lattice which nobody ever opened. Though the Squire used it every day, and had used it for five-and-thirty years, he had never altered its appointments, and his grandfather had not lived in it. Merchant Jack had furnished it handsomely for a library, and the Reverend John Clinton Smith, the historian of Kencote, had bought the books for him, and read most of them for him too. If he had returned from the tomb in which he had lain for a hundred years to this room where he had spent some of the happiest hours of his life, he would only have had to clear out a boxful or two of papers from the cupboards under the bookshelves and the drawers of the writing-tables, and remove a few photographs and personal knick-knacks, and there would have been nothing there that was not familiar, except the works of Surtees and a few score other books, which he would have taken up with interest and laid down again with contempt, in some new shelves by the fireplace. The Squire had no skill with a room. He hated any alteration in his house, and he had debated this question of a new bookcase to hold the few books he did read from time to time with as much care as the Reverend John Clinton Smith, book-lover as he was, had devoted to the housing of the whole library.

"Ah, my dear Tom," said the Squire heartily, "I'm glad you came up. I should have come down to you, but I've been so busy all the morning that I thought you wouldn't mind a summons. Have you brought Grace?"

"She is with Nina," said the Rector, and sat heavily down in the easy-chair opposite to that from which the Squire had risen. He was a big man, with a big face, clean shaven except for a pair of abbreviated side whiskers. He had light-blue eyes and a mobile, sensitive mouth. His clothes were rather shabby, and except for a white tie under a turned-down collar, not clerical. His voice, coming from so massive a frame, seemed thin, but it was of a pleasant tenor quality, and went well with the mild and attractive expression of his face. All the parishioners of Kencote liked the Rector, though he was not at all diligent in visiting them. Perhaps they liked him the better on that account.

The Rector was the Squire's half-brother. Colonel Thomas Clinton, the Squire's grandfather, had followed, amongst other traditions of his family, that of marrying early, and marrying money. His wife was a city lady, daughter of Alderman Sir James Banket, and brought him forty thousand pounds. Besides his six daughters, he had one son, who was delicate and could not support the fatigue of his own arduous pursuit of sport. He was sent to Eton and to Trinity College, and a cornetcy was bought for him in the Grenadier Guards. He also married early, and married, following an alternative tradition, not money, but blood. His wife was a sister of a brother officer, the Marquis of Nottingham, and they were happy together for a year. He died of a low fever immediately after the birth of his son, Edward, that Squire of Kencote with whom we have to do.

Colonel Thomas took a great deal more pride in his sturdy grandson than ever he had been able to take in his weakly son. He taught him to ride and to shoot, and to tyrannise over his six maiden aunts, who all took a hand in bringing him up. His own placid, uncomplaining wife had died years before, and Lady Susan Clinton, tired of living in a house where women seemed to exist on sufferance, had married again, but had not been allowed to take her child to her new home. She had the legal right to do so, of course, but was far too frightened of the weather-beaten, keen-eyed old man, who could say such cutting things with such a sweet smile upon his lips, to insist upon it. Her second husband was the Rector of a neighbouring parish, who grew hot to the end of his days when he thought of what he had undergone to gain possession of his bride. He did not keep her long, for she died a year later in giving him a son. That son was now the Reverend Thomas Beach, Rector of Kencote, to which preferment the Squire had appointed him nearly thirty years before, when he was only just of canonical age to receive it. And in the comfortable

Rectory of Kencote, except for a year's curacy to his father, he had lived all his clerical life.

The Squire and the Rector were not altogether unlike in appearance. They were both tall and well covered with flesh, and there was a family resemblance in their features. But the Squire's bigness and ruddiness were those of a man who took much exercise in the open air, the Rector's of a man physically indolent, who lived too much indoors, and lived too well.

But if they were not unlike in appearance, they were as dissimilar as possible in character. The Squire's well-carried, massive frame betokened a man who considered himself to have a right to hold his head high and plant his footsteps firmly; the Rector's big body disguised a sensitive, timorous character, and a soul never quite at ease in its comfortable surroundings. That ponderous weight of soft flesh, insistent on warmth and good food and much rest, had a deal to answer for. Spare and active, with adventures of the spirit not discouraged by the indolence of the flesh, the Rector of Kencote might have been anything in the way of a saint that his Church encourages. He would certainly not have been Rector of Kencote for thirty years, with the prospect of being Rector of Kencote for thirty years more if he lived so long. He had a simple, lovable soul. It told him that he did nothing to speak of in return for his good income and the fine house in which he lived in such comfort, and troubled him on this score more than it would have troubled a man with less aptitude for goodness; and it omitted to tell him that he had more direct influence for righteousness than many a man who would have consciously exercised all the gifts with which he might have been endowed. He simply could not bring himself to visit his parish regularly, two or three afternoons a week, as he had made up his mind to do when he was first ordained. The afternoons always slipped away somehow, and there were so many of them. The next would always do. So it had been for the first years of his pastorate, and he had long since given way altogether to his indolence and shyness in respect of visiting his flock; but his conscience still troubled him about it. He was a great reader, but his reading had become quite desultory, and he now read only for his own entertainment. His sermons were poor; he had no delivery and no gift of expression; he could not even give utterance to the ideas that did, not infrequently, act on his brain, nor hardly to the human tenderness which was his normal attitude towards mankind. But he did go on writing fresh ones, stilted and commonplace as they were. Mental activity was less of a burden to him than bodily activity, and he had kept himself up to that part of what he thought to be his clerical duty.

For the rest, he was fond of his books and his garden, fond of his opulent, well-appointed house, and all that it contained, and fond of the smaller distractions of a country life, but no sportsman. He had no children, but a graceful, very feminine wife, who reacted pleasantly on his intellect and looked well after the needs of his body. He sometimes went to London for a week or two, and had been to Paris; but he liked best to be at home. He watched the progress of the seasons with interest, and knew something about birds, something about flowers and trees, was a little of a weather prophet, and often thought he would study some branch of natural science, but had lacked the energy to do so. He liked the winter as well as the summer, for then his warm house called him more seductively. He liked to tramp home along muddy country roads in the gloaming, drink tea in his wife's pretty drawing-room, chat to her a little, and then go into his cosy, book-lined study and read till dinner-time. He would have been a happy man as a layman, relieved of that gnawing conviction that his placid, easy life was rather far from being apostolic. And nobody, not even his wife, had any idea that he was not quite contented, and grateful for the good things that he enjoyed.

"Well, Tom," said the Squire, "I'm infernally worried again. It's that boy Walter. What do you think he wants to do now?" He spoke with none of the heat of the morning. It might have been thought that he had already accepted the inevitable and was prepared to make the best of it.

"I don't know, Edward," said the Rector; and the Squire told him.

"And you have a particular objection to this place, Melbury Park?" inquired the Rector guilelessly.

"O my dear Tom," said the Squire impatiently, "have you ever seen the place?"

"From the railway only," admitted the Rector; "and chiefly its back-gardens. It left an impression of washing on my mind."

"It left an impression of *not* washing on mine," said the Squire, and leant back in his chair to laugh heartily at his witticism.

The Rector also did justice to it, perhaps more than justice, with a kind smile. "Well, Edward," he said, "it may be so, but it is, otherwise, I should say, respectable. It is not like a slum. Has Walter any particular reason for wishing to go there?"

The Squire gave a grudging summary of the reasons Walter had advanced for wishing to go there, and made them appear rather ridiculous reasons. He also produced again such of the arguments he had advanced at breakfast-time as seemed most weighty, and managed to work himself up into a fair return of his morning's feeling of being very badly treated.

"Well, Edward," said the Rector gently, when he had come to an end, "I think if I were you I should not make any objections to Walter's going to Melbury Park."

"You wouldn't?" asked the Squire, rather weakly.

"No, I don't think I would. You see, my dear Edward, some of us are inclined to take life too easily. I'm sometimes afraid that I do myself."

"You do your duty, Tom. Nobody is asked to do more than that."

"Well, you may be right, but I am not sure. However, what I was going to say was that one cannot help respecting—perhaps even envying—a young fellow like Walter who doesn't want to take life easily."

"He has stuck to his work," said the Squire. "I will say that for the boy; and he's never come to me for money to pay bills with, as Humphrey has, and even Dick—though, as far as Dick goes, he'll have the property some day, and I don't grudge him what he wants now within reason."

"You see, Edward, when a man has congenial work which takes up his time, he is not apt to get into mischief. I think, if I may say so, that you ought to admit now, however much you may have objected to Walter's choice of a profession in the first instance, that he has justified his choice. He put his hand to the plough and he has not looked back. That is a good deal to say for a young man with Walter's temptations towards an easy, perhaps idle, life."

"Well," said the Squire, "I do admit it. I do admit it, Tom. I have my natural prejudices, but I'm the last man in the world that any one has a right to call obstinate. I objected to Walter becoming a doctor in the first instance. It was natural that I should. He ought to have succeeded you, as Dick will succeed me. And none of our family have ever been doctors. But I gave way, and I've every wish, now, that he should succeed in his profession. And the reason I object to this move so strongly is that as far as my judgment goes it is not a step in the right direction. It might be so for the ordinary doctor—I don't know and I can't say—but I'm willing to help a son of mine over some of the drudgery, and it will be very disagreeable for me to have Walter settling down to married life in a place like Melbury Park, when he might do so much better. You must remember, Tom, that he is the first of the boys to get married. Dick will marry some day soon, I hope and trust, and Humphrey too, but until they do, Walter's son, if he has one, will be heir to this property, eventually. He ought *not* to be brought up in a place like Melbury Park."

"There is a good deal in what you say, Edward," replied the Rector, who privately thought that there was very little; "but the contingency you mention is a very unlikely one."

"I don't lay too much stress on it. If I thought that Walter was right from the point of rising in his profession to go to this place I would leave all that out of the question."

"Well, I'll tell you what, Edward," said the Rector, with an engaging smile, "supposing you keep an open mind on the question until you have heard what Walter has to say about it. How would that be?"

The Squire hummed and ha'd, and thought that on the whole it might be the best thing to do.

"You see," said the Rector in pursuance of his bright idea, "it is just possible that there may be reasons which Walter has considered, and may wish to urge, that *might* make it advisable for him, even with the exceptional advantages you could give him, to go through the training afforded by just such a practice as this. I should let him urge them, Edward, if I were you. I should let him urge them. You can but repeat your objections, if they do not appeal to your judgment. You will be in a better position to make your own views tell, if you dispose your mind to listen to his. I should take a kindly tone, I think, if I were you. You don't want to set the boy against you."

"No, I don't want that," said the Squire. "And I should have done what you advise, in any case. It's the only way, of course. Let us go in and have some luncheon. Then you don't think, Tom, that there would be any serious objection to my giving way on this point, if Walter is reasonable about it?"

"Well, Edward, do you know, I really don't think there would," replied the Rector, as they crossed the hall to the dining-room.

The ladies were already there. Mrs. Beach was by the window talking to the twins, who adored her. She was getting on for fifty, but she was still a pretty woman, and moved gracefully as she came across the room to shake hands with her brother-in-law. "It is very nice to see you back again, Edward," she said, with a charming smile. "You do not look as if London had disagreed with you."

"My dear Grace," said the Squire, holding her white, well-formed hand in his big one. "I'll tell you my private opinion of London, only don't let it go any further. It can't hold a candle to Kencote." Then he gave a hearty laugh, and motioned her to a seat on his right. The twins cast a look of intelligence at one another, and Cicely glanced at her mother. The Squire had recovered his good humour.

"For these an' all his mercies," mumbled the Squire, bending his head.—"Oh, beg your pardon, Tom," and the Rector said grace.

"Have you heard what that silly fellow Walter wants to do, Grace?" asked the Squire.

"Nothing except that he hopes to get married next month," replied Mrs. Beach, helping herself to an omelette, "and I hope that he will make a better husband than Tom."

The Rector, already busy, spared her a glance of appreciation, and the twins giggled at the humour of their favourite.

"Yes, he is going to be married, and he proposes to take Muriel to live at Melbury Park, of all places in the world."

"Then in that case," replied Mrs. Beach equably, "Tom and I will not give them the grand piano we had fixed upon for a wedding present. They must content themselves with the railway whistles."

The twins laughed outright and were ineffectively rebuked by Miss Bird. That they were to be seen and not heard at table was a maxim she had diligently instilled into them. But they were quite right to laugh. Aunt Grace was surpassing herself. She always kept the Squire in a good humour, by her ready little jokes and the well-disguised deference she paid him. The deference was not offered to him alone, but to all men with whom she came in contact, even her husband, and men liked her immensely. She teased them boldly, but she deferred to their manhood. Women sometimes grew tired of her sweetness of manner, which was displayed to them too, and quite naturally. She was a sweet woman, if also, in spite of her ready tongue, rather a shallow one. Mrs. Clinton did not like her, but did not show it, except in withholding her confidence, and Mrs. Beach had no idea that they were not intimate. Cicely was indifferent towards her, but had loved her as a child, for the same reason that the twins thought her the most charming of womankind, because she treated them as if they were her equals in intelligence, as no doubt they were. It had never occurred to them to mimic her, which was a feather in her cap if she had known it. And another was that Miss Bird adored her, being made welcome in her house, and, as she said, treated like anybody else.

By the time luncheon was over the Squire had so overcome his bitter resentment at the idea of Walter's going to live at Melbury Park, that he could afford to joke about it. Aunt Grace had suggested that they should all go and live there, and had so amused the Squire with a picture of himself coming home to his villa in the evening and eating his dinner in the kitchen in his shirt sleeves, with carpet slippers on his feet, which was possibly the picture in her mind of "how the poor live," that he was in the best of humours, and drank two more glasses of port than his slightly gouty tendency usually permitted.

The twins persuaded Miss Bird to take them to the station to meet Walter in the afternoon. They were not allowed to go outside the park by themselves, and walked down the village on either side of the old starling, each of them over-topping her by half a head, like good girls, as she said herself. They wore cool white dresses, and shady hats trimmed with poppies, and looked a picture. When they reached the by-road to the station, Joan said, "One, two, three, and away," and they shot like darts from the side of their instructress, arriving on the platform flushed and laughing, not at all like good girls, while Miss Bird panted in their rear, clucking threats and remonstrances, to the respectful but undisguised amusement of the porter, and the groom who had preceded them with the dog-cart.

Walter got out of a third-class carriage when the train drew up and said, "Hullo, twanky-diddleses! Oh, my adorable *Sturna vulgaris vetus*, embrace me! Come to my arms!"

"Now, Walter, do behave," said Miss Bird sharply. "What will people think and Joan 'n Nancy I shall certainly tell Mrs. Clinton of your *disgraceful* behaviour I am quite ashamed of you running off like that which you *know* you are not allowed to do you are very *naughty* girls and I am seriously displeased with you."

"Ellen Bird," said Walter, "don't try and put it on to the twankies. I looked out of the carriage window and saw you sprinting along the station road yourself. You have had a little race and are annoyed at being beaten. I shall put you up in the cart and send you home, and I will walk back with the twankies." And in spite of Miss Bird's almost frenzied remonstrances, up into the cart she was helped, and driven off at a smart pace, with cheers from the twins, now entirely beyond her control.

"Well, twanky dears," said Walter, starting off at a smart pace with a twin on either side, "I suppose there's a deuce of a bust up, eh? Look here, you can't hang on. It's too hot."

"It wouldn't be too hot for Muriel to hang on," said Joan, her arm having been returned to her.

"There was a bust up this morning at breakfast," said Nancy. "Edward came in purple with passion two minutes late for prayers."

"Eh?" said Walter sharply. "Look here, you mustn't speak of the governor like that."

"It's only her new trick," said Joan. "She'll get tired of it."

"You're not to do it, Nancy, do you hear?" said Walter.

"Oh, all right," said Nancy. "Mr. Clinton of Kencote, J.P., D.L., was so put out that he wouldn't kneel down to say his prayers."

"Annoyed, eh?" said Walter.

"Yes," said Joan, "but he's all right now, Walter. Aunt Grace came to lunch, and beat Bogey."

"What!"

"It's only her new trick," said Nancy. "She'll get tired of it. She means put him in a good humour."

"Really, you twankies do pick up some language. Then there's nothing much to fear, what?"

"No, we are all coming to live at Melbury Park, and Aunt Grace is going to take in our washing."

"Oh, that's the line taken, is it?" said Walter. "Well, I dare say it's all very funny, but I can't have you twankies giving yourselves airs, you know. I don't know why they talk over things before you. The governor might have kept it to himself until he had seen me."

"Mr. Clinton doesn't keep things to himself," said Nancy. "You might know that by this time; and Joan and I are quite old enough to take an intelligent interest in family affairs. We do take the deepest interest in them, and we know a lot. Little pitchers have long ears, you know."

"So have donkeys, and they get them pinched if they're not careful," retorted Walter. "How are you getting on with your lessons, twankies?"

"I believe our progress is quite satisfactory, thank you, Dr. Clinton," replied Joan. "Perhaps you would like to hear us a few dates, so that our afternoon walk may not pass entirely unimproved."

"You had much better look at Joan's tongue," said Nancy. "Starling said last night that her stomach was a little out of order, and we rebuked her for her vulgarity."

"You are a record pair, you two," said Walter, looking at them with unwilling admiration. "I don't believe any of us led that poor old woman the dance that you do. Do you want some jumbles, twankies?"

"Ra-*ther*," said the twins with one voice, and they turned into the village shop.

The tea-table was spread on the lawn, and the Squire came out of the window of the library as Walter reached the garden. "Well, my boy," he said, "so you're going to settle down at Melbury Park, are you? That's a nice sort of thing to spring on us; but good luck to you! You can always come down here when you want a holiday."

CHAPTER VIII

BY THE LAKE

Whitsuntide that year fell early in June, and the weather was glorious. Cicely awoke on Friday morning with a sense of happiness. She slept with her blinds up, and both her windows were wide open. She could see from her pillow a great red mass of peonies backed by dark shrubs across the lawn, and in another part of the garden laburnums and lilacs and flowering thorns, and all variations of young green from trees and grass under a sky of light blue. Thrushes and blackbirds were piping sweetly. She loved these fresh mornings of early summer, and had often wakened to them with that slight palpitation of happiness.

But, when she was fully awake, it had generally happened that the pleasure had rather faded, at any rate of late years, since she had grown up. In her childhood it had been enough to have the long summer day in front of her, especially in holiday time, when there would be no irksome schoolroom restraint, nothing but the pleasures and adventures of the open air. But lately she had needed more, and more, at Kencote, had seldom been forthcoming. Moreover she had hardly known what the "more" was that she had wanted. She had never been unhappy, but only vaguely dissatisfied, and sometimes bored.

This morning her waking sense of well-being did not fade as she came to full consciousness, but started into full pleasure as she remembered that her cousins, Angela and Beatrice Birket, with their father and mother, were in the house. And Dick and Humphrey had come down with them the evening before. Guests were so rare at Kencote that to have a party of them was a most pleasurable excitement. Dick and Humphrey would see that there was plenty of amusement provided, quiet enough amusement for them, no doubt, but for Cicely high pleasure, with something to do all the day long, and people whom she liked to do it with.

And—oh yes—Jim had returned home from his travels the day before, and would be sure to come over, probably early in the morning.

She jumped out of bed, put on her dressing-gown, and went to the window. The clock from the stable turret struck six, but she really could not lie in bed on such a morning as this, with so much about to happen. She would dress and go out into the garden. A still happier thought—she would go down to the lake and bathe from the Temple of Melancholy. It was early in the year, but the weather had been so warm for the last month that it was not too early to begin that summer habit. Perhaps the twins would come with her. They were early risers.

She was just about to turn away from the window when she saw the twins themselves steal round the corner of the house. Their movements were mysterious. Although there was nobody about, they trod on tiptoe across the broad gravel path and on to the dewy lawn. Joan—she could always tell them apart, although to the outside world they were identical in form and feature—carried a basket which probably contained provisions, a plentiful supply of which was generally included in the elaborate arrangements the twins made for their various games of adventure. There was nothing odd in this, but what was rather odd was that she also held a long rope, the other end of which was tied around Nancy's neck, while Nancy's hands were knotted behind her.

When they got on to the grass they both turned at the same moment to glance up at the windows of the house, and caught sight of Cicely, who then perceived that Joan's features were hidden by a mask of black velvet. She saw them draw together and take counsel, and then, without speaking, beckon her insistently to join them. She nodded her head and went back into the room, smiling to herself, while the twins pursued their mysterious course towards the shrubberies. She thought she would not bathe after all; but she dressed quickly and went down into the garden, a little curious to learn what new invention the children were busying themselves with.

It proved to be nothing more original than the old game of buccaneers. Nancy had awakened to find herself neatly trussed to her bed and Joan in an unfinished state of attire, but wearing the black velvet mask, brandishing in her face a horse pistol, annexed from the collection of old-fashioned weapons in the hall. Thus overpowered she had succumbed philosophically. It was the fortune of war, and if she had thought of it she might just as well have been kneeling on Joan's chest, as Joan was kneeling, somewhat oppressively, on hers. Given her choice of walking the plank from the punt on the lake or being marooned on the rhododendron island, she had accepted the latter alternative, stipulating for an adequate supply of food; and a truce having been called, while pirate and victim made their toilets and raided together for the necessary rations, she had then allowed herself to be bound and led off to the shore where the pirate ship was beached.

All this was explained to Cicely—the search for provisions having no particular stress laid on it—when she joined them, and she was awarded the part of the unhappy victim's wife, who was to gaze across the water and tear her hair in despair at being unable to go to the rescue.

"You must rend the air with your cries," Joan instructed her, "not too loud, because we don't want any one to hear. The pirate king will then appear on the scene, and stalking silently up behind you— well, you'll see. I won't hurt you."

Nancy was already comfortably marooned. She could be seen relieved of her bonds seated amongst the rhododendrons, which were in full flower on the island and all round the lake, making her first solitary meal off cold salmon and a macedoine of fruit, and supporting her painful situation with fortitude.

Cicely accepted her rôle, but dispensed with the business of tearing her hair. "O my husband!" she cried, stretching her arms across the water. "Shall I never see thee more? What foul ruffian has treated thee thus?"

"Very good," said Nancy, with her mouth full—she was only twenty yards away—"keep it up, Sis."

"I will not rest until I have discovered the miscreant and taken his life," proceeded Cicely.

"Shed his blood," corrected Nancy. "Say something about my bones bleaching on the shore."

"Thy bones will bleach on the shore," Cicely obeyed. "And I, a disconsolate widow, will wander up and down this cruel strand — oh, don't, Joan, you are hurting."

For she found herself in the grip of the pirate king, who hissed in her ear, "Ha, ha, fair damsel! Thou art mine at last. 'Twas for love of thee I committed this deed. Thy lily-livered husband lies at my mercy, and once in Davy Jones's locker will be out of my path. Then the wedding bells shall ring and we will sail together over the bounding main. Gently, gently, pretty dove! Do not struggle. I will not hurt thee."

"Unhand me, miscreant," cried Cicely. "Think you that I would forget my brave and gallant husband for such as thou, steeped in crime from head to foot? Unhand me, I say. Help! Help!"

"Peace, pretty one!" cooed the pirate king. "Thou art in my power and thy cries do not daunt me. I have only to lift my voice and my brave crew will be all around me. Better come with me quietly. There is a cabin prepared for thee in my gallant barque. None shall molest thee. Cease struggling and come with me."

Urged towards the shore by the pirate king, Cicely redoubled her cries for assistance, but no one was more surprised than she to see an elderly gentleman in a grey flannel suit and a straw hat bound from behind the bushes, level a latch-key at the head of the masked bandit, and cry, "Loose her, perjured villain, or thy brains shall strew the sand."

Nancy's clear, delighted laugh came from the island, Joan giggled and said, "O Uncle Herbert!"

"Uncle me no Herberts," said Mr. Birket. "Put up your hands or I shoot. (Cicely, if you will kindly swoon in my arms — Thank you.) Know, base buccaneer, that I represent his Britannic Majesty on these seas, and wherever the British flag flies there is liberty. Allow me to disarm you of your weapon."

"I yield to superior force," said the bold buccaneer in stately tones.

"Very wise of you. I should fold my arms and scowl if I were you. Behold, the lady cometh to. She is, yes she is, the daughter I have mourned these many years. And you, base marauder, though you know it not, are the long-lost brother of that luckless wight starving, if I mistake not, to death on the island. Well for you that your hands are not imbrued in his gore. Put off at once in your stout ship—and be careful not to tumble overboard—and restore him to his hapless bride."

"I will obey your bidding," said the pirate king proudly. "The claims of relationship are paramount."

"Well put. I have hopes of you yet. I am also hungry. Bring back the victim's basket, and we will eat together and forget this unfortunate occurrence."

Joan punted across to the island and the marooned Nancy was brought to the mainland with her somewhat depleted store of provisions. Mr. Birket dropped his rôle while the embarkation proceeded, and mopped his brow with a bandana handkerchief. He was a short, grey-haired man with a keen lawyer's face. "Well, my dear," he said to Cicely, "I think that went off very well, but it is somewhat exhausting."

Cicely laughed. "The twins will never forget it," she said. "Did you see them come out?"

"I saw them come on to the lake. I was in the Temple, getting through a little work."

"What ever time did you get up?"

"Oh, half-past five. My regular hour in the summer. I'm kept pretty busy, my dear. But I don't generally have such a charming place as this to work in. Now then, pirate, hurry up with those victuals. Your uncle is hungry."

They picnicked on the shore—the twins' provisioning having fortunately been ample—and Mr. Birket proved himself an agreeable companion. Joan said to Nancy afterwards that the practice of the law seemed to brighten people's brains wonderfully. He smoked a cigar, told them stories, and made them laugh. At half-past eight he fetched his papers from the Temple and they went indoors to get ready for breakfast. "I think," he said, as they crossed the lawn, "we had better say nothing about the startling occurrences of the morning. They might come as a shock to our elders and betters." And Joan and Nancy, remembering the contents of the basket and the source from which they had been derived, agreed.

Herbert Birket was Mrs. Clinton's only brother. Their father had been a Colonel in the Indian Army, and had retired to end his days in a little house on the outskirts of Bathgate, desiring nothing more than to read the *Times* through every morning and find something in it to disagree with, walk so many miles a day, see his son well started in the profession he had chosen, and his daughter well, but not splendidly, married. He had gained his desires in all but the last item. The young Squire of Kencote, in all the glory of his wide inheritance and his lieutenancy in the Household Cavalry, had ridden past the little house on his way to Bathgate and seen a quiet, unassuming, fair-haired girl watering her flowers in the garden, had fallen in love with her, met her at a county ball, fallen still more deeply in love, and finally carried her off impetuously from the double-fronted villa in the Bathgate Road to rule over his great house at Kencote.

South Meadshire had rung with the romance, and old Colonel Birket had not been altogether delighted with his daughter's good fortune, wishing to spend his last days in peace and not in glory. The wedding had taken place in London, with a respectable show of relations on the bride's side and all the accompaniments of semi-military parade on the bridegroom's. There was no talk of a misalliance on the part of his friends, nor was there a misalliance, for the Birkets were good enough people; but the young Squire's six maiden aunts had returned to the dower-house at Kencote after the wedding and shaken their respective heads. No good would come of it, they said, and had, perhaps, been a little disappointed ever afterwards that no harm had come of it, at any rate to their nephew.

The old Colonel had long since been laid in his grave, and the little house in the Bathgate Road, now in the respectable occupancy of a retired druggist, would have seemed as strange a dwelling-place to the daughters of Herbert Birket, who had prospered exceedingly, as to the children of Mrs. Clinton of Kencote.

Angela and Beatrice Birket were handsome girls, both of them younger than Cicely, but with their assured manners and knowledge of the world, looking older. They had been brought up strictly by their mother, who had paid great attention to their education. They might have been seen during their childhood on any reasonably fine afternoon walking in Kensington Gardens or Hyde Park with a highly priced French governess, two well, but plainly dressed children with long, straight hair and composed faces. They never appeared in their mother's drawing-room when visitors were there, being employed in a room upstairs either at lessons, or consuming the plainest variety of schoolroom tea. They were taken sometimes to an afternoon concert, and on very rare occasions to a play. When they were at home in London, their days were given to their lessons, with the requisite amount of regular exercise to keep them in good health. In holiday time, in the summer, at Christmas and at Easter, they were allowed to run quite wild, in old clothes at some out-of-the-way seaside place, in country farmhouses, where they scrambled about on ponies and amongst ducks and chickens, or in the country houses of their friends and relations, where there were other children of their age for them to play with. So they had loved the country and hated London, and had never been so surprised in their lives as when they were duly presented and launched in society to find that London was the most amusing place in the world and that all the pains and drudgery to which they had been put there had prepared them for the enjoyment of the manifold interests and pleasures that came in their way. They had developed quickly, and those who had known them in their rather subdued childhood would hardly have known them now.

Of all the places in which they had spent their holidays in days gone by they had liked Kencote best. It had been a paradise of fun and freedom for them; they and Cicely had been happy from morning till night. The elder boys home from school or college had been kind to them, and Frank, the sailor, who was about their own age, and not too proud to make a companion of his sister and cousins, had led the way in all their happy adventures. And they had loved the twins, whom they had seen grow up from babyhood. No, there had been no place like Kencote in the old days, and the pleasure of a visit there still persisted, although it was no longer the most congenial house at which they visited.

All the party assembled for prayers in the dining-room. That was understood to be the rule. The twins were there, very clean and well brushed and very demure. Mr. Birket wished them good-morning solemnly and hoped that they had slept well, at which they giggled and were rebuked by Miss Bird, when their uncle turned away to ask the same question of Cicely. As Miss Bird said, — What would their uncle think of them if they could not answer a civil question without behaving in that silly fashion? At which they giggled again. Angela and Beatrice, tall and glossy-haired, dressed in white, made a handsome quartet with Dick and Humphrey, the one in smart grey flannel, the other in white.

"This little rest will do you both good," said Dick. "You shall lie about, and Miss Bird shall read to you. You will go back to the excitements of the metropolis thoroughly refreshed."

"Oh, we are going to be very energetic," said Angela. "We want to play lawn tennis, for one thing. One never gets a chance nowadays, and we both hate croquet."

"We'll get up a tournament," said Humphrey, "and invite the neighbourhood. You'll see some queer specimens. I hear you're writing a book, Trixie."

Beatrice laughed, and blushed a little. "I've left off," she said.

"Ah, I've heard stories about you," said Dick. "Soon have something else to do, eh? Don't blush. I won't tell anybody. Look here, we'll play golf this morning. We laid out quite a decent little course in the park last autumn. And in the afternoon we'll have a picnic."

"Oh, preserve us!" said Humphrey.

"Oh, do let us have a picnic," said Angela.

"It will be like old times," said Beatrice.

"We'll go to Blackborough Castle," said Dick, "and take the twankies. We must give them a little fun. Siskin, how about a picnic?"

Mrs. Birket was telling Mrs. Clinton that Beatrice's engagement would be announced when they returned to London. "She is young," she said, "but both the girls are older in mind than in age."

"You have educated them well," Mrs. Clinton said. She looked across the room at the two handsome, smiling girls, and at her own pretty daughter, who had not been very well educated and was not older in mind than in age. But just then the gong sounded, every one took their seats, the Squire came in with a hearty "Good-morning! Good-morning!" which greeting his assembled family and guests might take and divide amongst them, and the proceedings of the day began.

Later in the morning Angela and Beatrice, Dick and Humphrey were actively engaged at lawn tennis. Cicely was sitting under a great lime on the lawn waiting for her turn. The twins, having discovered an unusually congenial companion in their uncle, had carried him off somewhere out of sight, and Cicely was alone for the moment. A voice behind her, "Hullo, Cicely!" made her start, and then she sprang up. "Jim!" she cried. "How jolly to see you back! I thought you would come over this morning."

The game had to be interrupted while the returned traveller was welcomed. "You look as fit as a fiddle, old boy," said Dick. "You'll be able to stay at home and enjoy yourself now, I hope. Will you play when we've finished this? I can lend you a pair of shoes."

"No thanks," said Jim. "I'll talk to Cicely." So the others went back on to the lawn.

"Come and have a stroll round," Jim suggested; and Cicely, with a half-regretful glance at the tennis lawn, rose to go with him.

They went to the rhododendron dell round the lake. It was where every one went naturally if they wanted to walk and talk at the same time. Jim's honest, weathered face was very frequently turned towards Cicely's fair, young one, and there was a light in his eyes which made her turn hers away a little confusedly when they met it. But Jim's voice was level enough, and his speech ordinary. "I'm jolly glad to get back again," he said. "I've never liked Mountfield half so well. I was up at six o'clock this morning, and out and about."

"So was I," said Cicely, and she told him, laughing, of the events of the morning.

"I expect they've grown, those young beggars," said Jim, alluding thus disrespectfully to the twins. "I've often thought of them while I've been away, and of everybody at Kencote—you especially."

"We've all thought of you, too," said Cicely, "and talked about you. You haven't been forgotten, Jim."

"I hoped I shouldn't be," he said simply. "By Jove, how I've looked forward to this—coming over here the first moment I could. I wish you hadn't got all these people here, though."

"All these people!" echoed Cicely. "Why, Jim, you know them as well as we do."

"Yes, I'm a selfish beggar. I wanted to have you all to myself."

Cicely was a little disturbed in her mind. Jim had not talked to her like this for five years. Ever since that long, happy summer when he and she had been together nearly every day, when he had made love to her in his slow, rather ponderous way, and she, her adolescence flattered, had said "yes" when he had asked her to marry him—or rather ever since he had written to her from Oxford to say that he must wait for some years before he could expect to marry and that she was to consider herself quite free—he had never by word or sign shown whether he also considered himself free, or whether he intended, when the time came, to ask her again to be his wife. When he had come back to Mountfield at Christmas he had been in all respects as he had been up to six months before, friendly and brotherly, and no more. It made it easier for her, for her pride had been a little wounded. If he had held aloof, but shown that, although he had given her her freedom, he hoped she had not accepted it, she would have felt irked, and whatever unformed love she had for Jim would quickly have disappeared. But, as it was, his equable friendship kept alive the affection which she had always felt for him; only it seemed to make the remembrance of their love passages a little absurd. She was not exactly ashamed of what had happened, but she never willingly thought of it, and after a year or so it became as much a part of her past life as the short frocks and pinafores of her childhood. She had been mildly chaffed about Jim on occasions, and there was no doubt that in the minds both of her family and of Jim's the expectation of an eventual marriage had never altogether subsided. Nor, strangely enough, had it altogether subsided in hers, although if she had ever asked herself the question as to whether she was in love with Jim in the slightest degree she would have answered it forcibly in the negative. But—there it was, as it is with every young girl—some day she would be married; and it might happen that she would be married to Jim.

"Do you remember," Jim asked her when they had walked the length of the lake and come out in front of the Temple, "how you used to try to teach me to draw here?"

Yes, it was obviously Jim's intention to open up a buried subject, and she was not by any means prepared for that. The sketching lessons had been a shameless subterfuge for obtaining privacy, for Jim had about as much aptitude for the arts as a dromedary, and his libels on the lake and the rhododendrons would have made old Merchant Jack and his landscape gardener turn in their graves.

Cicely laughed. "Have you brought back any sketches from your travels?" she asked.

"No. I've got lots of photographs, though." Jim was always literal.

"Angela and Beatrice paint beautifully," Cicely said. "We are going to make sketches at Blackborough this afternoon. Will you come with us, Jim? We are all going."

"Yes, I'll come," said Jim. "Cicely, are you glad to see me home again?"

"Yes, of course, I'm glad. We have all missed you awfully, Jim."

"You can't think how bucked up I am to think that I need never leave Mountfield again as long as I live. That's what's so jolly about having a place of your own. It's part of you. You feel that, don't you, Cicely?"

"Well, as I haven't got a place of my own, Jim, I don't know that I do."

"When those beastly death duties are paid off," Jim began, but Cicely would not let him finish. "Anyhow," she said, "I should hate to think I was going to stay in one place all my life, however much I liked it. Of course, it is natural that you should feel as you do when you have been travelling for a year. If I ever have the chance of travelling for a year perhaps I shall feel like that about Kencote." She laughed and looked him in the face, blushing a little. "Let us go back and play tennis," she said.

His face fell, and he walked by her side without speaking. Cicely little knew how keen was his disappointment. This was the hour he had been looking forward to every day for the last year, and this the place, with the sun glinting through the young green of beech and ash and lighting up those masses and drifts of brilliant colour everywhere about them. It was true that he had meant to come to no conclusions with the girl he loved with all his heart. The time for that would not be for another year at least, according to the decision he had long since come to. But he had so hungered for her during his long exile, for such it had seemed to him in spite of the various enjoyments and interests he had gained from it, that the thought had grown with him that he would take just a little of the sweetness that a word from her, to show that she was his as he was hers, would give him. She had not spoken the word, and Jim's heart was heavy as he walked back to the garden by her side.

CHAPTER IX

THE QUESTION OF MARRIAGE

"Blackborough Castle?" said the Squire at luncheon. "Well, if you like—but you'll take your tea in the company of Dick, Tom and Harry, and I think you would be more comfortable at home."

"I don't suppose there'll be anybody else there to-day," said Dick, "and the spirit of youth cries aloud for tea on the floor." So it was settled. Mrs. Clinton and Mrs. Birket went in the carriage, Angela rode with Humphrey, and Dick drove the rest of the party, which did not include the Squire, in the brake.

"You look like bean-feasters," said Humphrey, as they drove past him and Angela. "But you need not behave as such," said Miss Bird to the twins, who, one on each side of their uncle, were inclined to be a trifle uproarious.

They had the old keep of the castle pretty well to themselves, spread their cloth on the green turf by the battlements, where centuries ago men-at-arms had tramped the now covered stones, and made merry in true picnic style. There was a footman to clear away, and the party broke up into little groups, and explored the ruins, and wandered in the thick woods which surrounded them.

Jim looked a little wistfully at Cicely as she went away with her arm in that of Beatrice Birket, but made no attempt to join her, and presently allied himself to the storming party which Joan was collecting to rescue Miss Bird, confined in the deepest dungeon.

"Now, Trixie, you have got to tell me all about it," Cicely said, when the two girls were out of hearing of the rest.

"My dear," said Beatrice, laughing, "I told you last night that he had asked me and I had said yes, and that I am very happy."

"Oh, I know. But that was before Angela, and she said we were to have no raptures. I want raptures, please."

"Well, I'm afraid you won't get them. I'm too well drilled. You know, Cicely, I rather envy you being brought up as you were. You're more natural, somehow, than Angela and I."

"Well, I envy *you*; so we're quits. But never mind about that now. Trixie, is Angela just the least bit jealous?"

"No, not a bit," said Beatrice loyally. "But you see she's a year older, and ever so much cleverer, and prettier too."

"She's none of those things except a year older. But she's a dear all the same, and so are you. I don't wonder at anybody falling in love with you. Are you very much in love too?"

"Well, Cicely, I don't mind telling you in strict confidence that I am. But, perhaps, it's in a way you would not sympathise with particularly."

"Tell me in what way, and you'll see."

"Of course George isn't especially good-looking; in fact he isn't good-looking at all, except for his eyes. I used to think I should never love anybody unless he was as handsome as—as, well, Dick is, for instance—that sort of man—you know—smart and well set up, and"—with a laugh—"rather ignorant."

"Dick isn't ignorant," said Cicely indignantly.

"My dear, compared to George he is a monument of ignorance, a pyramid of it; so are most men. It was just that; George is so clever, and he's making such use of his brains too. He is one of the youngest men in parliament, and is in office already. It was looking up to him as a pillar of wisdom, and then finding that he looked to me of all people, to help him on."

"I'm sure you will help him on. I heard some one say in London that many politicians owed a great deal of their success to their wives."

"I don't mean quite in that way. I don't think George is ambitious, though I am for him. He wants to get things done. Father says it is because he is so young. He tells me about everything, and it makes me grateful—you know, I think when you are very grateful, that is being in love."

"You dear thing!" said Cicely, squeezing her arm. "Does Uncle Herbert like him? They are not on the same side in politics, are they?"

"No. But it doesn't seem to matter. It doesn't matter in the least to me. Of course, there *are* things. George is a tremendous churchman, you know, and I have never thought much about religion—not deeply, I mean. But it is a real thing with him, and I'm learning. You see, Cicely, we are rather a different engaged couple from most, although we don't appear so to the world at large. Outside our two selves, George is a coming man, and I am a lucky girl to be making such a match."

"I'm glad you have told me about it all," Cicely said. "It must be splendid to be looking forward to helping your husband in all the good things he is going to do."

"Oh, it is. I am ever so happy. And George is the dearest soul—so kind and thoughtful, for all his cleverness. Cicely, you must meet him."

"I should love to," said Cicely simply. "I never meet anybody interesting down here." Her incipient sense of revolt had died down for the time; she was young enough to live in the present, if the present was agreeable enough, as it was with this mild, unwonted, holiday stir about her. She only felt, vaguely, a little sorry for herself.

"It is lovely," said Beatrice; "but I own I shouldn't care for it all day and every day. It is rather jolly to feel you're in the middle of things."

"Oh, I know it is," said Cicely, laughing. "*I* was in the middle of things in London, and I enjoyed it immensely."

Beatrice's engagement was the subject of another conversation that evening. When the party got back from the picnic, Cicely set out for the dower-house. Nobody had been near the old aunts that day; it was seven o'clock, and there was just time to pay them a short visit.

Mr. Birket was in the hall as she passed through, and she asked him to go with her.

"I should like to pay my respects to those two admirable ladies," he said. "They make me feel that I am nobody, which is occasionally good for the soul of man."

"Ah," said Cicely, as they went across the garden together, "you are a wicked Radical, you see, and you want to disestablish their beloved Church."

"Do I?" said Mr. Birket. "How truly shocking of me. My dear, don't believe everything you hear. I am sure that my chief fault is that I don't possess land. Cicely, how much land must you possess if you really want to hold your head up? Would a hundred acres or so do the trick? I suppose not. Two hundred acres, now! I might run to that if the land was cheap."

"Two hundred acres, I should think, uncle," said Cicely, "with a manor-house, and, say, a home farm. And if you could get the advowson of a living, it would be all to the good."

"Would it? Thank you for telling me. But then I should have to ask the parson to dinner, and we might not get on. And I should have to go to church. I like going to church when I'm not obliged to—that is if they'll preach me a good sermon. I insist upon a good sermon. But if I had to go to set an example—well, I shouldn't go; and then I should get into trouble."

"Yes, I think you would, uncle. You can't live your own life entirely in the country. There are responsibilities."

"Ah, you've thought of that, have you? You do think things over?"

"Yes. I do think things over. There's nothing much else to do."

Mr. Birket cast a side glance at her. The sun striking through the trees of the park flushed translucently the smooth, fair flesh of her cheek and her ungloved hand. In her white frock, moving freely, with the springy grace of a young animal, she attracted the eye. Her head, under her wide hat-brim, was pensive, but she looked up at him with a smile. "If you could bring yourself to it, you know," she began, and broke off. "I mean," she began again, "I think you must either be a man, or—or very young, or not young at all."

Mr. Birket was a man of very quick perception. His face softened a little. "My dear," he said, "when you are very young things are happening every day, when you are a little older anything may happen, and when you are older still happenings don't matter. But you haven't got to the third stage yet."

"No," Cicely said, "I suppose not. Happenings do matter to me; and there aren't enough of them."

The two old ladies received Mr. Birket courteously. He was accidentally allied to the Clintons, and in his own path of life had striven, not without success, to make himself worthy of the alliance. He came to see them, two old ladies who had lived all their long lives in a small country village, had hardly ever been to London, and never out of England, who had been taught to read and write and to add up pounds, shillings and pence, and had never felt the lack of a wider education. He came with his great reputation, his membership of Parliament, his twenty thousand a year of income earned by the exercise of his brain, and a judgeship looming in the near future, and as far as they were concerned he came straight out of the little house on the Bathgate Road, now fitly occupied by a retired chemist. But far be it from them to show a brother of their nephew's wife that he was not welcome among them.

They talked of the weather, of Blackborough Castle, of Jim Graham's return, and of Walter's coming marriage with Muriel.

"Well, that will be the first wedding in the new generation," said Mr. Birket. "But there will be another very soon. Have you heard that my girl, Beatrice, is going to be married?"

The old ladies had not heard this piece of news and expressed their interest. Privately they thought it a little odd that Mr. Birket should talk as if there were any connection between the two events, although, of course, it was true that Walter was of the new Birket generation as well as the new Clinton generation.

"She is rather young," pursued Mr. Birket, "but George Senhouse is a steady fellow as well as a successful one. It is George Senhouse she is going to marry—you have heard of him?"

"Any relation, if I may ask, to Sir George Senhouse of whom we read in the House of Parliament?" asked Aunt Ellen.

"Yes—George Senhouse—that's the man. Not on my side, you know, Miss Clinton, but I'm sure you won't think that a drawback."

Indeed it was not. Mr. Birket was a Liberal, and therefore a deadly foe to the true religion of the Church of England as by compromise established, and to all the societies for raising mankind to a just appreciation of that religion which the Misses Clinton supported. And Sir George Senhouse, a capable and earnest young man, with an historic name, had early devoted his powers to the defence of those things in the outside world which they held dear. It was, indeed, a surprising piece of good fortune for Mr. Birket—and no wonder that he was so evidently pleased.

"I hope your daughter will be strengthened to assist him in all the good work he does," said Aunt Ellen.

"I sincerely hope she will," said Mr. Birket. "The engagement is not announced yet; but I tell *you*, Miss Clinton—and Miss Laura."

"Oh, we should not say a word before the proper time," said Aunt Laura.

When Cicely and Mr. Birket had gone, Aunt Ellen said, "You may take my word for it, sister, that it is owing to the Clinton connection. We have lived a retired life, but I know very well how these things tell."

As Cicely dressed for dinner—it was the first time she had been alone during the day—she thought about Jim, and what he had said to her, or tried to say to her, early in the morning. He had disturbed her mind and given her something that she had to think about. She had told Mr. Birket that she thought things over, and it was true; she had courage in that way. With but little in her education or scope of life to feed it, her brain was active and inquiring. It worked on all matters that came within her ken, and she never shirked a question. She was affectionate, loyal, and naturally light-hearted, but she was critical too, of herself no less than of others. It would have been easy for her, if she had had less character, to put away from her, as she had done for the last five years, the consideration of her relationship to Jim, to have ignored his approach to her, since she had stopped him from coming closer, and to have deferred searching her own mind until he should have approached her again and in such a way that she could no longer have avoided it. But she had locked up the remembrance of the happenings of five years before in a cupboard of her brain, and locked the key on it. If she had thought of it at all, she would have had to think of herself as having made a present to Jim which he had returned to her. And because she could not altogether escape from the memory of it, she had come to look upon herself as a rather foolish and very immature young person in those days, who had not in the least known what she was about when she allowed herself to be made love to.

With regard to Jim her thoughts had been even less definite. His attitude to her had been so entirely brotherly that she had never felt the necessity of asking herself whether he was still keeping his expressed love for her alive, although he would not show it, or whether he, too, thought of their love-making as a piece of rather childish folly, and had put it completely behind him. Beyond the first slight awkwardness of meeting him when he came back from Oxford after his letter to her, she had felt none in his presence, and until this very morning her attitude towards him had been frank and her feelings affectionate. He had made that possible by showing the same attitude and apparently the same feelings.

But what she now had to consider was whether he had actually been so frank towards her as she to him; whether he had not been keeping something back, and, in effect, playing a part. If it were so, their relationship was not as she had thought it, and would have to be adjusted.

She turned her mind to this point first. It would really be rather surprising if Jim had been in love with her all this time and she had not known it. She thought she must have known if it were so, and she rejected the idea. What she could not get away from—it hardly needed stating in her mind—was that he had tentatively made love to her that morning. Or rather—and here she rather congratulated herself on making the distinction, as a process of pure thought—he had seemed to show her that marriage was in his mind, perhaps as a thing already settled between them, although she, for her part, had long since given up thinking of it as a matter to be considered, however loosely, settled. Of course she knew he was fond of her, as she was of him. If he was not in love with her, as once he had been, he might still want to marry her, as the nicest person he could find, and the requisite impulsion might come from his return after a long absence. She would be included in his heightened appreciation of all his home surroundings. These considerations passed through her mind, in no logical sequence of thought, but at various points of her self-questioning, and when she was also thinking further of her own part in what might follow, trying to discover what she wanted and to decide what she should do. The fact that he had opened and would probably open again the subject of their marriage was all that really mattered, and she knew that without thinking.

She knew, too, without thinking, that she did not want to engage herself again to marry Jim, at any rate not yet; and, in fact, she would not do so. What her honesty of mind impelled her to was the discovery of the root from which this femininely instinctive decision had flowered. What were her reasons for not wanting to marry Jim now, or soon; and would they take from her, when examined, that always present but always unstated possibility of some day finding herself living at Mountfield as his wife? She a little dreaded the conclusion, which may have shown that she had already made up her mind; but it was here that an answer had to be found, and she faced it bravely.

She was not ready to marry Jim now, or soon, because in the first place she did not love him—not in that way—and in the second place because she did not love, in any way, what he stood for.

When she said to herself that she did not love Jim her mind recoiled a little. He was such a good sort, so kind, so reliable. It was just as if she had said that she did not love her brothers. It was ungracious, and ungrateful. She did love him. Dear old Jim! And she would be sorry to cause him pain. But, if she did not want him to make love to her—and certainly she didn't—she couldn't possibly love him as a girl ought to love her prospective husband—as Beatrice, for instance, loved her young parliamentarian. That seemed settled. And because she did think things over, and was no longer very young indeed, she saw that the change of circumstances in a girl's life when she was going to be married counted for something, something of the pleasure, something of the excitement. It was so with Beatrice, and with Muriel. They loved the men they were going to marry, but they also got a great deal of satisfaction out of the change in their surroundings, quite apart from that. What sort of change would she have as Jim's wife? She would step straight out of one large house into another, and she would no more be the mistress of Mountfield than she had been of Kencote. So she told herself. For the mistresses of houses like Kencote and Mountfield were really a sort of superior housekeeper, allowed to live with the family, but placed where they were with the sole object of serving their lords and masters, with far less independence than a paid housekeeper, who could take her money and go if she were dissatisfied with her position.

What a prospect! To live out the rest of her life in the subjection against which she had already begun to rebel, in exactly similar surroundings and in exactly the same atmosphere! If she married Jim she would not even have the pleasure of furnishing her own house. It would be Jim's house, and the furniture and all the appurtenances of it were so perfect in Jim's eyes that she knew he would never hear of her altering a thing. She would not be able to rearrange her drawing-room without his permission. That was what it meant to marry a country gentleman of Jim's sort, who disliked "gadding about," and would expect his wife to go through the same dull round, day after day, all her life long, while he amused himself in the way that best suited him.

When she had reached this point, and the end of her toilet together, Cicely suddenly determined that she would *never* marry Jim, and if he pressed her she would tell him so. She didn't want to marry anybody. If only she could get away from Kencote and be a hospital nurse, or something of the sort, that was all she wanted. With this rather unsatisfactory conclusion she cleared her mind, ran downstairs, and found Jim himself alone in the drawing-room.

CHAPTER X

TOWN *versus* COUNTRY

"Hullo!" said Jim. "You're down early."

"I didn't know you were here," said Cicely, and was annoyed at herself, and blushed in consequence.

But whatever conclusion Jim may have drawn from her hurried, rather eager entrance, her denial, and her blush, he only said, "Mother and Muriel are upstairs."

"I wonder why Muriel didn't come to my room," said Cicely. "I think I'll go and find her."

"All right," said Jim, and Cicely went out of the room again.

Jim took up a book from a table, turned over a few leaves, and then threw it down and went to the window, where he stood looking out, with his hands in his pockets.

By and by Mr. Birket came in, and joined him. "Shame to be indoors on an evening like this," he said. "I should like to dine at nine o'clock in the summer."

"What about the servants?" asked Jim.

"Ah, yes," said Mr. Birket. "Is it true you are a Free Trader, Graham?"

"Yes, I am," said Jim, with a shade of defiance.

"So am I," said Mr. Birket.

Jim smiled. "Well, you've got to be in your party," he said.

"Not at all. It isn't a question of party. It's a question of common-sense."

"That's just what I think. I've looked into it with as much intelligence as I'm capable of—they say about here that isn't much—and I can't see why you shouldn't be a Tory as good as any of 'em and still stick to Free Trade."

"Nor can I," said Mr. Birket. "But they won't let you. You had better join us, Graham. Anybody with any dawning of sense must be very uncomfortable where you are."

"I should be a jolly sight more uncomfortable with you," said Jim. "And I've got keen on the Empire since I've been travelling."

"Oh, if you've seen it," said Mr. Birket, somewhat cryptically, and then the door opened, and Mrs. Clinton and Mrs. Birket came in together.

Mrs. Birket was a tall, good-looking woman, who held herself upright, was well dressed and well informed. She had a good manner, and in mixed company never allowed a drop in the conversation. But as she talked well this was not so tiresome as it might have been. She was quoted amongst her circle, which was a wide one, as an excellent hostess, and the tribute was deserved, because, in addition to her conversational aptitude, she had the art of looking after her guests without apparent effort. She had been strict with her daughters, but they were now her companions, and devoted to her. Mrs. Clinton talked to her, perhaps more than to any other woman she knew, and the two were friends, although the circumstances of their lives were wide apart.

The two ladies were followed by the four girls, who came in chattering, and by Mrs. Graham, who, even in evening clothes, with a necklace of diamonds, looked as if she liked dogs. Then came Humphrey, extraordinarily well dressed, his dark hair very sleek; and Dick, very well dressed too, but with less of a town air; and then the Squire, just upon the stroke of eight, obviously looking forward to his dinner.

"Nina, what on earth can have become of Tom and Grace?" he asked when he had greeted Mrs. Graham and Muriel. "No sign of 'em anywhere. We can't wait, you know."

Mrs. Clinton glanced at the ormolu clock, representing Time with a scythe and hour-glass, on the mantelpiece, but said nothing. As it began to chime the door opened and the Rector and Mrs. Beach were announced.

"Grace! Grace!" said the Squire, holding up a warning finger, but smiling affably. "I've never known you run it so fine before."

"My dear Edward," said Mrs. Beach, with her sweet smile, "Tom broke a collar stud. It is one of those little accidents that nobody can foresee and nobody can guard against."

"Except by laying in a stock," said Mrs. Graham.

"Well, my dear Grace, you were just *not* late," said the Squire, "I will forgive you."

So they all went in to dinner amicably, and a very good dinner it was, although there was an entire absence of what the Squire called French fal-lals. English *versus* French cooking was a favourite dinner-table topic of his, and he expatiated on it this evening. "It stands to reason," he said, "that natural food well cooked—of course it must be well cooked, before an open range, and so on—is better than made-up stuff. Now what have we got this evening?" He put on his gold-rimmed glasses and took up a menu-card. A shade of annoyance passed over his face when he discovered that it was written in French. "Who wrote this rubbish?" he asked, looking over his glasses at Mrs. Clinton.

"I did, father," said Cicely, blushing.

"Good for you, Siskin!" broke in Dick. "Very well done. It gives the entertainment an air."

"I helped with the accents," said Angela.

"Well," said the Squire, "I don't like it. As far as I can make out it's a purely English dinner, except, perhaps, the soup, and it ought to be described in English. What's the good of calling roast lamb 'agneau rôti'?" He pronounced it "rotty," with an inflection of scorn. "There's no sense in it. But as I was saying—where are you going to find better food than salmon and roast lamb, new potatoes, asparagus, peas—of course they're forced, but they're English—and so on?" He

99

threw down the card and took off his glasses. "Everything grown on the place except the salmon, which old Humphrey Meadshire sent me."

"You've left out the 'Pêche à la Melba'," said Mrs. Beach. "It is the crowning point of the whole dinner. But I quite agree with you, Edward, you couldn't have a better one anywhere."

"Rather on the heavy side," commented Humphrey.

"Not at all," said Mr. Birket. "The fruits of the earth in due season, or, if possible, a little before it; that's the best dinner any man can have."

"Every country has its own cooking," said Mrs. Birket. "I really think the English is the best if it is well done."

"Which it very seldom is," said Mrs. Graham.

"Of course this is the very best time of all the year for it," said the Rector. "Did you bring back any new curry recipes from India, Jim?"

Jim replied that he had not, and the Squire said, "By the bye, Jim, I see that fellow Mackenzie came home in the *Punjaub*. The papers are full of him this evening. Did you happen to meet him?"

Jim said that he had shared the same cabin, and that Mackenzie had promised to spend a week-end at Mountfield some time or other.

"We are going to make a lion of him in London," said Humphrey. "We haven't had an explorer for a long time. I believe he's shaggy enough to be a great success."

"You must bring him over to dine, Jim," said the Squire. "It's interesting to hear about these fellows who trot all over the world. But heavens, what a life!"

"A very good life, I think," said Mr. Birket. "Not much chance to get moss-grown."

"Now, I'm sure that is a dig at us people who live in the country," said Mrs. Beach. "Because *you* don't get moss-grown, Mr. Birket."

"He would if he lived in the country," said Mrs. Birket. "He would lie on his back all day long and do nothing at all. He has an unequalled power of doing nothing."

"Not at all," said Mr. Birket. "I'm a very hard worker. Cicely caught me at it at six o'clock this morning, didn't you, my dear?"

"You've no responsibilities, Herbert," the Squire broke in. "If you owned land you wouldn't want to lie on your back."

"He is trying to make the land lie on *our* backs," said Dick. "We shan't have any left soon."

"All you Radicals," began the Squire; but Mrs. Beach had something to say: "Mr. Birket, you despise us country folk at the bottom of your heart. I'm sure you do."

"Not at all," said Mr. Birket. "I think you live a peaceful and idyllic existence, and are much to be envied."

"Peaceful!" the Squire snorted. "That's all you Radicals know about it. I assure you we work as hard as anybody, and get less return for it. I wish you'd tell your precious leaders so, Herbert."

"I will," said Mr. Birket.

"What with one thing and another," proceeded the Squire, "the days are gone as soon as they are begun."

"But when they are finished something has always been done," said Mrs. Beach. "That is the difference between a town life and a country life. In London you are immensely busy and tire yourself to death, but you've nothing to show for it."

"Your brains are sharpened up a bit," said Humphrey.

"If you have any," suggested Mrs. Graham.

"Mother, don't be rude," said Muriel.

"The remark had no personal bearing," said Humphrey, with a grin.

"I didn't say so," retorted Mrs. Graham.

"I think it is a matter of temperament," said Mrs. Birket. "Everybody who lives in London likes the country, and everybody who lives in the country likes London—for a change. But if you had to live in one or the other all the year round——"

"I would choose the country," said Mrs. Beach, "and I'm sure you would, Edward."

"Of course I would," said the Squire. "I do live in the country all the year round. I've had enough of London to last me all my life."

"Two for the country," said Dick. "Now we'll go round the table. Mother, where do your tastes lie?"

Mrs. Clinton did not reply for a moment; then she said, "I don't think I should mind which it was if I had my family round me."

"Oh, come now, Nina," said the Squire, "that's no answer. Surely *you* don't want to become a town madam."

"You mustn't bring pressure, Edward," said Mrs. Beach. "We shall have quite enough on our side."

"Mother neutral," said Dick. "Jim?"

"Oh, the country," said Jim.

"Three for the country. Angela?"

"London."

"You must give a reason," said Mrs. Beach.

Angela laughed. "I like music, and plays," she said, "and hearing people talk."

"Well, surely you can hear people talk in the country," said the Squire.

"And such talk!" added Mrs. Graham, at which everybody laughed except the Squire, who saw no humour in the remark.

"Three to one," said Dick. "Aunt Grace, you've had your turn. Now it's mine. I don't want to bury myself yet awhile, but when the time comes I expect I shall shy at London as the governor does. I'm country."

"Why?" asked Angela.

"Oh, because there's more to do. Now then, Beatrice. You're London, I suppose."

"Yes," said Beatrice. "Because there's more to do."

"Good for you! That's four to two. Mrs. Graham!"

"Can you ask?" said that lady. "And I won't give any reasons. I like the country best because I like it best."

"Father is country. Five to two."

"And my reason," said the Squire, "is that every man who doesn't like the country best, when he can get it, isn't a man at all. He's a popinjay."

"Well, at the risk of being called the feminine for popinjay," said Mrs. Birket, with a smile, "I must choose London."

"Oh, but I don't include the women, my dear Emmeline," said the Squire. "And I don't include men like Herbert either, who've got their work to do. I'm thinking of the fellows who peacock about on pavements when they might be doing 'emselves good hunting, or some such pursuit. It's country sport that's good for a man, keeps him strong and healthy; and he sees things in the proper light too. England was a better country than it is now when the House of Commons was chiefly made up of country gentlemen. You didn't hear anything about this preposterous socialism then. I tell you, the country gentlemen are the backbone of England, and your party will find it out when you've turned them out of the country."

"Oh, but we shan't do that," said Mr. Birket. "That would be too dreadful."

"No politics," said Dick. "We're five to three. Tom, you're a country man, I'm sure."

But the Rector was not at all sure that he was. He sometimes thought that people were more interesting than Nature. On the whole, he thought he would choose the town.

"Then I change round," said Mrs. Beach. "Where thou goest, Tom, I will go. Dick, I'm town."

"Then that changes the game. Town's one up. Muriel, be careful."

"Certainly not country," said Muriel. "I've had enough of it. I think the best place to live in is a suburb."

"Melbury Park!" laughed the Squire. "Ha! ha!"

"That's town," said Dick. "Four to six. We yokels are getting worsted."

"I'll come to your rescue," said Humphrey. "I don't want to be cut off with a shilling. Give me a big country house and a season ticket, and I'm with you."

"Five to six then. Now, Siskin, make it all square."

"No," said Cicely. "I hate the country."

"What!" exclaimed the Squire.

"It's so dreadfully dull," said Cicely. "There's nothing in the world to do."

"But this is a revolt!" said Dick.

"Nothing to do!" echoed the Squire, in a voice of impatient censure. "There's everything to do. Don't talk nonsense, Cicely. You have got to live in the country whether you like it or not, so you had better make the best of it."

"Very sound advice," said Mr. Birket. "I follow it myself. It may surprise the company, but I'm for the country. Cows enrapture me, and as for the buttercups, there's no flower like 'em."

"Town has it," said Dick. "Seven to six—a very close match."

When Mr. and Mrs. Birket were alone together that night, Mr. Birket said, "My dear, I think Edward Clinton gets more intolerable every time I see him. I hope I have succeeded in disguising that opinion."

"Perfectly, Herbert," said his wife. "And you must please continue to do so for Nina's sake."

Mr. Birket sighed. "Poor dear Nina!" he said. "She was so bright as a girl. If she hadn't married that dunderhead she'd have been a happy woman. I bet she isn't now. He has crushed every bit of initiative out of her. And I'll tell you what, my dear, he'll crush it out of Cicely if she doesn't get away from these deadly surroundings. Heavens, what a life for a clever girl!"

"Do you think Cicely clever?"

"She doesn't know anything, because they have never let her learn anything. But she thinks for herself, and she's beginning to kick at it all. If she'd had the chances our girls have had, she'd have made use of them. Can't we give her a chance, Emmeline? She's a particularly nice girl. Have her up to London for a month or two. The girls are fond of her—and you're fond of her too, aren't you?"

"Yes, I'm very fond of her," said Mrs. Birket.

"Well—then, why not?"

"Do you think Edward would let her come?"

"My private opinion of Edward would probably surprise him, if he could hear it, but I don't think even he would go so far as to deny his children a pleasure so long as it didn't put him out personally."

"Well, I'll ask, if you like. I should be very glad to have her. But some one might fall in love with her, you know, Herbert. She's very pretty, and there's always the chance."

"And why on earth not? He doesn't want to keep her an old maid, does he?"

"He wants her to marry Jim Graham."

"I thought that was all over years ago."

"As far as she is concerned, perhaps. I'm sure Edward still looks upon it as going to happen some day."

"I don't believe she'll marry Graham, even if he wants her. He's just such another as Edward, with a trifle more sense."

"No, Herbert, he is quite different. I like him. I think it would be a good thing for Cicely to marry him."

"She ought to have the chance of seeing other fellows. Then, if she likes to embark afresh on a vegetable existence, it will be her own choice. Of course, you needn't vegetate, living in the country, but the wife of Jim Graham probably would. Give her her chance, anyway."

But this particular chance was denied to Cicely. The Squire wouldn't hear of it. "My dear Emmeline," he said, "it is very kind of you — very kind of you indeed. But she'd only get unsettled. She's got maggots in her head already. I hope some day to see her married to a country gentleman, like her mother before her. Though I say it, no women could be better off. Until the time comes, it's best for Cicely to stay at home."

"Idiot!" said Mr. Birket, when the decision was conveyed to him. "I was mistaken in him. I think now he would be capable of any infamy. Don't tell Cicely, Emmeline."

But the Squire told her, and rebuked her because the invitation had been offered. "What you have to do," he said, "is to make yourself happy at home. Heaven knows there's enough to make you so. You have everything that a girl can want. For goodness' sake be contented with it, and don't always want to be gadding about."

Cicely felt too sore to answer him, and retired as soon as his homily was over. In the afternoon — it was on Sunday — she went for a walk with her uncle. He did not express himself to her as he had done to

Mrs. Birket, but gave her the impression that he thought her father's refusal unfortunate, but not unreasonable, smiling inwardly to himself as he did so.

"I should have loved to come, you know, Uncle Herbert," she said.

"And we should have loved to have you, my dear," he said. "But, after all, Kencote is a very jolly place, and it's your own fault if you're bored in it. Nobody ought to be bored anywhere. I never am."

"Well then, please tell me what to do with myself."

"What do you do, as it is?"

"I read a little, and try to paint, and — — "

"Then read more, and try to paint better. Effort, my dear, — that's the secret of life. Give yourself some trouble."

He gave her more advice as they walked and talked together, and she listened to him submissively, and became interested in what he said to her.

"I should like to make myself useful in some way," she said. "I don't want to spend all my life amusing myself or even improving myself."

"Oh, improving yourself! That's not quite the way to put it. Expressing yourself—that's what you want to do—what everybody ought to do. And look here, my dear, when you say you want to make yourself useful—I suppose you mean hospital nursing or something of that sort, eh?"

Cicely laughed. "I have thought of that," she said.

"Well then, don't think of it any more. It's not the way—at least not for you. You make yourself useful when you make yourself loved. That's a woman's sphere, and I don't care if all the suffragettes in the country hear me say it. A woman ought to be loved in one way or another by everybody around her; and if she is, then she's doing more in the world than ninety-nine men out of a hundred. Men want opportunities. Every woman has them already. Somebody is dependent on her, and the more the better for her—and the world. What would your old aunts do without you, or your mother, or indeed anybody in the place? They would all miss you, every one. Don't run away with the idea you're not wanted. Of course you're wanted. *We* want you, only we can't have you because they want you here."

"You give me a better conceit of myself," she said gratefully.

"Keep it, my dear, keep it," said Mr. Birket. "The better conceit we have of ourselves the more we accomplish. Now I think we'd better be turning back."

CHAPTER XI

A WEDDING

The London newspapers devoted small space, if any, to the wedding of Walter Clinton, Esq., M.D., third son of Edward Clinton, Esq., of Kencote, Meadshire, and Muriel, only daughter of the late Alexander Graham, Esq., and the Honourable Mrs. Graham of Mountfield, Meadshire, but the *Bathgate Herald and South Meadshire Advertiser* devoted two of its valuable columns to a description of the ceremony, a list of the distinguished guests present, and a catalogue of the wedding presents. No name that could possibly be included was left out. The confectioner who supplied the cake, the head gardeners at Kencote and Mountfield who—obligingly—supplied the floral decorations; the organist who presided, as organists always do, at the organ, and gave a rendering, a very inefficient one, of Mendelssohn's Wedding March; the schoolmaster who looked after the children who strewed flowers on the churchyard path; the coachman who drove the happy pair to the station; the station-master who arranged for them a little salvo of his own, which took the form of fog-signals, as the train came in—they were all there, and there was not an error in their initials or in the spelling of their names, although there were a good many in the list of distinguished guests, and still more in the long catalogue of presents.

There was a large number of presents, more than enough to open the eyes of the readers of the *Melbury Park Chronicle and North London Intelligencer*, which, by courtesy of its contemporary, printed the account in full, except for the omission of local names, and in *minion* instead of *bourgeois* type. Some of the presents were valuable and others were expensively useless, and the opinion expressed in Melbury Park was that the doctor couldn't possibly find room for them all in his house and would have to take a bigger one. Melbury Park opened its eyes still wider at the number of titles represented amongst the donors, for the Clintons, as has been said, had frequently married blood, and many of their relations were represented, Walter had been popular with his school and college friends, and on Muriel's side the Conroys and their numerous connections had come down handsomely in the way of Georgian sugar-sifters, gold and enamelled umbrella tops, silver bowls and baskets and bridge boxes, writing-sets, and candlesticks, and other things more or less adapted to the use of a doctor's wife in a rather poor suburb of London.

The wedding, if not "a scene of indescribable beauty, fashion and profusion," as the Bathgate reporter, scenting promotion, described it, was a very pretty one. The two big houses produced for the occasion a sufficient number of guests, and the surrounding country of neighbours, to fill Mountfield church with a congregation that was certainly well dressed, if not noticeably reverent. The bride looked beautiful, if a trifle pale, under her veil and orange blossoms, and the bridegroom as gallant as could be expected under the circumstances. There were six bridesmaids, the Honourable Olivia and Martha Conroy and Miss Evelyn Graham, cousins of the bride, and the Misses Cicely, Joan, and Nancy Clinton, sisters of the bridegroom, who were attired—but why go further into these details, which were so fully gone into in the journals already mentioned? Suffice it to say that the old starling, in a new gown and the first *toque* she had ever worn, wept tears of pride at the appearance of her pupils, and told them afterwards, most unwisely, that the Misses Olivia and Martha Conroy could not hold a candle to them in respect of good looks.

The twins—there is no gainsaying it—did look angelic, with their blue eyes and fair hair, and the Misses Conroy, who were of the same sort of age, were not so well favoured by nature; but that was no reason why Joan should have told them that they were a plain-headed pair, and Nancy that they had spoilt the whole show, when some trifling dispute arose between them at the close of a long day's enthusiastic friendship. The Misses Conroy, though deficient in beauty, were not slow in retort, and but for the fine clothes in which all four were attired, it is to be feared that the quarrel would have been pushed to extremes. It was a regrettable incident, but fortunately took place in a retired corner of the grounds, and stopped short of actual violence.

Jim Graham gave his sister away, and Dick acted as best man to his brother, piloting him through the various pitfalls that befall a bridegroom with the same cool efficiency as he displayed in all emergencies, great or small. It was this characteristic which chiefly differentiated him from his father, who may have been efficient, but was not cool.

Jim Graham's eyes often rested on Cicely during the wedding ceremony. She was by far the prettiest of the bridesmaids, and it was little wonder if his thoughts went forward to the time when he and she would be playing the leading part in a similar ceremony. But there was some uneasiness mixed with these anticipations. Cicely was not quite the same towards him as she had been before his journey, although since that morning by the lake he had made no attempt to depart from the brotherly intimacy which he had told himself was the best he had a right to until he could claim her for his own. She had never seemed quite at her ease with him, and he was beginning to follow up the idea, in his slow, tenacious way, that his wooing, when he should be ready for it, would have to be done all over again—that it might not be easy to claim her for his own. And, of course, that made him desire her all the more, and added in his eyes to her grace and girlish beauty.

Afterwards, in the house and on the lawn, where a band played and a tent for refreshments had been put up, he talked to her whenever he could and did his best to keep a cheerful, careless air, succeeding so well that no one observing him would have guessed that he had some difficulty in doing so. Except Cicely; she felt the constraint. She felt that he was in process of marking the difference in her attitude towards him, and was impatient of the slow, ruminating observation of which she would be the object. As long as he was natural with her she would do her best to keep up the same friendly and even affectionate relations which had existed between them up to a year ago, but she could not help a slight spice of irritation creeping into her manner in face of that subtle change behind his ordinary address. She was trying to clear up her thoughts on many matters, and Jim was the last person in the world to help her. She wanted to be left alone. If only he would do that! It was the only possible way by which he could gain the end which, even now, she was not quite sure that she would refuse him in the long-run.

"Well, you needn't be snappy," Jim said to her, with a good-humoured smile on his placid face when he had asked her for further details of her visit to London.

She made herself smile in return. "Was I?" she said. "I didn't mean to be; but I have been home nearly a month now, and I'm rather tired of talking about London."

"All right," replied Jim. "I agree that this is a better place. Come and have a look at the nags. There has been such a bustle that I haven't been near them to-day."

But Cicely refused to go and look at the nags. Nags were rather a sore point with her, and the constant inspection and weighing of the qualities of those at Kencote was enough for her without the addition of the stables at Mountfield. So they went back from the rose-garden where they were standing to join the crowd on the lawn.

Aunt Ellen and Aunt Laura sat in the shade of a big cedar and held a small reception. During their long lives they had been of scarcely any account in the ebb and flow of Clinton affairs, but the tide of years had shelved them on a little rock of importance, and they were paid court to because of their age. Old Lord Meadshire was the only other member of their generation left alive. He was their first cousin. His mother had been the youngest of Merchant Jack's five daughters. He had never failed to pay them courteous attention whenever he had been at Kencote, and he was talking to them now, as Cicely joined them, of the days when they were all young together. The two old ladies had quite come to believe that they and their cousin Humphrey had spent a large part of their childhood together, although he was fifteen years younger than Aunt Ellen, and his visits to Kencote during his youth had been extremely rare. Colonel Thomas had been too busy with his chosen pursuits to have much time for interchange of social duties, proclaimed himself a fish out of water, and behaved like one, whenever he went to the house of his youngest sister, and had little to offer a lady of high social importance and tastes in a visit to his own.

"Well, my dear," Lord Meadshire said to Cicely, as she approached, "I was reminding your aunts of the time when we used to drive over from Melford to Kencote in a carriage with postillions. Very few railways in those days. We old people like to put our heads together and talk about the past sometimes. I recollect my grandfather—*our* grandfather," and he bowed to the two old ladies—"Merchant Jack they used to call him here, because he had made his money in the city as younger sons used to do in those days, and are beginning to do again now, but they don't go into trade as they did then; and he was born in the year of the Battle of Culloden. That takes you back— what?"

"I recollect," said Aunt Ellen in a slow, careful voice, "when our Uncle John used to come down to Kencote by the four-horse coach, and post from Bathgate."

"Ah," said Lord Meadshire sympathetically, "I never saw my Uncle John, to my knowledge, though he left me a hundred pounds in his will. I recollect I spent it on a tie-pin. I was an extravagant young dog in those days, my dear. You wouldn't have suspected me of spending a hundred pounds on a tie-pin, would you?"

"Uncle John was very kind to us," said Aunt Laura. "There were six of us, but he never came to the house without bringing us each a little present."

"He was always dressed in black and wore a tie-wig," said Aunt Ellen. "Our dear father and he were very dissimilar, but our father relied on his judgment. It was he who advised him to send Edward to Bathgate Grammar School."

"He would take a kind interest in our pursuits," said Aunt Laura, "and would always walk with us and spend part of the day with us, however occupied he might be with our father."

"Edward was very high-spirited as a child," said Aunt Ellen, "and our dear father did not sufficiently realise that if he encouraged him to break away from his lessons, which we all took it in turns to give him, it made him difficult to teach."

"And when Uncle John went away in the morning he gave us each one a present of five new sovereigns wrapped in tissue paper," said Aunt Laura, "and he would say, 'That is to buy fal-lals with.'"

"So our Uncle John and our Uncle Giles, the Rector, persuaded our father to send Edward to Bathgate Grammar School, where he remained until he went to Eton, riding over there on Monday morning and returning home on Saturday," concluded Aunt Ellen.

Lord Meadshire took his leave of the old ladies, and Aunt Ellen said, "I am afraid that our cousin Humphrey is ageing. We do not see him as much as we used to do. He was very frequently at Kencote in the old days, and we were always pleased to see him. With the exception of your dear father, there is no man for whom I have a greater regard."

"He is a darling," said Cicely. "He is as kind as possible to everybody. Would you like me to get you anything, Aunt Ellen? I must go to Muriel now."

"No thank you, my dear," said Aunt Ellen. "Your Aunt Laura and I have had sufficient. We will just rest quietly in the shade, and I have no doubt that some others of our kind friends will come and talk to us."

It was getting towards the time for the bride and bridegroom to depart for their honeymoon, which they were to spend in Norway. Walter had had no holiday of any sort that year and had thought the desire for solitude incumbent on newly married couples might reasonably be conjoined with the desire for catching salmon; and Muriel had agreed with him.

The men were beginning to show a tendency to separate from the ladies. The Rector of Kencote and the Vicar of Melbury Park, a new friend of Walter's who happened, as the Squire put it, to be a gentleman, were talking together by the buffet under the tent. The Vicar, who was thin and elderly, and looked jaded, was saying that the refreshment to mind and spirit, to say nothing of body, which came from living close to Nature was incalculable, and the Rector was agreeing with him, mentally reserving his opinion that the real refreshment to mind and spirit, to say nothing of body, was to be found, if a man were strong enough to find it, in hard and never-ending work in a town.

At the other end of the buffet Dick and Humphrey and Jim Graham were eating sandwiches and drinking champagne. They were talking of fishing, with reference to Walter's approaching visit to a water which all four of them had once fished together.

"It is rather sad, you know," said Humphrey. "Remember what a good time we had, Jim? It'll never happen again. I hate a wedding. It'll be you next."

Jim looked at him inscrutably. "Or Dick," he said.

Dick put down his glass. "I'm not a starter," he said. "I must go and see that Walter doesn't forget to change his tie."

The Squire and Mrs. Clinton and Lord Conroy were in a group together on the lawn. Lord Conroy, bluff and bucolic, was telling Mrs. Clinton about his own marriage, fifteen years before. "Never thought I should do it," he said, "never. There was I, forty and more, but sound, Mrs. Clinton, mind you, sound as a bell, though no beauty—ha, ha! And there was my lady, twenty odd, as pretty as paint, and with half the young fellows in London after her. I said, 'Come now, will you have me? Will you or won't you? I'm not going near London,' I said, 'not once in five years, and I don't like soup. Otherwise you'll have your own way and you'll find me easy to get on with.' She took me, and here we are now. I don't believe there's a happier couple in England. I believe in marrying, myself. Wish I'd done it when I was a young fellow, only then I shouldn't have got my lady. I'm very glad to see my niece married to such a nice young fellow as your son—very glad indeed; and my sister tells me there's likely to be another wedding in both families before long—eh? Well, I mustn't be too inquisitive; but Jim's a nice young fellow too, a very nice young fellow, though as obstinate as the devil about this Radical kink he's got in his brain."

"Oh, he'll get over that," said the Squire. "It isn't sense, you know, going against the best brains in the country; I tell him we're not *all* likely to be wrong. And he's got a stake, too. It don't do to play old Harry with politics when you've got a stake."

"Gad, no," assented Lord Conroy. "We've got to stand together. I'm afraid your brother's against us, though, eh, Mrs. Clinton?"

"Oh, Herbert!" said the Squire. "He's a lawyer, and they can always make white black if it suits 'em."

Mrs. Clinton flushed faintly, and Lord Conroy said, "He's a very rising man, though, and not so advanced as some. He told me a story just now about a judge and one of those Suffragettes, as they call 'em, and I haven't heard such a good story for many a long day." And Lord Conroy laughed very heartily, but did not repeat the story.

The carriage drove round to the door, the coachman and the horses adorned with white favours, and the guests drifted towards the house and into the big hall. Walter and Dick came down the staircase, and Muriel and her mother and Cicely followed immediately afterwards. Muriel's eyes were wet, but she was merry and talkative, and Mrs. Graham was more brusque in her speech than usual, but very talkative too. Every one crowded round them, and Walter had some difficulty in leading his bride through the throng. There was laughter and hand-shaking and a general polite uproar. At last they got themselves into the carriage, which rolled away with them to their new life. It was really Joan and Nancy who had conceived the idea of tying a pair of goloshes on behind, but the Misses Conroy had provided them, one apiece, and claimed an equal share in the suggestion. It was arising out of this that their quarrel presently ensued, and they might not have quarrelled at all had not Miss Bird told the twins in the hearing of their friends that where they had learned such a vulgar notion passed her comprehension. It was really a dispute that did all four young ladies very great credit.

CHAPTER XII

FOOD AND RAIMENT

The Rector gave out his text, "Is not the life more than meat and the body more than raiment?" and proceeded to read his homily in a monotonous, sweet-toned voice which had all the good effects of a sleeping-draught and none of the bad ones.

Kencote church was old, and untouched by modern restoration or Catholic zeal. The great west door was open, and framed a bright picture of trees and grass and cloudless sky. The hot sunshine of an August morning shone through the traceried windows in the nave, and threw a square of bright colour from the little memorial window in the chancel on to the wide, uneven stone pavement. But the church was cool, with the coolness of ancient, stone-built places, which have resisted for centuries the attacks of sun and storm alike, and gained something of the tranquil insensibility of age.

The congregation was penned, for the most part, in high pews. When they stood up to sing they presented a few score of heads and shoulders above the squares and oblongs of dark woodwork; when they sat or knelt the nave seemed to be suddenly emptied of worshippers, and the drone of the responses mounting up to the raftered roof had a curious effect, and seemed to be the voice of the old church itself, paying its tribute to the unseen mysteries of the long ages of faith.

On the north side of the chancel, which was two steps higher than the nave, was the Squire's pew. Its occupants were shielded from the gaze of those in the body of the church by a faded red curtain hung on an iron rail, but the Squire always drew it boldly aside during the exhortation and surveyed the congregation, the greater part of which was dependent on him for a livelihood and attended church as an undergraduate "keeps chapels," for fear of unpleasant consequences.

The Squire's pew occupied the whole of the space usually devoted to the organ and the vestry in modern built churches, and had a separate entrance from the churchyard. It had a wooden floor, upon which was a worn blue carpet sprinkled with yellow fleurs de lis. The big hassocks and the seat that ran along the north wall were covered with the same material. In front of the fixed bench was a row of heavy chairs; in the wall opposite to the curtain was a fireplace. Mrs. Clinton occupied the chair nearest to the fire, which was always lit early on Sunday morning in the winter, but owing partly to the out-of-date fashion of the grate and partly to the height and extent of the church, gave no more heat than was comfortable to those immediately within its radius, and none at all to those a little way from it. The Squire himself remained outside its grateful influence. His large, healthy frame, well covered with flesh, enabled him to dispense with artificial warmth during his hour and a half's occupation of the family pew, and also to do his duty by using the last of the row of chairs and hassocks, and so to command the opportunities afforded by the red curtain.

On the stone walls above the wainscoting were hung great hatchments, the canvas of some fraying away from the black quadrangular frames after a lapse of years, and none of them very recently hung there. The front of the pew was open to the chancel, and commanded a full view of the reading-desk and a side glimpse of the pulpit through the bars of the carved, rather battered rood-screen. Flanked by the reading-desk on one side and the harmonium on the other were the benches occupied by the school-children who formed the choir, and behind them were other benches devoted to the use of the Squire's household, whose devotions were screened from the gaze of the common worshippers by no curtain, and who, therefore—maids, middle-aged women, and spruce men-servants— provided a source of interested rumination when heads were raised above the wooden partitions, and bonnets, mantles, and broadcloth could be examined, and perhaps envied, at leisure.

Cicely had played the Rector up into the pulpit with the last verse of a hymn, had found the place from which she would presently play him down again with the tune of another, had propped the open book on the desk of the harmonium, and had then slid noiselessly into a chair on a line with the front choir bench, where she now sat with her hands in her lap, facing the members of her assembled family, sometimes looking down at the memorial brass of Sir

Richard Clinton, knight, obiit 1445, which was let into the pavement at her feet, sometimes, through the open doors of the rood screen, to where that bright picture of sunlit green shone out of the surrounding gloom at the end of the aisle.

"Is not the life more than meat and the body than raiment?" The text had been given out twice and carefully indexed each time. The Squire had fitted his gold-rimmed glasses on to his nose and tracked down the passage in his big Bible. Having satisfied himself that the words announced were identical with the words printed, he had put the Bible on the narrow shelf in front of him and closed his eyes. His first nod had followed, as usual, about three minutes after the commencement of the sermon. He had then opened his eyes wide, met the fascinated gaze of a small singing-girl opposite to him, glared at her, and, having reduced her to a state of cataleptic terror, pushed aside the red curtain and transferred his glare to the body of the church. The bald head of a respectable farmer and the bonnet of his wife, which were all he could see of the congregation at the moment, assured him that all was well. He drew the curtain again and went comfortably to sleep without further ado.

Mrs. Clinton, at the other end of the row, sat quite still, with no more evidence of mental effort on her comely, middle-aged face than was necessary for the due reception of the Rector's ideas, and that was very little. Joan and Nancy sat one on either side of Miss Bird, Joan next to her mother. They looked about everywhere but at the preacher, and bided with what patience they possessed the end of the discourse, aided thereto by a watchful eye and an occasional admonitory peck from the old starling. Dick had come in late and settled himself upon the seat behind the row of chairs. Upon the commencement of the sermon he had put his back against the partition supporting the curtain, and his long legs up on the bench in front of him, and by the look on his lean, sunburnt face was apparently resting his brain as well as his body.

"Is not the life more than meat and the body than raiment?" The technique of the Rector's sermons involved the repetition of his text at stated intervals. Cicely thought, as the words fell on her ears for the third or fourth time, that she could have supplied a meaning to them which had escaped the preacher. Food and raiment! That represented all the things amongst which she had been brought up, the large, comfortable rooms in the big house, the abundant, punctual meals, the tribe of servants, the clothes and the trinkets, the gardens and stables, well-stocked and well-filled, the home farm, kept up to supply the needs of the large household, everything that came to the children of a well-to-do country gentleman as a matter of course, and made life easy—but oh, how dull!

No one seeing her sitting there quietly, her slender, ungloved hands lying in her lap, prettily dressed in a cool summer frock and a shady, flower-trimmed hat, with the jewelled chains and bracelets and brooches of a rich man's daughter rousing the admiring envy of the school-children, whose weekly excitement it was to count them up—nobody would have thought that under the plaited tresses of this young girl's shapely head was a brain seething in revolt, or that the silken laces of her bodice muffled the beatings of a heart suffocated by the luxurious dulness of a life which she now told herself had become insupportable. Cicely had thought a great deal since her visit to London and Muriel's wedding, and had arrived at this conclusion—that she was suffocating, and that her life was insupportable.

She raised her eyes and glanced at her father, wrapped in the pleasant slumber that overtakes healthy, out-of-door men when they are forced for a time into unwonted quiescence, and at her brother, calm and self-satisfied, dressed with a correct elaboration that was only unobtrusive because it was so expensively perfect. The men of the family—everything was done to bring them honour and gratification. They had everything they wanted and did what they would. It was to them that tribute and obedience were paid by every one around them, including their own womenfolk.

She looked at her two young sisters. They were happy enough in their free and healthy childhood; so had she been at their age, when the spacious house and the big gardens, the stables and the farm and the open country had provided everything she needed for her amusement. But even then there had been the irksome restraint exercised by "the old starling" and the fixed rules of the house to spoil her freedom, while her brothers had been away at Eton, or at Oxford or Cambridge, trying their wings and preparing for the unfettered delights of well-endowed manhood.

She looked at her mother, placid and motionless. Her mother was something of an enigma, even to her, for to those who knew her well she always seemed to be hiding something, something in her character, which yet made its mark in spite of the subjection in which she lived. Cicely loved her mother, but she thought of her now with the least little shade of contempt, which she would have been shocked to recognise as such. Why had she been content to bring all the hopes and ambitions that must have stirred her girlhood thus into subjection? What was the range of her life now? Ruling her large house with a single eye to the convenience of her lord and master, liable to be scolded before her children or her household if anything went wrong; blamed if the faults of any one of the small army of servants reached the point at which it disturbed his ease; driving out in her fine carriage to pay dull calls on dull neighbours; looking after the comfort of ungrateful villagers; going to church; going to dinner-parties; reading; sewing; gardening under pain of the head gardener's displeasure, which was always backed up by the Squire if complaint was brought to him that she had braved it; getting up in the morning and going to bed at night, at stated hours without variation; never leaving her cage of confined luxury, except when it suited his convenience that she should leave it with him. She was nothing but a slave to his whims and prejudices, and so were all the women of the family, slaves to wait upon and defer humbly and obediently to their mankind.

"Is not the life more than meat and the body than raiment?" It was the men who enjoyed the life, and the meat and raiment as well. While the women vegetated at home, they went out into the world. It was true that they were always pleased to come back again, and no wonder, when everything was there that could minister to their amusement. It was quite different for her, living at home all the year round. She was quite sick of it. Why was not her father like other men of his wealth and lineage, who had their country houses and their country sports, but did not spend the whole year over them? Daughters of men of far less established position than the Squire went to London, went abroad, visited constantly at other country houses, and saw many guests in their own houses. Her own brothers did all these things, except the last. They seldom brought their friends to Kencote, she supposed because it was not like other big country houses, at any rate not like the houses at which they stayed. It was old-fashioned, not amusing enough; shooting parties were nearly always made up from amongst neighbours, and if any one stayed in the house to shoot, or for the few winter balls, it was nearly always a relation, or at best a party of relations. And the very few visits Cicely had ever paid had been to the houses of relations, some of them amusing, others not at all so.

She was now rather ashamed of her diatribe to Muriel Graham about her London visit. She must have given Muriel the impression that what she hungered for was smart society. She remembered that she had compared the ball at the house of her aunt, Mrs. Birket, unfavourably with those at other houses at which she had danced, and blushed and fidgeted with her fingers when she thought of this. She liked staying with Mrs. Birket better than with any other of her relations, and she was still sore at her father's refusal to allow her to spend some months with her. She met clever, interesting people there, she was always made much of, and she admired and envied her cousins. They had travelled, they heard music, saw plays and pictures, read books; and they could talk upon all these subjects, as well as upon politics and upon what was going on in the big world that really mattered—not superficially, but as if they were the things that interested them most, as she knew they were. It was that kind of life she really longed for; she had only got her thoughts a little muddled in London because she had been rather humiliated in feeling herself a stranger where her brothers were so much at home. When she saw Muriel again she must put herself right there. Muriel would understand her. Muriel had cut herself adrift from the well-fed stagnation of country life and rejoiced to be the partner of a man who was doing something in the world. Life was more than food to her and the body than raiment. Cicely wished that such a chance had come to her.

But the Rector had repeated his text for the last time, and was drawing to the end of his discourse. She must slip back to her seat at the harmonium, and defer the consideration of her own hardships until later.

The congregation aroused itself and stood up upon the stroke of the word "now"; and, whilst the last hymn was being given out and played over, the Squire started on a collecting tour with the wooden, baize-lined plate which he drew from beneath his chair. The coppers clinked one by one upon the silver already deposited by himself and his family, and he closely scrutinised the successive offerings. His heels rang out manfully upon the worn pavement beneath which his ancestors were sleeping, as he strode up the chancel and handed the alms to the Rector. He was refreshed by his light slumber, his weekly duty was coming to an end, and he would soon be out in the open air inspecting his stables and looking forward to his luncheon. He sang the last verses of the hymn lustily, his glasses on his nose, a fine figure of a man, quite satisfied with himself and the state in life to which he had been called.

The congregation filed out of church into the bright sunshine. Dick, with Joan on one side of him and Nancy on the other, set out at a smart pace across the park, bound for the stables and the home farm. Cicely walked with the old starling, who lifted her flounced skirt over her square-toed kid boots, as one who expected to find dew where she found grass, even in the hot August noonday. The Squire and Mrs. Clinton brought up the rear, and the men and maids straggled along a footpath which diverged to another quarter of the house.

Cicely left the rest of the family to the time-honoured inspection of horses and live stock, always undertaken, summer and winter, after church on Sunday morning, as a permissible recreation on a day otherwise devoted to sedentary pursuits. It was one of the tiresome routine habits of her life, and she was sick of routine. She dawdled in her bedroom, a room at least twenty feet square, with two big windows overlooking the garden and the park and the church tower rising from amongst its trees, until the gong sounded, when she hurried downstairs and took her seat at the luncheon table on the right of her father.

The sweets and a big cake were on the table, of which the appointments were a mixture of massive silver plate and inexpensive glass and china. The servants handed round the first hot dish, placed a cold uncut sirloin of beef in front of the Squire and vegetable dishes on the sideboard, and then left the room. After that it was every one help yourself. This was the invariable arrangement of luncheon on Sundays, and allowing for the difference of the seasons the viands were always the same. If anybody staying in the house liked to turn up their noses at such Sunday fare—one hot *entrée*, cold beef, fruit tarts and milk puddings, a ripe cheese and a good bottle of wine, why they needn't come again. But very few people did stay in the house, as has been said, and none of those who did had ever been known to object. There were no week-end parties, no traffic of mere acquaintances using the house like an hotel and amusing themselves with no reference to their host or hostess. The Squire was hospitable in an old-fashioned way, liked to see his friends around him and gave them of his best. But they must be friends, and they must conform to the usages of the house.

The talk over the luncheon table began with the perennial topic of the breeding of partridges and pheasants, and was carried on between the Squire and Dick, while the women kept submissive silence in the face of important matters with which they had no concern. Then it took a more general turn, and drifted into a reminiscence of the conversation that had taken place over the dinner table the night before. Mrs. Graham and Jim had dined at Kencote and brought Ronald Mackenzie with them, who had arrived the evening before on his promised week-end visit.

Humphrey's prophecy had come true. Mackenzie had been the lion of the London season, and now that London was empty might have taken his choice of country houses for a week-end visit from whatever county he pleased. His visit was something of an honour, and was even chronicled in the newspapers, which had not yet lost interest in his movements. He was a star of considerable magnitude, liable to wane, of course, but never to sink quite into obscurity, and just now a planet within everybody's ken.

It was characteristic of the Clinton point of view that the parentage of this man, whose sole title to fame arose from the things that he had done, should be discussed. Dick knew all about him. He did not belong to any particular family of Mackenzies. He was the son of a Scots peasant, and was said to have tramped to London at the age of sixteen, and to have taken forcible shipment as a stowaway in the Black-Lyell Arctic Expedition; and afterwards to have climbed to the leadership of expeditions of his own with incredible rapidity. He had never made any secret of his lowly origin, and was even said to be proud of it. The Squire approved heartily of this.

It was also characteristic of the Squire that a man who had done big things and got himself talked about should be accepted frankly as an equal, and, outside the sphere of clanship, even as a superior. A great musician would have been treated in the same way, or a great painter, or even a great scholar. For the Squire belonged to the class of all others the most prejudiced and at the same time the most easily led, when its slow-moving imagination is once touched—a class which believes itself divinely appointed to rule, but will give political adherence and almost passionate personal loyalty to men whom in the type it most dislikes, its members following one another like sheep when their first instinctive mistrust has been overcome. Mackenzie was one of the most talked of men in England at this moment. It was a matter of congratulation that Jim had caught him for a two-days' visit, though Jim's catch had involved no more skill than was needed to answer an unexpected note from Mackenzie announcing his arrival on Friday afternoon. The Clintons had dined at Mountfield on Friday night, the Grahams and Mackenzie had dined at Kencote on Saturday, and it had been arranged that Jim and his guest should drive over this afternoon and stay to dine again.

When luncheon was over the Squire retired into the library with the *Spectator*, which it was known he would not read, Dick went into the smoking-room, Mrs. Clinton and Miss Bird upstairs, and the twins straight into the garden, where Cicely presently followed them with a book. She settled herself in a basket chair under a great lime tree on the lawn, and leaving her book lying unopened on her lap, gave herself over to further reverie.

Perhaps the sudden descent of this man from a strange world into the placid waters of her life had something to do with the surging up of her discontent, for she had not been so discontented since the Birkets' visit two months before, having followed out to some extent her uncle's advice and found life quite supportable in consequence. She knew she had waited for Mackenzie's name to be mentioned at luncheon and had blushed when she heard it, only, fortunately, nobody had seen her, not even the sharp-eyed twins. She would have resented it intensely if her interest and her blush had been noticed, and put down to personal attraction. It was not that at all. She rather disliked the man, with his keen, hawklike face, his piercing eyes, and his direct, unvarnished speech. He was the sort of man of whom a woman might have reason to be afraid if she were, by unaccountable mischance, attracted by him, and he by her. He would dominate her and she would be at least as much of a chattel as in the hands of a male Clinton. It was what he stood for that interested her, and she could not help comparing his life with that of her father and her brothers, or of Jim Graham, much to the disadvantage of her own kind.

Her resentment, if it deserved that name, had fixed itself upon her father and brothers, and Jim shared in it. He was just the same as they were, making the little work incumbent on him as easy as possible and spending the best part of his life in the pursuits he liked best. She had come to the conclusion that there was no place for her in such a life as that. When Jim proposed to her, as she felt sure he would do when he was ready, she would refuse him. She felt now that she really could not go through with it, and her determination to refuse to marry Jim rose up in her mind and fixed itself as she sat in her chair under the tree. If he had been a poor man, with a profession to work at, she would have married him and found her happiness in helping him on. She wanted the life. The food and the raiment were nothing to her, either at Kencote or Mountfield.

CHAPTER XIII

RONALD MACKENZIE

Cicely rose from her seat and strolled across the lawn, through an iron gate and a flower-garden, and on to another lawn verging on the shrubberies. Joan and Nancy were employed here in putting tennis balls into a hole with the handles of walking sticks. Cicely rebuked them, for, according to his lights, the Squire was a strict Sabbatarian.

"Darling!" expostulated Joan, in a voice of pleading, "we are not using putters and golf balls. There *can't* be any harm in this."

Cicely did not think there was, and passed on through the shrubbery walk to where a raised path skirting a stone wall afforded a view of the road along which Jim and Ronald Mackenzie would presently be driving.

She hardly knew why she had come. It was certainly not to watch for Jim. And if there was any idea in her mind of catching a glimpse of Ronald Mackenzie, herself unobserved by him, so that she might by a flash gain some insight into the character of a man who had interested her, she was probably giving herself useless trouble, for it was not yet three o'clock and the two men were not likely to arrive for another half-hour or more.

But she had no sooner taken her stand by the stone wall and looked down at the road from under the shade of the great beech which overhung it, than Jim's dog-cart swung round the corner, and Ronald Mackenzie, sitting by his side, had looked up and sent a glance from his bold dark eyes right through her. She had not had time to draw back; she had been fairly caught. She drew back now, and coloured with annoyance as she pictured to herself the figure she must have presented to him, a girl so interested in his coming and going that she must lie in wait for him, and take up her stand an hour or so before he might have been expected. At any rate, he should not find her submissively waiting for him when he drove up to the door. She would keep out of the way until tea-time, and he might find somebody else to entertain him.

The shrubbery walk, which skirted the road, wound for over a mile round the park, and if she followed it she would come, by way of the kitchen gardens and stableyard, to the house again, and could regain her bedroom unseen, at the cost of a walk rather longer than she would willingly have undertaken on this hot afternoon. But it was the only thing to do. If she went back by the way she had come, she might meet Jim and his friend in the garden, and of course they would think she had come on purpose to see them. If she crossed the park she ran the risk of being seen. So she kept to the shelter of the trees, and followed the windings of the path briskly, and in rather a bad temper.

At a point about half-way round the circle, the dense shrubbery widened into a spinney, and cut through it transversely was a broad grass ride, which opened up a view of the park and the house. When Cicely reached this point she looked to her right, and caught her breath in her throat sharply, for she saw Ronald Mackenzie striding down the broad green path towards her. He was about fifty yards away, but it was impossible to pretend she had not seen him, or to go on without waiting for him to catch her up. Indeed, the moment he caught sight of her he waved his hand and called out, "I thought I should catch you." He then came up with a smile upon his face, and no apparent intention of apologising for his obvious pursuit of her.

What was the right attitude to take up towards a man who behaved like that? Cicely blushed, and felt both surprised and annoyed. But she was powerless to convey a hint of those feelings to him, and all he knew was that she had blushed.

"You shouldn't have run away from me like that," he said, as he shook hands with her and looked her straight in the face. "I shan't do you any harm. We will go back this way"; and he walked on at a fairly smart rate by the way she had been going, and left her to adapt her pace to his, which she did, with the disgusted feeling that she was ambling along at an undignified trot.

She was aware that if she opened her mouth she would say just the one thing that she did not want to say, so she kept it closed, but was not saved by so doing, because he immediately said it for her. "How did I know where to find you? Well, I guessed you didn't expect to be spied under that tree, and that you'd keep away for a bit. I didn't want that, because I had come over on purpose to see you. So I cast my eye round the country—I've an eye for country—saw where you would be likely to go and the place to intercept you. So now you know all about it."

This was a little too much. Cicely found her tongue. "Thank you," she said, with dignity, "I didn't want to know all about it," and then felt like a fool.

"Then you have something you didn't want," he replied coolly. "But we won't quarrel; there's no time. Do you know what I think about you and about this place?"

He looked down at her and waited for an answer; and an answer had to be given. She was not quite prepared, or it would be more accurate to say that she hardly dared, to say, "No, and I don't want to," so she compromised weakly on "No."

"Well, I'll tell you. It seems to me just Paradise, this lovely, peaceful, luxurious English country, after the places I've been to and the life I've led. And as for you, you pretty little pink and white rose, you're the goddess that lives in the heart of it. You're the prettiest, most graceful creature on God's earth, and you're in the right setting."

Cicely felt like a helpless rabbit fascinated by a snake. Nothing that she had ever learned, either by direct precept from the old starling, or as the result of her own observation of life, had prepared her to cope with this. Outrageous as were his words and tone, she could only show that she resented them by implicitly accusing him of making love to her; and her flurried impulse was to shun that danger spot.

She laughed nervously. "You use very flowery language; I suppose you learned it in Tibet," she said, and felt rather pleased with herself.

"One thing I learned in Tibet," he answered, "if I hadn't learned it before, was that England is the most beautiful country in the world. I'm not sure that I wouldn't give up all the excitement and adventure of my life to settle down in a place like Graham's—or like this."

Cicely congratulated herself upon having turned the conversation. She was ready to talk on this subject. "You wouldn't care for it very long," she said. "It is stagnation. I feel sometimes as if I would give anything to get out of it."

He looked down at her with a smile. "And what would you like to do if you could get out of it?" he asked.

"I should like to travel for one thing," she said. "If I were a man I would. I wouldn't be content to settle down in a comfortable country house to hunt foxes and shoot pheasants and partridges all my life."

"Like Graham, eh? Well, perhaps you are right. You're going to marry Graham, aren't you?"

"No," she said shortly.

"He thinks you are," he said, with a laugh. "He's a good fellow, Graham, but perhaps he takes too much for granted, eh? But I know you are not going to marry Graham. I only asked you to see what you would say. You are going to marry me, my little country flower."

"Mr. Mackenzie!" She put all the outraged surprise into her voice of which she was capable, and stopped short in the path.

He stopped too, and faced her. His face was firmly set. "I have no time to go gently," he said. "I ask straight out for what I want, and I want you. Come now, don't play the silly miss. You've got a man to deal with. I've done things already and I'm going to do more. You will have a husband you can be proud of."

He was the type of the conquering male as he stood before her, dark, lean, strong and bold-eyed. His speech, touched with a rough northern burr, broke down defences. He would never woo gently, not if he had a year to do it in. Men of his stamp do not ask their wives in marriage; they take them.

Cicely went red and then white, and looked round her helplessly. "You can't run away," he said, and waited for her to speak.

His silence was more insolently compelling than any words could have been. Her eyes were drawn to his in spite of herself, fluttered a moment, and rested there in fascinated terror. So the women in ages of violence and passion, once caught, surrendered meekly.

"You are mine," he said, in a voice neither raised nor lowered. "I said you should be when I first saw you. I'll take care of you. And I'll take care of myself for your sake."

Suddenly she found herself trembling violently. It seemed to be her limbs that were trembling, not she, and that she could not stop them. He put his arm around her. "There, there!" he said soothingly. "Poor little bird! I've frightened you. I had to, you know. But you're all right now."

For answer she burst into tears, her hands to her face. He drew them away gently, mastering her with firm composure. "It was a shock, wasn't it?" he said in a low, vibrating monotone. "But it had to be done in that way. Jim Graham doesn't upset you in that way, I'll be bound. But Jim Graham is a rich, comfortable vegetable; and I'm not exactly that. You don't want to be either, do you?"

"No," she said, drying her eyes.

"You want a mate you can be proud of," he went on, still soothing her. "Somebody who will do big things, and do them for your sake, eh? That's what I'm going to do for you, little girl. I'm famous already, so I find. But I'll be more famous yet, and make you famous too. You'll like that, won't you?"

He spoke to her as if she were a little child. His boasting did not sound like boasting to her. His strength and self-confidence pushed aside all the puny weapons with which she might have opposed him. She could not tell him that she did not love him. He had not asked for her love; he had asked for herself; or rather, he had announced his intention of taking her. She was dominated, silenced, and he gave her no chance to say anything, except what he meant her to say.

He took his arms from her. "We must go back now," he said, "or they will wonder what has become of us." He laughed suddenly. "They were a little surprised when I ran away after you."

It occurred to her that they must have been considerably surprised. The thought added to her confusion. "Oh, I can't go back to them!" she cried.

"No, no," he said soothingly. "You shall slip into the house by a back way. I shall say I couldn't find you."

They were walking along the path, side by side. His muscular hands were pendant; he had attempted no further possession of her, had not tried to kiss her. Perhaps he knew that a kiss would have fired her to revolt, and once revolting she would be lost to him. Perhaps he was not guided by policy at all, but by the instinctive touch of his power over men—and women.

Cicely was beginning to recover her nerve, but her thoughts were in a whirl. She was not angry; her chief desire was to go away by herself and think. In the meantime she wanted no further food for thought. But that was a matter not in her hands.

"I'm going away in a fortnight, you know," he said. "Back to Tibet. I left some things undone there."

"You only came home a month ago," she said, clutching eagerly at a topic not alarmingly personal.

"I know. But I'm tired of it—the drawing-rooms and the women. I want to be doing. *You* know."

She thought she did know. The rough appeal thrown out in those two words found a way through her armour, which his insolent mastery had only dented and bruised. It gave her a better conceit of herself. This was a big man, and he recognised something of his own quality in her. At any rate, she would stand up to him. She would not be "a silly miss."

"Of course, you have surprised me very much," she said, with an effort at even speech, which probably came to him as hurried prattle. "I can't say what I suppose you want me to say at once. But if you will give me time—if you will speak to my father——"

He broke in on her. "Good heavens!" he said, with a laugh. "You don't think I've got time for all that sort of thing, do you?—orange flowers and church bells and all the rest of it. Don't you say a word to your father, or any one else. Do you hear?"

His roughness nerved her. "Then what do you want me to do?" she asked boldly.

"Do? Why, come to London and marry me, of course. You've got the pluck. Or if you haven't, you're not what I thought you, and I don't want you at all. There's no time to settle anything now, and I'm off to-morrow. If I stay longer, and come over here again with Graham, they will suspect something. Meet me to-night out here—this very spot, do you see? I'll get out of the house and be over here at two o'clock. Then I'll tell you what to do."

They had come to a little clearing, the entrance to a strip of planted ground which led to a gate in the walled kitchen garden, and so to the back regions of the house. She stood still and faced him. "Do you think I am going to do that?" she asked, her blue eyes looking straight into his.

He had aroused her indignant opposition. What would he do now, this amazing and masterful man?

He looked down at her with an odd expression in his face. It was protecting, tender, amused. "Little shy flower!" he said—he seemed to cling to that not very original metaphor—"I mustn't forget how you have been brought up, in all this shelter and luxury, must I? It is natural to you, little girl, and I'll keep you in it as far as I can. But you've got to remember what I am too. You must come out of your cotton wool sometimes. Life isn't all softness and luxury."

Food and raiment! What had she been thinking of all the morning? Her eyes fell.

"You can trust me, you know," he said, still speaking softly. "But you believe in daring, don't you? You must show a little yourself."

"It isn't at all that I'm afraid," she said weakly.

"Of course not. I know that," he answered. "It is simply that you don't do such things here." He waved his hand towards the corner of the big house, which could be seen through the trees. "But you want to get out of it, you said."

Did she want to get out of it? She was tired of the dull ease. She was of the Clintons, of the women who were kept under; but there were men Clintons behind her too, men who took the ease when it came to them, but did not put it in the first place, men of courage, men of daring. It was the love of adventure in her blood that made her answer, "Perhaps I will come," and then try to dart past him.

He put out his arm to stop her. "I'm not going to walk six miles here and back on the chance," he said roughly. But she was equal to him this time. "If you don't think it worth while you need not come," she said. "I won't promise." Then she was gone.

He walked back slowly to the garden. Jim Graham was lying back in a basket chair, dressed in smart blue flannel and Russian leather boots, talking to Joan and Nancy. Through the open window of the library the top of the Squire's head could be seen over the back of an easy-chair.

Mackenzie joined the little group under the lime. "Couldn't find her," he said shortly.

"She'll turn up at tea-time," said Jim equably.

The clear eyes of the twins were fixed on Mackenzie. They had run round to the front of the house on hearing the wheels of Jim's cart on the gravel. They wanted to see the great man he had brought with him, and they were not troubled with considerations of shyness. But the great man had taken no notice of them at all, standing on the gravel of the drive staring at him.

He had jumped down from the cart and made off, directly, round the corner of the house.

"Where is he going?" asked the twins.

"He wants to show Cicely some drawings," said Jim. "He saw her in the shrubbery. Want a drive round to the stables, twankies?"

Now the twins devoured Mackenzie with all their eyes. "I am Joan Clinton, and this is my sister Nancy," said Joan. "Nobody ever introduces us to anybody that comes here, so we always introduce ourselves. How do you do?"

Mackenzie seemed to wake up. He shook hands with both twins. "How do you do, young ladies," he said with a smile. "You seem very much alike."

"Not in character," said Nancy. "Miss Bird says that Joan would be a very well-behaved girl if it were not for me."

"I'm sure you are both well behaved," said Mackenzie. "You look as if you never gave any trouble to anybody."

"What we look and what we are are two very different things," said Joan. "Aren't they, Jim?"

"Good Lord, I should think they were," said Jim. He had been bustled off immediately after luncheon, and was lying back in his chair in an attitude inviting repose. He had rather hoped that Mackenzie, whose quick energy of mind and body were rather beyond his power to cope with, would have been off his hands for half an hour when he had announced his intention of going in search of Cicely. He would have liked to go in search of Cicely himself, but that was one of the things that he did no longer. He had nothing to do now but wait with what patience he could until his time came. He had a sort of undefined hope that Mackenzie might say something that would advance him with Cicely, praise him to her, cause her to look upon him with a little refreshment of her favour. But he had not welcomed the questions with which the twins had plied him concerning his guest.

"Jim wants to go to sleep," said Nancy. "Would you like to come up into the schoolroom, Mr. Mackenzie? We have a globe of the world."

"We can find Cicely if you want to see her," added Joan.

Mackenzie laughed his rough laugh. "We won't bother Miss Clinton," he said. "But I should like to see the globe of the world."

So the twins led him off proudly, chattering. Jim heard Joan say, "We have had a bishop in our schoolroom, but we would much rather have an explorer," but by the time they had crossed the lawn he was sleeping peacefully.

If he had known it, it was hardly the time for him to sleep.

"If you're ill, go to bed; if not, behave as usual," was a Clinton maxim which accounted for Cicely's appearance at the tea-table an hour later, when she would much rather have remained in her own room. The effort, no small one, of walking across the lawn in full view of the company assembled round the tea-table, as if nothing had happened to her within the last hour, braced her nerves. She was a shade paler than ordinary, but otherwise there was nothing in her appearance to arouse comment. Mackenzie sprang up from his chair as she approached and went forward to meet her. "I tried to find you directly I came, Miss Clinton," he said in his loud voice, which no course of civilisation would avail to subdue. "I've brought those sketches I told you about last night."

Cicely breathed relief. She had not been told the pretext upon which he had started off in pursuit of her immediately upon his arrival, and had had terrifying visions of a reception marked by anxious and inquiring looks. But Jim greeted her with his painfully acquired air of accepted habit, and immediately, she was sitting between him and Mackenzie, looking at the bundle of rough pencil drawings put into her hands, outlines of rugged peaks, desolate plains, primitive hillside villages, done with abundant determination but little skill. She listened to Mackenzie's explanations without speaking, and was relieved to hand over the packet to the Squire, who put on his glasses to examine them, and drew the conversation away from her.

Mackenzie spoke but little to her after that. He dominated the conversation, much more so than on the previous evening, when there had been some little difficulty in extracting any account of his exploits from him. Now he was willing to talk of them, and he talked well, not exactly with modesty, but with no trace of boastful quality, such as would certainly have aroused the prejudices of his listeners against him.

He talked like a man with whom the subject under discussion was the one subject in the world that interested him. One would have said that he had nothing else in his mind but the lust for strange places to conquer. He appeared to be obsessed by his life of travel, to be able to think of nothing else, even during this short interval in his years of adventure, and in this stay-at-home English company whose thoughts were mostly bound up in the few acres around them.

Cicely stole glances at him. Was he acting a carefully thought out plan, or had he really forgotten her very existence for the moment, while his thoughts winged their way to cruel, dark places, whose secrets he would wrest from them, the only places in which his bold, eager spirit could find its home? He radiated power. She was drawn to him, more than half against her will. He had called to her to share his life and his enterprise. Should she answer the call? It was in her mind that she might do so.

He made no attempt to claim her after tea; but when the church bells began to ring from across the park, and she had to go to play for the evening service, he joined the little party of women—the Clinton men went to church once on Sundays, but liked their women to go twice—and sat opposite to her in the chancel pew, sometimes fixing her with a penetrating look, sometimes with his head lowered on his broad chest, thinking inscrutable thoughts, while the dusk crept from raftered roof to stone floor, and the cheap oil lamps and the glass-protected candles in the pulpit and reading-desk plucked up yellow courage to keep off the darkness.

The congregation sang a tuneful, rather sentimental evening hymn in the twilight. They sang fervently, especially the maids and men in the chancel pews. Their minds were stirred to soothing and vaguely aspiring thoughts. Such hymns as this at the close of an evening service were the pleasantest part of the day's occupations.

The villagers went home to their cottages, talking a little more effusively than usual. The next morning their work would begin again. The party from the great house hurried home across the park. The sermon had been a little longer than usual. They would barely have time to dress for dinner.

Jim Graham's dog-cart came round at half-past ten. The Squire, who had been agreeably aroused from his contented but rather monotonous existence by his unusual guest, pressed them to send it back to the stable for an hour. "The women are going to bed," he said—they were always expected to go upstairs punctually at half-past ten—"we'll go into my room."

But Mackenzie refused without giving Jim the opportunity. "I have a lot of work to do to-night," he said. "Don't suppose I shall be in bed much before four; and I must leave early to-morrow."

So farewells were said in the big square hall. Mrs. Clinton and Cicely were at a side-table upon which were rows of silver bedroom candlesticks, Mrs. Clinton in a black evening dress, her white, plump neck and arms bare, Cicely, slim and graceful, in white. The men stood between them and the table in the middle of the hall, from which Dick was dispensing whisky and soda water; the Squire, big and florid, with a great expanse of white shirt front, Jim and Mackenzie in light overcoats with caps in their hands. Servants carried bags across from behind the staircase to the open door, outside of which Jim's horse was scraping the gravel, the bright lamps of the cart shining on his smooth flanks.

The Squire and Dick stood on the stone steps as the cart drove off, and then came back into the hall. Mrs. Clinton and Cicely, their candles lighted, were at the foot of the staircase.

"Well, that's an interesting fellow," said the Squire as the butler shut and bolted the hall door behind him. "We'll get him down to shoot if he's in England next month."

"And see what he can do," added Dick.

Cicely went upstairs after her mother. The Squire and Dick went into the library, where a servant relieved them of their evening coats and handed them smoking-jackets, and the Squire a pair of worked velvet slippers.

CHAPTER XIV

THE PLUNGE

When Cicely had allowed the maid who was waiting for her to unfasten her bodice, she sent her away and locked the door after her. During the evening she had sketched in her mind a portrait of herself sitting by the open window and thinking things over calmly. It seemed to be the thing to do in the circumstances.

But she could not think calmly. She could not even command herself sufficiently to go on with her undressing. The evening had been one long strain on her nerves, and now she could only throw herself on her bed and burst into tears. She had an impulse to go in to her mother and tell her everything, and perhaps only the fact that for the moment her physical strength would not allow her to move held her back.

After a time she became quieter, but did not regain the mastery of her brain. She seemed to be swayed by feeling entirely. The picture of her mother, calm and self-contained, kneeling at her long nightly devotions, faded, and in its place arose the image of the man who had suddenly shouldered his way into her life and with rude hands torn away the trappings of convention that had swathed it.

He attracted her strongly. He stood for a broad freedom, and her revolt against the dependence in which she lived was pointed by his contempt for the dull, easy, effortless life of the big country house. Her mind swayed towards him as she thought of what he had to offer her in exchange—adventure in unknown lands; glory, perhaps not wholly reflected, for there had been women explorers before, and her strong, healthy youth made her the physical equal of any of them; comradeship in place of subjection. She weighed none of these things consciously; she simply desired them.

There came to her the echo of her brother's speech as she had come up the stairs: "And let us see what he can do." He stood before her in his rugged strength, not very well dressed, his greying head held upright, his nostrils slightly dilated, his keen eyes looking out on the world without a trace of self-consciousness; and beside him stood Dick in his smart clothes and his smoothed down hair, coolly ignoring all the big things the man had done, and proposing to hold over his opinion of him till he saw whether he could snap off a gun quickly enough to bring down a high pheasant or a driven partridge. If he could pass that test he would be accepted without further question as "a good fellow." His other achievements, or perhaps more accurately the kind of renown they had brought him, would be set against his lack of the ordinary gentleman's upbringing. If he could not, he would still be something of an outsider though all the world should acclaim him. Dick's careless speech—she called it stupid—affected her strangely. It lifted her suitor out of the ruck, and made him bulk bigger.

She got up from her bed and took her seat by the open window, according to precedent. She had seen herself, during the evening, sitting there looking out on to the moonlit garden, asking herself quietly, "What am I going to do?" weighing the pros and cons, stiffening her mind, and her courage. And she tried now to come to a decision, but could not come anywhere near to laying the foundation of one. She had not the least idea what she was going to do, nor could she even discover what she wanted to do.

She got up and walked about the room, but that did not help her. She knelt down and said her prayers out of a little well-worn book of devotions, and made them long ones. But it was nothing more than repeating words and phrases whose meaning slipped away from her. She prayed in her own words for guidance, but none came. There existed only the tumult of feeling.

She heard her father and brother come up to bed and held her breath in momentary terror, then breathed relief at the thought that if they should, unaccountably, break into her room, which they were not in the least likely to do, they could not know what was happening to her, or make her tell them. They went along the corridor talking loudly. She had often been disturbed from her first sleep by the noise the men made coming up to bed. She heard a sentence from her father as they passed her door. "They would have to turn out anyhow if anything happened to me."

Dick's answer was inaudible, but she knew quite well what they were discussing. It had been discussed before her mother and herself, and even the twins and Miss Bird, though not before the servants, during the last few days. Lord and Lady Alistair MacLeod, she a newly wed American, had motored through Kencote, lunched at the inn and fallen in love with the dower-house. Lady Alistair—*he* would have nothing to do with it—had made an offer through the Squire's agent for a lease of the house, at a rental about four times its market value. The Squire did not want the money, but business was business. And the MacLeods would be "nice people to have about the place." All that stood in the way was Aunt Ellen and Aunt Laura. They could not be turned out unless they were willing to go, but the Squire knew very well that they *would* go if he told them to. There was a nice little house in the village which would be the very thing for them if he decided to accept the tempting offer. He would do it up for them. After all, the dower-house was much too large and there were only two of them left. So it had been discussed whether Aunt Ellen, at the age of ninety-three, and Aunt Laura, at the age of seventy-five, should be notified that the house in which they had spent the last forty years of their lives, and in which their four sisters had died, was wanted for strangers.

That was not the only thing that had been discussed. The question of what would be done in various departments of family and estate business when the Squire should have passed away—his prospective demise being always referred to by the phrase, "if anything should happen to me"—was never shirked in the least; and Dick, who would reign as Squire in his stead, until the far off day when something should happen to *him*, took his part in the discussion as a matter of course. These things were and would be; there was no sense in shutting one's eyes to them. And one of the things that would take place upon that happening was that Mrs. Clinton, and Cicely, if she were not married, and the twins, would no longer have their home at Kencote, unless Dick should be unmarried and should invite them to go on living in his house. He would have no legal right to turn Aunt Ellen and Aunt Laura out of the dower-house, if they still remained alive, but it had been settled ever since the last death amongst the sisters that they would make way. It would only be reasonable, and was taken for granted.

And now, as it seemed, her father and brother had made up their minds to exercise pressure—so little would be needed—to turn out the poor old ladies, not for the sake of those who might have a claim on their consideration, but for strangers who would pay handsomely and would be nice people to have about the place. Cicely burned with anger as she thought of it.

Two o'clock struck from the clock in the stable turret. Cicely opened her door softly, crept along the corridor and through a baize door leading to a staircase away from the bedrooms of the house. At the foot of it was a door opening into the garden, which she was prepared to unlock and unbolt with infinite care to avoid noise. But the carelessness of a servant had destroyed the need of such caution. The door was unguarded, and with an unpleasant little shock she opened it and went out.

The night was warm, and the lawns and trees and shrubs of the garden lay in bright moonlight. She hurried, wrapped in a dark cloak, to the place from which she had fled from Mackenzie in the afternoon. She felt an impulse of shrinking as she saw his tall figure striding up and down on the grass, but she put it away from her and went forward to meet him.

He gave a low cry as he turned and saw her. "My brave little girl!" he said, and laid his hands on her shoulders for a moment, and looked into her face. He attempted no further love-making; his tact seemed equal to his daring. "We have come here to talk," he said. "When we have made our arrangements you shall go straight back. I wouldn't have asked you to come out here like this if there had been any other way."

She felt grateful. Her self-respect was safe with him. He understood her.

"Will you come with me?" he asked, and she answered, "Yes."

A light sprang into his eyes. "My brave little queen of girls!" he said, but held himself back from her.

"What time can you get out of the house without being missed for an hour or two?" he asked.

She stood up straight and made a slight gesture as if brushing something away, and thenceforward answered him in as matter-of-fact a way as he questioned her.

"In the afternoon, after lunch," she said.

"Very well. There is a train from Bathgate at four o'clock. Can you walk as far as that?"

"Oh yes."

"You can't go from here, and you can't drive. So you must walk. Is there any chance of your being recognised at Bathgate?"

"I am very likely to be recognised."

He thought for a moment. "Well, it can't be helped," he said. "If there is any one in the train you know you must say you are going up to see Mrs. Walter Clinton. Graham has told me all about her and your brother."

"I shan't be able to take any luggage with me," she said.

"No. That is a little awkward. We must trust to chance. Luck sides with boldness. You can buy what you want in London. I have plenty of money, and nothing will please me better than to spend it on you, little girl." His tone and his eyes became tender for a moment. "I shall be on the platform in London to meet you," he said. "I shall be surprised to see you there until you tell me there is nobody to fear. I hate all this scheming, but it can't be helped. We must get a start, and in two days we shall be married. Don't leave any word. You can write from London to say you are going to marry me. I'll do the rest when we are man and wife."

Cicely's eyes dropped as she asked, "Where shall I be till—till——"

"Till we're married? My little girl! It won't be very long. There is a good woman I know. I'll take you there and she will look after you. I shall be near. Leave it all to me and don't worry. Have you got money for your journey?"

"Yes, I have enough."

"Very well. Now go back, and think of me blessing the ground you walk on. You're so sweet, and you're so brave. You're the wife for me. Will you give me one kiss?"

She turned her head quickly. "No," he said at once. "I won't ask for it; not till you are mine altogether."

But she put up her face to him in the moonlight. "I'm yours now," she said. "I have given myself to you," and he kissed her, restraining his roughness, turning away immediately without another word to stride down the grass path into the darkness of the trees.

Cicely looked after him for an instant and then went back to the house and crept up to her room.

CHAPTER XV

BLOOMSBURY

Mackenzie met her at the London terminus. She had seen no one she knew either at the station at Bathgate or in the train. She was well dressed, in a tailor-made coat and skirt and a pretty hat. She got out of a first-class carriage and looked like a young woman of some social importance, travelling alone for once in a way, but not likely to be allowed to go about London alone when she reached the end of her journey. She was quite composed as she saw Mackenzie's tall figure coming towards her, and shook hands with him as if he were a mere acquaintance.

"I have seen nobody I know," she said, and then immediately added, "I must send a telegram to my mother. I can't leave her in anxiety for a whole night."

He frowned, but not at her. "You can't do that," he said, "you don't want the post-office people to know."

"I have thought of that. I will say 'Have come up to see Muriel. Writing to-night.' It isn't true, but I will tell them afterwards why I did it."

"Will that satisfy them?"

"I am deceiving them anyhow."

"Oh, I don't mean that. Will they think it all right—your coming up to your sister-in-law?"

"No, they will be very much surprised. But the post-office people will not gather anything."

"They will wire at once to your brother. You had much better leave it till to-morrow."

"No, I can't do that," she said. "I will wire just before eight o'clock. Then a return wire will not go through before the morning."

"Yours might not get through to-night."

"Oh yes, it will. They would take it up to the house whatever time it came."

"Very well," he said. "Now come along," and he hailed a hansom.

"Please don't think me tiresome," she said, when they were in the cab, "but there is another thing I must do. I must write to my mother so that she gets my letter the very first thing to-morrow morning."

He gave an exclamation of impatience. "You can't do that," he said again. "The country mails have already gone."

"I can send a letter by train to Bathgate. I will send it to the hotel there with a message that it is to be taken over to Kencote the first thing in the morning."

"You are very resourceful. It may give them time to get on to our track, before we are married."

"I have promised to marry you," she said simply. It was she who now seemed bold, and not he.

"I don't see how they could get here in time," he said grudgingly. "Graham only knows the address of my club, and they don't know there where I live." He brightened up again. "Very well, my queen," he said, smiling down at her. "You shall do what you like. Write your letter—let it be a short one—when you get in, and we will send that and the wire when we go out to dinner."

They drove to a dingy-looking house in one of the smaller squares of Bloomsbury. During the short journey he became almost boisterous. All the misgivings that had assailed her since they had last parted, the alternate fits of courage and of frightened shrinking, had passed him by. This was quite plain, and she was right in attributing his mood partly to his joy in having won her, partly to his love of adventure. It was an added pleasure to him to surmount obstacles in winning her. If his wooing had run the ordinary course, the reason for half his jubilation would have disappeared. She felt his strength, and, woman-like, relinquished her own doubts and swayed to his mood.

"You have begun your life of adventure, little girl," he said, imprisoning her slender hand in his great muscular one, and looking down at her with pride in his eyes. She had an impulse of exhilaration, and smiled back at him.

The rooms to which he took her, escorted by a middle-aged Scotswoman with a grim face and a silent tongue, were on the first floor—a big sitting-room, clean, but, to her eyes, inexpressibly dingy and ill-furnished, and a bedroom behind folding doors.

"Mrs. Fletcher will give you your breakfast here," he said, "but we will lunch and dine out. We will go out now and shop when you are ready."

She went into the bedroom and stood by the window. Fright had seized her again. What was she doing here? The woman who had come from her dark, downstairs dwelling-place to lead the way to these dreadful rooms, had given her one glance but spoken no word. What must she think of her? She could hear her replying in low monosyllables to Mackenzie's loud instructions, through the folding doors.

Again the assurance and strength and determination which he exhaled came to her aid. She had taken the great step, and must not shrink from the consequences. He would look after her. She washed her hands and face—no hot water had been brought to her—and went back to the sitting-room. "I am hoping you will be comfortable here, miss," the woman said to her. "You must ask for anything you want."

She did not smile, but her tone was respectful, and she looked at Cicely with eyes not unfriendly. And, after all, the rooms were clean—for London.

Mackenzie took her to a big shop in Holborn and stayed outside while she made her purchases. She had not dared to bring with her even a small hand-bag, and she had to buy paper on which to write her letter to her mother.

"I lived in Mrs. Fletcher's rooms before I went to Tibet," Mackenzie said as they went back to the house. "I tried to get them when I came back—but no such luck. Fortunately they fell vacant on Saturday. We'll keep them on for a bit after we're married. Must make ourselves comfortable, you know."

She stole a glance at him. His face was beaming. She had thought he had taken her to that dingy, unknown quarter as a temporary precaution. Would he really expect her to make her home in such a place?

She wrote her letter to her mother at the table in the sitting-room. Mrs. Fletcher had brought up a penny bottle of ink and a pen with a J nib suffering from age. Mackenzie walked about the room as she wrote, and it was difficult for her to collect her thoughts. She gave him the note to read, with a pretty gesture of confidence. It was very short.

"MY OWN DARLING MOTHER,—I have not come to London to see Muriel, but to marry Ronald Mackenzie. I said what I did in my telegram because of the post-office. I am very happy, and will write you a long letter directly we are married.—Always your very loving daughter,

"CICELY."

"Brave girl!" he said as he returned it to her.

She gave a little sob. "I wish I had not had to go away from her like that," she said.

"Don't cry, little girl," he said kindly. "It was the only way."

She dried her eyes and sealed up the note. She had wondered more than once since he had carried her off her feet why it was the only way.

They carried through the business of the letter and the telegram and drove to a little French restaurant in Soho to dine. The upstairs room was full of men and a few women, some French, more English. Everybody stared at her as she entered, and she blushed hotly. And some of them recognised Mackenzie and whispered his name. The men were mostly journalists, of the more literary sort, one or two of them men of note, if she had known it. But to her they looked no better than the class she would have labelled vaguely as "people in shops." They were as different as possible from her brothers and her brothers' friends, sleek, well-dressed men with appropriate clothes for every occasion, and a uniform for the serious observance of dinner which she had never imagined a man without, except on an unavoidable emergency. She had never once in her life dined in the same frock as she had worn during the day and hardly ever in the company of men in morning clothes.

This cheap restaurant, where the food and cooking were good but the appointments meagre, struck her as strangely as if she had been made to eat in a kitchen. That it did not strike Mackenzie in that way was plain from his satisfaction at having introduced her to it. "Just as good food here as at the Carlton or the Savoy," he said inaccurately, "at about a quarter of the price; and no fuss in dressing-up!"

She enjoyed it rather, after a time. There was a sense of adventure in dining in such a place, even in dining where nobody had thought of dressing, although dressing for dinner was not one of the conventions she had wished to run away from; it was merely a habit of cleanliness and comfort. Mackenzie talked to her incessantly in a low voice—they were sitting at a little table in a corner, rather apart from the rest. He talked of his travels, and fascinated her; and every now and then, when he seemed furthest away, his face would suddenly soften and he would put in a word of encouragement or gratitude to her. She felt proud of having the power to make such a man happy. They were comrades, and she wanted to share his life. At present it seemed to be enough for him to talk to her. He had not as yet made any demand on her for a return of confidence. In fact, she had scarcely spoken a word to him, except in answer to speech of his. He had won her and seemed now to take her presence for granted. He had not even told her what arrangements he had made for their marriage, or where it was to be; nor had he alluded in any way to the course of their future life or travels, except in the matter of Mrs. Fletcher's room in Bloomsbury.

"When are we going to Tibet again?" She asked him the question point blank, as they were drinking their coffee, and Mackenzie was smoking a big briar pipe filled with strong tobacco.

He stared at her in a moment's silence. Then he laughed. "Tibet!" he echoed. "Oh, I think now I shan't be going to Tibet for some months. But I shall be taking you abroad somewhere before then. However, there will be plenty of time to talk of all that." Then he changed the subject.

He drove her back to her rooms and went upstairs with her. It was about half-past nine o'clock. "I have to go and meet a man at the Athenæum at ten," he said. "Hang it! But I will stay with you for a quarter of an hour, and I dare say you won't be sorry to turn in early."

He sat himself down in a shabby armchair on one side of the fireless grate. He was still smoking his big pipe. Cicely stood by the table.

He looked up at her. "Take off your hat," he said, "I want to see your beautiful hair. It was the first thing I noticed about you."

She obeyed, with a blush. He smiled his approval. "Those soft waves," he said, "and the gold in it! You are a beautiful girl, my dear. I can tell you I shall be very proud of you. I shall want to show you about everywhere."

He hitched his chair towards her and took hold of her hand. "Do you think you are going to love me a little bit?" he asked.

She blushed again, and looked down. Then she lifted her eyes to his. "I don't think you know quite what you have made me do," she said.

He dropped her hand. "Do you regret it?" he asked sharply.

She did not answer his question, but her eyes still held his. "I have never been away from home in my life," she said, "without my father or mother. Now I have left them without a word, to come to you. You seem to take that quite as a matter of course."

The tears came into her eyes, although she looked at him steadily. He sprang up from his chair and put his hand on her shoulder. "My poor little girl!" he said, "you feel it. Of course you feel it. You've behaved like a heroine, but you've had to screw up your courage. I don't want you to think of all that. That is why I haven't said anything about it. You mustn't break down."

But she had broken down, and she wept freely, while he put his arm round her and comforted her as he might have comforted a child. Presently her sobbing ceased. "You are very kind to me," she said. "But you won't keep me away from my own people, will you—after—after——"

"After we are married? God bless me, no. And they won't be angry with you—at least, not for long. Don't fear that. Leave it all to me. We shall be married to-morrow. I've arranged everything."

"You have not told me a word about that," she said forlornly.

"I didn't mean to tell you a word until to-morrow came," he said. "You are not to brood."

"You mean to rush me into everything," she said. "If I am to be the companion to you that I want to be, you ought to take me into your confidence."

"Why, there!" he said, "I believe I ought. You're brave. You're not like other girls. You can imagine that I have had a busy day. I have a special license, signed by no less a person than the Archbishop of Canterbury. Think of that! And we are going to be married in a church. I knew you would like that; and I like it better too. You see I have been thinking of you all the time. Now you mustn't worry any more." He patted her hand. "Go to bed and get a good sleep. I'll come round at ten o'clock to-morrow morning, and we're to be married at eleven. Then a new life begins, and by the Lord I'll make it a happy one for you. Come, give me a smile before I go."

She had no difficulty in doing that now. He took her chin in his fingers, turned her face up to his and looked into her eyes earnestly. Then he left her.

She had finished her breakfast, which had been cleared away, when he came in to her the next morning. She was sitting in a chair by the empty grate with her hands in her lap, and she looked pale.

Mackenzie had on a frock coat, and laid a new silk hat and a new pair of gloves on the table as he greeted her with unsentimental cheerfulness.

"Will you sit down?" she said, regarding him with serious eyes. "I want to ask you some questions."

He threw a shrewd glance at her. "Ask away," he said in the same loud, cheerful tone, and took his seat opposite to her, carefully disposing of the skirts of his coat, which looked too big even for his big frame.

"I have been thinking a great deal," she said. "I want to know exactly what my life is to be if I marry you."

"*If* you marry me!" he took up her words. "You *are* going to marry me."

"You said something last night," she went on, "which I didn't quite understand at the time; and I am not sure that you meant me to. Are you going to take me with you to Tibet, and on your other journeys, or do you want to leave me behind—here?" There was a hint of the distaste she felt for her surroundings in the slight gesture that accompanied the last word. But she looked at him out of clear, blue, uncompromising eyes.

He did not return her look. "Here?" he echoed, looking round him with some wonder. "What is the matter with this?"

"Then you do mean to leave me here."

"Look here, my dear," he said, looking at her now. "I am not going to take you to Tibet, or on any of my big journeys. I never had the slightest intention of doing so, and never meant you to think I had. A pretty thing if I were to risk the life of the one most precious to me, as well as my own, in such journeys as I take!"

"Then what about me?" asked Cicely. "What am I to do while you are away, risking your own life, as you say, and away perhaps for two or three years together?"

"Would you be very anxious for me?" he asked her, with a tender look, but she brushed the question aside impatiently.

"I am to live alone, while you go away," she said, "live just as dull a life as I did before, only away from my own people, and without anything that made my life pleasant in spite of its dulness. Is that what you are offering me?"

"No, no," he said, trying to soothe her. "I want you to live in the sweetest little country place. We'll find one together. You needn't stay here a minute longer than you want to, though when we are in London together it will be convenient. I want to think of you amongst your roses, and to come back to you and forget all the loneliness and hardships. I want a home, and you in it, the sweetest wife ever a man had."

"I don't want that," she said at once. "You are offering me nothing that I didn't have before, and I left it all to come to you—to share the hardships and—and—I would take away the loneliness."

"You are making too much of my big journeys," he broke in on her eagerly. "That is the trouble. Now listen to me. I shall be starting for Tibet in March, and ——"

"Did you know that when you told me you were going in a fortnight?" she interrupted him.

"Let me finish," he said, holding up his hand. "It is settled now that I am going to Tibet in March, and I shan't be away for more than a year. Until then we will travel together. I want to go to Switzerland almost directly to test some instruments. You will come with me, and you can learn to climb. I don't mind that sort of hardship for you. At the end of October we will go to America. I hadn't meant to go, but I want money now—for you—and I can get it there. That's business; and for pleasure we will go anywhere you like—Spain, Algiers, Russia—Riviera, if you like, though I don't care for that sort of thing. When I go to Tibet I'll leave you as mistress of a little house that you may be proud of, and you'll wait for me there. When I get back we'll go about together again, and as far as I can see I shan't have another big job to tackle for some time after that—a year, perhaps two years, perhaps more."

She was silent for a moment, thinking. "Come now," he said, "that's not stagnation. Is it?"

"No," she said unwillingly. "But it isn't what I came to you for." She raised her eyes to his. "You know it isn't what I came to you for."

His face grew a little red. "You came to me," he said in a slower, deeper voice, looking her straight in the eyes, "because I wanted you. I want you now and I mean to have you. I want you as a wife. I will keep absolutely true to you. You will be the only woman in the world to me. But my work is my work. You will have no more say in that than I think good for you. You will come with me wherever I think well to take you, and I shall be glad enough to have you. Otherwise you will stay behind and look after my home—and, I hope, my children."

Her face was a deep scarlet. She knew now what this marriage meant to him. What it had meant to her, rushing into it so blindly, seemed a foolish, far off thing. Her strongest feeling was a passionate desire for her mother's presence. She was helpless, alone with this man, from whom she felt a revulsion that almost overpowered her.

He sat for a full minute staring at her downcast face, his mouth firmly set, a slight frown on his brows.

"Come now," he said more roughly. "You don't really know what you want. But I know. Trust me, and before God, I will make you happy."

She hid her face in her hands. "Oh, I want to go home," she cried.

He shifted in his chair. The lines of his face did not relax. He must set himself to master this mood. He knew he had the power, and he must exercise it once for all. The mood must not recur again, or if it did it must not be shown to him.

And there is no doubt at all that he would have mastered it. But as he opened his mouth to speak, Cicely sitting there in front of him, crying, with a white face and strained eyes, there were voices on the stairs, the door opened, and Dick and Jim Graham came into the room.

CHAPTER XVI

THE PURSUIT

Cicely had not been missed from home until the evening. At tea-time she was supposed to be at the dower-house, or else at the Rectory. It was only when she had not returned at a quarter to eight, that the maid who waited upon her and her mother told Mrs. Clinton that she was not in her room.

"Where on earth can she be?" exclaimed Mrs. Clinton. Punctuality at meals being so rigidly observed it was unprecedented that Cicely should not have begun to dress at a quarter to eight. At ten minutes to eight Mrs. Clinton was convinced that some accident had befallen her. At five minutes to, she tapped at the door of the Squire's dressing-room. "Edward," she called, "Cicely has not come home yet."

"Come in! Come in!" called the Squire. He was in his shirt sleeves, paring his nails.

"I am afraid something has happened to her," said Mrs. Clinton anxiously.

"Now, Nina, don't fuss," said the Squire. "What can possibly have happened to her? She must be at the dower-house, though, of course, she ought to be home by this time. Nobody in this house is ever punctual but myself. I am always speaking about it. You *must* see that the children are in time for meals. If nobody is punctual the whole house goes to pieces."

Mrs. Clinton went downstairs into the morning-room, where they were wont to assemble for dinner. Dick was there already, reading a paper. "Cicely has not come home yet," she said to him.

"By Jove, she'll catch it," said Dick, and went on reading his paper.

Mrs. Clinton went to the window and drew the curtain aside. It was not yet quite dark and she could see across the park the footpath by which Cicely would come from the dower-house. But there was no one there. Mrs. Clinton's heart sank. She knew that something *had* happened. Cicely would never have stayed out as late as this if she could have helped it. She came back into the room and rang the bell. "I must send down," she said.

Dick put his paper aside and looked up at her. "It *is* rather odd," he said.

The butler came into the room, and the Squire immediately behind him. "Edward, I want some one to go down to the dower-house and see if Cicely has been there," Mrs. Clinton said. "I am anxious about her."

The Squire looked at her for a moment. "Send a man down to the dower-house to ask if Miss Clinton has been there this afternoon," he said, "and if she hasn't, tell him to go to the Rectory."

The butler left the room, but returned immediately with Cicely's telegram. It was one minute to eight o'clock. He hung on his heel after handing the salver to Mrs. Clinton and then left the room to carry out his previous instructions. It was not his place to draw conclusions, but to do as he was told.

Mrs. Clinton read the telegram and handed it to the Squire, searching his face as he read it. "What, the devil!" exclaimed the Squire, and handed it to Dick.

The big clock in the hall began to strike. Porter threw open the door again. "Dinner is served, ma'am," he said.

"You needn't send down to the dower-house," Dick said, raising his eyes from the paper. "Miss Clinton has gone up to stay with Mrs. Walter." Then he offered his arm to his mother to lead her out of the room.

"Shut the door," shouted the Squire, and the door was shut. "What on earth does it mean?" he asked, in angry amazement.

"Better have gone in to dinner," said Dick. "I don't know."

Mrs. Clinton was white, and said nothing. The Squire turned to her. "What does it mean, Nina?" he asked again. "Did you know anything about this?"

"Of course mother didn't know," said Dick. "There's something queer. It's too late to send a wire. I'll go up by the eleven o'clock train and find out all about it. Better go in now." He laid the telegram carelessly on a table.

"Don't leave it about," said the Squire.

"Better leave it there," said Dick, and offered his arm to his mother again.

They went into the dining-room, only a minute late.

"Tell Higgs to pack me a bag for two nights," said Dick when the Squire had mumbled a grace, "and order my cart for ten o'clock. I'm going up to London. I shan't want anybody."

Then, as long as the servants were in the room they talked as usual. At least Dick did, with frequent mention of Walter and Muriel and some of Cicely. The Squire responded to him as well as he was able, and Mrs. Clinton said nothing at all. But that was nothing unusual.

When they were alone at last, the Squire burst out, but in a low voice, "What on earth does it mean? Tell me what it means, Dick."

"She hasn't had a row with any one, has she, mother?" asked Dick, cracking a walnut.

Mrs. Clinton moistened her lips. "With whom?" she asked.

"I know it's very unlikely. I suppose she's got some maggot in her head. Misunderstood, or something. You never know what girls are going to do next. She *has* been rather mopy lately. I've noticed it."

"She has not seen Muriel since she was married," said Mrs. Clinton. "She has missed her."

"Pah!" spluttered the Squire. "How dare she go off like that without a word? What on earth can you have been thinking of to let her,

Nina? And what was Miles doing? Miles must have packed her boxes. And who drove her to the station? When did she go? Here we are, sitting calmly here and nobody thinks of asking any of these questions."

"It was Miles who told me she had not come back," said Mrs. Clinton. "She was as surprised as I was."

"Ring the bell, Dick," said the Squire.

"I think you had better go up, mother, and see what she took with her," said Dick. "Don't say anything to anybody but Miles, and tell her to keep quiet."

Mrs. Clinton went out of the room. Dick closed the door which he had opened for her, came back to the table, and lit a cigarette. "There's something queer, father," he said, "but we had better make it seem as natural as possible. I shouldn't worry if I were you. I'll find out all about it and bring her back."

"Worry!" snorted the Squire. "It's Cicely who is going to worry. If she thinks she is going to behave like that in this house she is very much mistaken."

Dick drove into Bathgate at twenty minutes to eleven. He always liked to give himself plenty of time to catch a train, but hated waiting about on the platform. So he stopped at the George Hotel and went into the hall for a whisky-and-soda.

"Oh, good evening, Captain," said the landlord, who was behind the bar. "If you are going back to Kencote you can save me sending over. This letter has just come down by train." He handed Dick a square envelope which he had just opened. On it was his name and address in Cicely's writing, and an underlined inscription, "Please send the enclosed letter to Kencote by special messenger as early as possible to-morrow morning." Dick took out the inner envelope which was addressed to his mother, and looked at it. "All right," he said, "I'll take it over," and slipped it into the pocket of his light overcoat. He ordered his whisky-and-soda and drank it, talking to the landlord as he did so. Only a corner of the bar faced the hall, which was otherwise empty, and as he went out he took the letter from his pocket and opened it.

"The devil you will!" he said, as he read the few words Cicely had written. Then he went out and stood for a second beside his cart, thinking.

"I'm going to Mountfield," he said as he swung the horse round and the groom jumped up behind. The groom would wonder at his change of plan and when he got back he would talk. If he told him not to he would talk all the more. Wisest to say nothing at present. So Dick drove along the five miles of dark road at an easy pace, for he could catch no train now until seven o'clock in the morning and there was no use in hurrying, and thought and thought, as he drove. If he failed in stopping this astonishing and iniquitous proceeding it would not be for want of thinking.

Mountfield was an early house. Jim himself unbarred and unlocked the front door to the groom's ring. The chains and bolts to be undone seemed endless. "Take out my bag," said Dick, as he waited, sitting in the cart. "I'm going to stay here for the night. There'll be a note to take back to Mrs. Clinton. See that it goes up to her to-night."

He spoke so evenly that the groom wondered if, after all, there was anything going on under the surface at all.

"Hullo, old chap," Dick called out, directly Jim's astonished face appeared in the doorway. "Cicely has bolted off to see Muriel, and the governor has sent me to fetch her back. I was going up by the eleven o'clock train, but I thought I'd come here for to-night, and take you up with me in the morning. There's nothing to hurry for."

Then he got down from the cart and gave the reins to the groom. "I just want to send a note to the mater so that she won't worry," he said, as he went into the house.

He went across the hall into Jim's room, and Jim, who had not spoken, followed him. "Read that," he said, putting the letter into his hand.

Jim read it and looked up at him. There was no expression on his face but one of bewilderment.

"You think it over," said Dick, a little impatiently, and went to the writing-table and scribbled a note.

"DEAR MOTHER,—I thought I would come on here first on the chance of hearing something, and glad I did so. There is a letter from Cicely. It is all right. Jim and I are going up to-morrow morning. Don't worry.

"DICK."

Then, without taking any notice of Jim, still standing gazing at the letter in his hand with the same puzzled expression on his face, he went out and despatched the groom, closing the hall door after him.

He went back into the room and shut that door too. "Well!" he said sharply. "What the devil does it mean?"

Jim's expression had changed. It was now angry as well as puzzled. "It was when he went after her on Sunday," he said. "*Damn* him! I thought——"

"Never mind what you thought," said Dick. "When did he see her alone?"

"I was going to tell you. When we came over yesterday afternoon he saw her over the wall, and directly we got to the house he bolted off after her. He said he had promised to show her some sketches."

"But he didn't find her. He said so at tea-time—when she came out."

Jim was silent. "Perhaps that was a blind," said Dick. "How long was it before he came back and said he couldn't find her?"

"About half an hour, I should think. Not so much."

"He *must* have found her. But, good heavens! he can't have persuaded her to run away with him in half an hour! He had never been alone with her before."

"No."

"And he didn't see her alone afterwards."

Jim's face suddenly went dark. "He—he—went out after we went up to bed," he said.

"What?"

"He asked me to leave the door unlocked. He said he might not sleep, and if he didn't he should go out."

The two men looked at one another. "That's a nice thing to hear of your sister," said Dick bitterly.

"It's a nice thing to hear of a man you've treated as a friend," said Jim.

"How long have you known the fellow?"

"Oh, I told you. I met him when I was travelling, and asked him to look me up. I haven't seen him since until he wrote and said he wanted to come for a quiet Sunday."

"Why did he want to come? I'll tell you what it is, Jim. She must have met him in London, and you were the blind. Yes, that's it. She's been different since she came back. I've noticed it. We've all noticed it."

"I don't believe they met before," said Jim slowly.

"Why not?"

"I don't believe they did. Dick, do you think they can be married already? Is there time to stop it?"

"Yes, there's time. I've thought it out. We'll go up by the seven o'clock train. Where does the fellow live?"

Jim thought a moment. "I don't know. He wrote from the Royal Societies Club."

"Well, we'll find him. I'm not going to talk about it any more now. I'm too angry. Cicely! She ought to be whipped. If it *is* too late, she shall never come to Kencote again, if I have any say in the matter, and I don't think my say will be needed. Let's go to bed. We shall have plenty of time to talk in the train."

"I'll go and get hold of Grove," said Jim. "He must get a room ready, and see that we get to the station in the morning," and he went out of the room.

Dick walked up and down, and then poured himself out whisky-and-soda from a table standing ready. He lit a cigarette and threw the match violently into the fireplace. When Jim returned he said, "I've managed to keep it pretty dark so far. The governor would have blurted everything out—everything that he knew. I'm glad I intercepted that letter to the mater. I haven't any sort of feeling about opening it. *I'm* going to see to this. If we can get hold of her before it's too late, she must go to Muriel for a bit; I must keep it from the governor as long as I can—until I get back and can tackle him. He'll be so furious that he'll give it away all round. He wouldn't think about the scandal."

"Pray God we shan't be too late," said Jim. "What a fool I've been, Dick! I took it all for granted. I never thought that she wasn't just as fond of me as I was of her."

Dick looked at him. "Well, I suppose that's all over now," he said, "a girl who behaves like that!"

Jim turned away, and said nothing, and by and by they went up to bed.

They drove over to Bathgate the next morning and caught the seven o'clock train to Ganton, where they picked up the London express. Alone in a first-class smoking-carriage they laid their plans. "I have an idea that is worth trying before we do anything else," said Jim. "When we were travelling together that fellow told me of some rooms in Bloomsbury he always went to when he could get them."

"Do you know the address?"

"Yes," said Jim, and gave it. "He said they were the best rooms in London, and made me write down the address. I found it last night."

"Why on earth didn't you say so before?"

"I had forgotten. I didn't suppose I should ever want to take rooms in Bloomsbury."

"It's a chance. We'll go there first. If we draw blank, we will go to his club, and then to the Geographical Society. We'll find him somewhere."

"We can't do anything to him," said Jim.

"I'm not thinking much of him," Dick confessed. "It would be a comfort to bruise him a bit—though I dare say he'd be just as likely to bruise me. He's got an amazing cheek; but, after all, a man plays his own hand. If she had behaved herself properly he couldn't have done anything."

He flicked the ash of his cigar on to the carpet and looked carelessly out of the window, but turned his head sharply at the tone in which Jim said, "If I could get him alone, and it couldn't do her any harm afterwards, I'd kill him." And he cursed Mackenzie with a deliberate, blasphemous oath.

Dick said nothing, but looked out of the window again with an expression that was not careless.

Jim spoke again in the same low voice of suppressed passion. "I told him about her when I was travelling. I don't know why, but I did. And after you dined on Friday we spoke about her. He praised her. I didn't say much, but he knew what I felt. And he had got this in his mind then. He must have had. He was my friend, staying in my house. He's a liar and a scoundrel. For all he's done, and the name he's made, he's not fit company for decent men. Dick, I'd give up everything I possess for the chance of handling him."

"I'd back you up," said Dick. "But the chief thing is to get her away from him."

"I know that. It's the only thing. We can't do anything. I was thinking of it nearly all night long. And supposing we don't find him, or don't find him till too late."

"We won't think of that," said Dick coolly. "One thing at a time. And we'll shut his mouth, at any rate. I feel equal to that."

They were silent for a time, and then Jim said, "Dick, I'd like to say one thing. She may not care about seeing me. I suppose she can't care for me much—now—or she wouldn't have let him take her away. But I'm going to fight for her—see that? I'm going to fight for her, if it's not too late."

Dick looked uncomfortable in face of his earnestness. "If you want her," he began hesitatingly, "after——"

"Want her!" echoed Jim. "Haven't I always wanted her? I suppose I haven't shown it. It isn't my way to show much. But I thought it was all settled and I rested on that. Good God, I've wanted her every day of my life—ever since we fixed it up together—years ago. I wish I'd taken her, now, and let the beastly finance right itself. It wouldn't have made much difference, after all. But I wanted to give her everything she ought to have. If I've seemed contented to wait, I can tell you I haven't been. I didn't want to worry her. I—I—thought she understood."

"She's behaved very badly," said Dick, too polite to show his surprise at this revelation. Jim had always been rather a queer fellow. "If you want her still, she ought to be precious thankful. The whole thing puzzles me. I can't see her doing it."

"I couldn't, last night," said Jim, more quietly. "I can now. She's got pluck. I never gave her any chance to show it."

They were mostly silent after this. Every now and then one of them said a word or two that showed that their thoughts were busy in what lay before them. The last thing Jim said before the train drew up at the same platform at which Cicely had alighted the day before was, "I can't do anything to him."

They drove straight to the house in Bloomsbury. Mrs. Fletcher opened the door to them. "Mr. Mackenzie is expecting us, I think," said Dick suavely, and made as if to enter.

Mrs. Fletcher looked at them suspiciously, more because it was her way than because, in face of Dick's assumption, she had any doubts of their right of entrance. "He didn't say that he expected anybody," she said. "I can take your names up to him."

"Oh, thanks, we won't trouble you," said Dick. "We will go straight up. First floor, as usual, I suppose?"

It was a slip, and Mrs. Fletcher planted herself in the middle of the passage at once.

"Wait a moment," she said. "What do you mean by 'as usual'? Neither of you have been in the house before. You won't go up to Mr. Mackenzie without I know he wants to see you."

"Now, look here," said Dick, at once. "We are going up to Mr. Mackenzie, and I expect you know why. If you try to stop us, one of us will stay here and the other will fetch the policeman. You can make up your mind at once which it shall be, because we've no time to waste."

"Nobody has ever talked to me about a policeman before; you'll do it at your peril," she said angrily, still standing in the passage, but Dick saw her cast an eye towards the door on her left.

"I'm quite ready to take the consequences," said Dick, "but whatever they are it won't do you any good with other people in your house to have the police summoned at half-past ten in the morning. Now will you let us pass?"

She suddenly turned and made way for them. Dick went upstairs and Jim followed him. The door of the drawing-room was opposite to them. "I'll do the talking," said Dick, and opened the door and went in.

CHAPTER XVII

THE CONTEST

Mackenzie sprang up and stood facing them. His face had changed in a flash. It was not at all the face of a man who had been caught and was ashamed; it was rather glad. Even his ill-made London clothes could not at that moment disguise his magnificent gift of virility. So he might have looked—when there was no one to see him—face to face with sudden, unexpected danger in far different surroundings, dauntless, and eager to wrest his life out of the instant menace of death.

Dick had a momentary perception of the quality of the man he had to deal with, which was instantly obliterated by a wave of contemptuous dislike—the dislike of a man to whom all expression of feeling, except, perhaps, anger, was an offence. He had looked death in the face too, but not with that air. Assumed at a moment like this it was a vulgar absurdity. He met Mackenzie's look with a cool contempt.

But the challenge, and the reply to it, had occupied but a moment. Cicely had looked up and cried, "O Dick!" and had tried to rise from her chair to come to him, but could not. The tone in which she uttered that appeal for mercy and protection made Jim Graham wince, but it did not seem to affect her brother. "Go and get ready to come with us," he said.

Jim had never taken his eyes off Cicely since he had entered the room, but she did not look at him. She sat in her chair, trembling a little, her eyes upon her brother's face, which was now turned toward her with no expression in it but a cold authority.

She stood up with difficulty, and Jim took half a step forward. But Mackenzie broke in, with a gesture towards her. "Come now, Captain Clinton," he said. "You have found us out; but I am going to marry your sister. You are not going to take her away, you know." He spoke in a tone of easy good humour. The air, slightly theatrical, as it had seemed, with which he had faced their intrusion, had disappeared.

Dick took no notice of him whatever. "I am going to take you up to Muriel," he said to Cicely. "There's a cab waiting. Have you anything to get, or are you ready to come now?"

She turned to go to her room, but Mackenzie interposed again. "Stay here, please," he said. "We won't take our orders from Captain Clinton. Look here, Clinton, I dare say this has been a bit of a shock to you, and I'm sorry it had to be done in such a hurry. But everything is straight and honest. I want to marry your sister, and she wants to marry me. She is of age and you can't stop her. I'm going to make her a good husband, and she's going to make me the best of wives."

He still spoke good-humouredly, with the air of a man used to command who condescends to reason. He knew his power and was accustomed to exercise it, with a hand behind his back, so to speak, upon just such young men as these; men who were socially his superiors, and on that very account to be kept under, and taught that there was no such thing as social superiority where his work was to be done, but only leader and led.

But still Dick took no notice of him. "Come along, Cicely," he said, with a trifle of impatience.

Mackenzie shrugged his shoulders angrily. "Very well," he said, "if you've made up your mind to take that fool's line, take it and welcome. Only you won't take *her*. She's promised to me. My dear, tell them so."

He bent his look upon Cicely, the look which had made her soft in his hands. Dick was looking at her too, standing on the other side of the table, with cold displeasure. And Jim had never looked away from her. His face was tender and compassionate, but she did not see it. She looked at Dick, searching his face for a sign of such tenderness, but none was there, or she would have gone to him. Her eyes were drawn to Mackenzie's, and rested there as if fascinated. They were like those of a frightened animal.

"Come now," said Mackenzie abruptly. "It is for you to end all this. I would have spared you if I could—you know that; but if they must have it from you, let them have it. Tell them that I asked you to come away and marry me, and that you came of your own accord. Tell them that I have taken care of you. Tell them that we are to be married this morning."

She hesitated painfully, and her eyes went to her brother's face again in troubled appeal. He made no response to her look, but when the clock on the mantelpiece had ticked half a dozen audible beats and she had not spoken, he turned to Mackenzie.

"I see," he said. "You have— —"

"Oh, let her speak," Mackenzie interrupted roughly, with a flashing glance at him. "You have had your say."

"It is quite plain, sir," proceeded Dick in his level voice, "that you have gained some sort of influence over my sister."

"Oh, that is plain, is it?" sneered Mackenzie.

"Excuse me if I don't express myself very cleverly," said Dick. "What I mean is that somehow you have managed to *bully* her into running away with you."

They looked into one another's eyes for an instant. The swords were crossed. Mackenzie turned to Cicely. "Did I do that?" he asked quietly.

"If I might suggest," Dick said, before she could reply, "that you don't try and get behind my sister, but speak up for yourself— —"

"Did I do that?" asked Mackenzie again.

"O Dick dear," said Cicely, "I said I would come. It was my own fault."

"Your own fault—yes," said Dick. "But I am talking to this—this gentleman, now."

Mackenzie faced him again. "Oh, we're to have all that wash about gentlemen, are we? I'm not a gentleman. That's the trouble, is it?"

"It is part of the trouble," said Dick. "A good big part."

"Do you know what I do with the *gentlemen* who come worrying me for jobs when I go on an expedition, Captain Clinton—the gentlemen who want to get seconded from your regiment and all the other smart regiments, to serve under me?"

"Shall we stick to the point?" asked Dick. "My cab is waiting."

Mackenzie's face looked murderous for a moment, but he had himself in hand at once. "The point is," he said, "that I am going to marry your sister, with her consent."

"The point is how you got her consent. I am here in place of my father—and hers. If she marries you she marries you, but she doesn't do it before I tell her what she is letting herself in for."

"Then perhaps you will tell her that."

"I will." Dick looked at Cicely. "I should like to ask you to begin with when you first met—Mr. Mackenzie," he said.

"Dear Dick!" cried Cicely, "don't be so cruel. I—I—was discontented at home, and I——"

"We met first at Graham's house," said Mackenzie, "when you were there. I first spoke to her alone on Sunday afternoon, and she promised to come away and marry me on Sunday night. Now go on."

"That was when you told Graham that you couldn't sleep, I suppose, in the middle of the night."

"I walked over from Mountfield, and she came to me in the garden, as I had asked her to. We were together about three minutes."

Dick addressed Cicely again, still with the same cold authority. "You were discontented at home. You can tell me why afterwards. You meet this man and hear him bragging of his great deeds, and when he takes you by surprise and asks you to marry him, you are first of all rather frightened, and then you think it would be an adventure to go off with him. Is that it?"

"It's near enough," said Mackenzie, "except that I don't brag."

"I've got my own ears," said Dick, still facing Cicely. "Well, I dare say the sort of people you're used to don't seem much beside a man who gets himself photographed on picture postcards, but I'll tell you a few of the things we don't do. We don't go and stay in our friends' houses and then rob them. You belonged to Jim. You'd promised him, and this man knew it. We don't go to other men's houses and eat their salt and make love to their daughters behind their backs. We don't tell mean lies. We don't ask young girls to sneak out of their homes to meet us in the middle of the night. We respect the women we want to marry, we don't compromise them. If this man had been a fit husband for you, he would have asked for you openly. It's just because he knows he isn't that he brings all his weight to bear upon you, and you alone. He doesn't dare to face your father or your brothers."

Cicely had sunk down into her chair again. Her head was bent, but her eyes were dry now. Mackenzie had listened to him with his face set and his lips pressed together. What he thought of the damaging indictment, whether it showed him his actions in a fresh light, or only heightened his resentment, nobody could have told. "Have you finished what you have to say?" he asked.

"Not quite," replied Dick. "Listen to me, Cicely."

"Yes, and then listen to me," said Mackenzie.

"What sort of treatment do you think you're going to get from a man who has behaved like that? He's ready to give you a hole-and-corner marriage. He wants you for the moment, and he'll do anything to get you. He'll get tired of you in a few weeks, and then he'll go off to the other side of the world and where will *you* be? How much thought has he given to *your* side of the bargain? He's ready to cut you off from your own people—*he* doesn't care. He takes you from a house like Kencote and brings you here. He's lied to Jim, who treated him like a friend, and he's behaved like a cad to us who let him into our house. He's done all these things in a few days. How are you going to spend your life with a fellow like that?"

Cicely looked up. Her face was firmer, and she spoke to Mackenzie. "We had begun to talk about all these things," she said. "I asked you a question which you didn't answer. Did you know when you told me you were going back to Tibet in a fortnight and there wasn't time to—to ask father for me, that you weren't going until next year?"

"No, I didn't," said Mackenzie.

"When did he tell you that?" asked Dick.

"On Sunday."

"I can find that out for you easily enough. I shouldn't take an answer from him."

Again, for a fraction of a second, Mackenzie's face was deadly, but he said quietly to Cicely, "I have answered your question. Go on."

"You know why I did what you asked me," she said. "I thought you were offering me a freer life and that I should share in all your travels and dangers. You told me just before my brother came in that you didn't want me for that."

"I told you," said Mackenzie, speaking to her as if no one else had been in the room, "that you *would* have a freer life, but that I shouldn't risk your safety by taking you into dangerous places. I told you that I would do all that a man could do to protect and honour his chosen wife, and that's God's truth. I told you that I would make you happy. That I know I can do, and I will do. Your brother judges me by the fiddling little rules he and the like of him live by. He calls himself a gentleman, and says I'm not one. I know I'm not his kind of a gentleman. I've no wish to be; I'm something bigger. I've got my own honour. *You* know how I've treated you. Your own mother couldn't have been more careful of you. And so I'll treat you to the end of the chapter when you give me the right to. You can't go back now; it's too late. You see how this precious brother of yours looks at you, after what you have done. You'll be sorry if you throw yourself into *his* hands again. Show some pluck and send him about his business. You can trust yourself to me. You won't regret it."

The shadow of his spell was over her again. She hesitated once more and Dick's face became hard and angry. "Before you decide," he said, "let me tell you this, that if you do marry this fellow you will never come to Kencote again or see any of us as long as you live."

"You won't see your eldest brother," said Mackenzie. "I'll take care of that. But you *will* see those you want to see. I'll see to that too. It's time to end this. I keep you to your word. You said you were mine, and you meant it. I don't release you from your promise."

Cicely's calm broke down. "Oh, I don't know what to do," she cried. "I did promise."

"I keep you to your promise," said Mackenzie inexorably.

Then Jim, who had kept silence all this time, spoke at last. "Cicely," he said, "have you forgotten that you made *me* a promise?"

"O Jim," she said, without looking at him, "don't speak to me. I have behaved very badly to you."

"You never wanted to marry him," said Mackenzie roughly. "He's not the husband for a girl of any spirit."

Jim made no sign of having heard him. His face was still turned towards Cicely. "It has been my fault," he said. "I've taken it all for granted. But I've never thought about anybody else, Cicely."

Mackenzie wouldn't allow him to make his appeal as he had allowed Dick. "He has had five years to take you in," he said. "He told me so. And he hasn't taken you because he might have less money to spend on himself, till he'd paid off his rates and taxes. He told me that too. He can afford to keep half a dozen horses and a house full of servants. He can't afford a wife!"

He spoke with violent contempt. Dick gazed at him steadily with contemptuous dislike. "This is the fellow that invited himself to your house, Jim," he said.

"Let me speak now, Dick," said Jim, with decision. "He can't touch me, and I don't care if he does. He's nothing at all. I won't bother you. Cicely, my dear. I've always loved you and I always shall. But— —"

"No, he won't bother you," interrupted Mackenzie with a sneer. "He's quite comfortable."

"But you will know I'm there when you are ready to be friends again. If I haven't told you before I'll tell you now. I've kept back all I've felt for you, but I've never changed and I shan't change. This won't make any difference, except that— —"

"Except that he's lost you and I've won you," Mackenzie broke in. "He's had his chance and he's missed it. You don't want to be worried with his drivel."

Cicely looked up at Mackenzie. "Let him speak," she said, with some indignation. "I have listened to all you have said."

Mackenzie's attitude relaxed suddenly. After a searching glance at her he shrugged his shoulders and turned aside. He took up his grey kid gloves lying on the table and played with them.

"I don't blame you for this—not a bit," said Jim, "and I never shall. Whatever you want I'll try and give you."

"O Jim, I can't marry you now," said Cicely, her head turned from him. "But you are very kind." She broke into tears again, more tempestuous than before. Her strength was nearly at an end.

"I've told you that I shan't worry you," Jim said. "But you mustn't marry this man without thinking about it. You must talk to your mother—she'll be heart-broken if you go away from her like this."

"Oh, does she want me back?" cried Cicely.

"Yes, she does. You must go up to Muriel now. She'll want you too. And you needn't go home till you want to."

"I shall never be able to go home again," she said.

Mackenzie threw his gloves on to the table. "Do you want to go home?" he asked her. His voice had lost that insistent quality. He spoke as if he was asking her whether she would like to take a walk, in a tone almost pleasant.

"I want to go away," she said doggedly.

"Then you may go," said Mackenzie, still in the same easy voice. "I wanted you, and if we had been in a country where men behave like men, I would have had you. But I see I'm up against the whole pudding weight of British respectability, and I own it's too strong for me. We could have shifted it together, but you're not the girl to go in with a man. I'll do without you."

"You had better come now, Cicely," said Dick.

Mackenzie gave a great laugh, with a movement of his whole body as if he were throwing off a weight.

"Shake hands before you go," he said, as she rose obediently. "You're making a mistake, you know; but I don't altogether wonder at it. If I'd had a day longer they should never have taken you away. I nearly got you, as it was."

Cicely put her hand into his and looked him squarely in the face. "Good-bye," she said. "You thought too little of me after all. If you had really been willing for me to share your life, I think I would have stayed with you."

His face changed at that. He fixed her with a look, but she took her hand out of his and turned away. "I am ready, Dick," she said, and again he shrugged his broad shoulders.

"I wish I had it to do over again," he said. "Well, gentlemen, you have won and I have lost. I don't often lose, but when I do I don't whine about it. You can make your minds easy. Not a word about this shall pass my lips."

Dick turned round suddenly. "Will you swear that?" he asked.

"Oh, yes, if you like. I mean it."

Dick and Cicely went out of the room. "Well, Graham, I hope you'll get her now I've lost her," said Mackenzie.

Jim took no notice of him, but went out after the other two.

CHAPTER XVIII

AFTER THE STORM

Cicely had an air at once ashamed and defiant as she stepped up into the cab. Dick gave the cabman the address. "See you to-night, then," he said to Jim. It had been arranged between them that when Cicely had been rescued Jim should fall out, as it were, for a time. "Good-bye, Cicely," he said. "Give my love to Walter and Muriel," and walked off down the pavement.

"You can tell me now," said Dick, when the cab had started, "what went wrong with you to make you do such a thing as that."

"I'm not going to tell you anything," said Cicely. "I know I have made a mistake, and I know you will punish me for it—you and father and the boys. You can do what you like, but I'm not going to help you."

Tears of self-pity stood in her eyes, and her face was now very white and tired, but very childish too. Dick was struck with some compunction. "I dare say you have had enough for the present," he said, not unkindly. "But how you could!—a low-bred swine like that!"

Cicely set her lips obstinately. She knew very well that this weapon would be used freely in what she had called her punishment. Men like Dick sifted other men with a narrow mesh. A good many of those whom a woman might accept and even admire, if left to herself, would not pass through it. Certainly Mackenzie wouldn't. She would have had to suffer for running away, but she would suffer far more for running away with "a bounder." And what made it harder was that, although she didn't know it yet, in the trying battle that had just been waged over her, the sieve of her own perceptions had narrowed, and Mackenzie, now, would not have passed through that. She would presently be effectually punished there, if Dick and the rest should leave her alone entirely.

Dick suddenly realised that he was ravenously desirous of a cigarette, and having lit one and inhaled a few draughts of smoke, felt the atmosphere lighter.

"By Jove, that was a tussle," he said. "He's a dangerous fellow, that. You'll thank me, some day, Cicely, for getting you away from him."

"You didn't get me away," said Cicely. "You had nothing whatever to do with it."

"Eh?" said Dick.

"If you had been just a little kind I would have come with you the moment you came into the room. I was longing for some one from home. You made it the hardest thing in the world for me to come. If I had stayed with him it would have been your fault. I'll never forgive you for the way you treated me, Dick. And you may do what you like to me now, and father may do what he likes. Nothing can be worse than that."

She poured out her words hurriedly, and only the restraint that comes with a seat in a hansom cab within full view of the populace of Camden Town prevented her bursting into hysterical tears.

Dick would rather have ridden up to the mouth of a cannon than drive through crowded streets with a woman making a scene, so he said, "Oh, for God's sake keep quiet now," and kept quiet himself, with something to think about.

Presently he said, "No one knows at home yet that you aren't with Muriel. You've got me to thank for that, at any rate."

Cicely blushed with her sudden great relief, but went pale again directly. "I wrote to mother," she said. "She would get the letter early this morning."

"I've got the letter in my pocket," said Dick. "She hasn't seen it."

"You opened my letter to mother!" she exclaimed.

"Yes, I did, and lucky for you too. It was how we found you."

She let that pass. It was of no interest to her then to learn by what chance they had found her. "Then do you really mean that they don't know at home?" she asked eagerly.

"They know you have gone to Muriel—you'll be there in half an hour—and nothing else."

"O Dick, then you won't tell them," she cried, her hand on his sleeve. "You can't be so cruel as to tell them."

She had the crowded streets to thank for Dick's quick answer, "I'm not going to tell them. Do, for Heaven's sake, keep quiet."

She leant back against the cushions. She had the giddy feeling of a man who has slipped on the verge of a great height, and saved himself.

"You'll have plenty to answer for as it is," said Dick, with a short laugh. "You've run away, though you've only run away to Muriel. You won't get let down easily."

She was not dismayed at that. The other peril, surmounted, was so crushingly greater. And there had been reasons for her running away, even if she had not run away to Mackenzie. She stood by them later and they helped her to forget Mackenzie's share in the flight. But now she could only lean back and taste the blessed relief that Dick had given her.

"Do Walter and Muriel know I am coming?" she asked.

"I sent them a wire from Ganton this morning to say that I should probably bring you, and they weren't to answer a wire from home, if one came, till they had heard from me. You've made me stretch my brains since last night, Cicely. You'd have been pretty well in the ark if it hadn't been for me."

"You didn't help me for my own sake though," said Cicely.

Both of them spoke as if they were carrying on a conversation about nothing in particular. Their capacity for disturbing discussion was exhausted for the time. Cicely felt a faint anticipatory pleasure in going to Muriel's new house, and Dick said, "This must be Melbury Park. Funny sort of place to find your relations in!"

But Adelaide Avenue, to which the cabman had been directed, did not quite bear out the Squire's impressions, nor even the Rector's, of the dreary suburb; and lying, as it did, behind the miles of shop-fronts, mean or vulgarly inviting, which they had traversed, and away from the business of the great railway which gave the name of Melbury Park, its sole significance to many besides the Squire, it seemed quiet, and even inviting. It curved between a double row of well-grown limes. Each house, or pair of houses, had a little garden in front and a bigger one behind, and most of the houses were of an earlier date than the modern red brick suburban villa. They were ugly enough, with their stucco fronts and the steps leading up to their front doors, but they were respectable and established, and there were trees behind them, and big, if dingy, shrubs inside their gates.

Walter's house stood at a corner where a new road had been cut through. This was lined on each side with a row of two-storied villas behind low wooden palings, of which the owner, in describing them, had taken liberties with the name of Queen Anne. But Walter's house and the one adjoining it in the Avenue, though built in the same style, or with the same lack of it, were much bigger, and had divided between them an old garden of a quarter of an acre, which, although it would have been nothing much at Kencote, almost attained to the dignity of "grounds" at Melbury Park.

There was a red lamp by the front gate, and as they drew up before it, Muriel came out under a gabled porch draped with Virginia creeper and hurried to welcome them to her married home.

She looked blooming, as a bride should, even on this hot August day in London. She wore a frock of light holland, and it looked somehow different from the frocks of holland or of white drill which Cicely had idly observed in some numbers as she had driven through the streets and roads of the suburb. She had a choking sensation as she saw Muriel's eager face, and her neat dress, just as she might have worn it at home.

"Hullo, Dick," said Muriel. "Walter will be in to lunch. O Cicely, it *is* jolly to see you again. But where's your luggage? You've come to stay. Why, you're looking miserable, my dear! What on earth's the matter? And what did Mr. Clinton's telegram mean, and Dick's? We haven't wired yet, but we must."

They had walked up the short garden path, leaving Dick to settle with the cabman, who had been nerving himself for a tussle, and was surprised to find it unnecessary.

"I'm in disgrace, Muriel," said Cicely. "I'll tell you all about it when we are alone, if Dick doesn't first."

Muriel threw a penetrating look at her and then turned to Dick, who said, with a grin, "This is the drive, is it, Muriel?"

"You are not going to laugh at my house, Dick," said Muriel. "You'll be quite as comfortable here as anywhere. Come in. This is the hall."

"No, not really?" said Dick. "By Jove!"

It was not much of a hall, the style of Queen Anne as adapted to the requirements of Melbury Park not being accustomed to effloresce in halls; but a green Morris paper, a blue Morris carpet, and white enamelled woodwork had brought it into some grudging semblance of welcoming a visitor. The more cultured ladies of Melbury Park in discussing it had called it "artistic, but slightly *bizarre*," a phrase which was intended to combine a guarded appreciation of novelty with a more solid preference for sanitary wallpaper, figured oilcloth and paint of what they called "dull art colours."

"Look at my callers," said Muriel, indicating a china bowl on a narrow mahogany table that was full to the brim with visiting cards. "I can assure you I'm the person to know here. No sniffing at a doctor's wife in Melbury Park, Dick."

"By Jove!" said Dick. "You're getting into society."

"My dear Dick, don't I tell you, I *am* society. Oh, good gracious, I was forgetting. Walter told me to send a telegram to Kencote the very moment you came. Mr. Clinton wired at eight o'clock this morning and it's half-past twelve now."

Cicely turned away, and Dick became serious again. "Where's the wire?" he asked. "I'll answer it."

"Come into Walter's room," said Muriel, "there are forms there."

"I wonder he hasn't wired again," said Dick, and as he spoke a telegraph boy came up to the open door.

"Cannot understand why no reply to telegram. Excessively annoyed. Wire at once.—EDWARD CLINTON," ran the Squire's second message, and his first, which Muriel handed to Dick: "Is Cicely with you. Most annoyed. Wire immediately.—EDWARD CLINTON."

"I'll soothe him," said Dick, and he wrote, "Cicely here. Wanted change. Is writing. Walter's reply must have miscarried.—DICK." "Another lie," he said composedly.

"I want some clothes sent, please, Dick," said Cicely in a constrained voice.

"Better tell 'em to send Miles up," said Dick, considering.

"No, I don't want Miles," said Cicely, and Dick added, "Please tell Miles send Cicely clothes for week this afternoon."

"I suppose you can put her up for a week, Muriel," he said.

"I'll put her up for a month, if she'll stay," said Muriel, putting her arm into Cicely's, and the amended telegram was despatched.

"Now come and see my drawing-room," said Muriel, "and then you can look after yourself, Dick, till Walter comes home, and I will take Cicely to her room."

The drawing-room opened on to a garden, wonderfully green and shady considering where it was. The white walls and the chintz-covered chairs and sofa had again struck the cultured ladies of Melbury Park as "artistic but slightly *bizarre*," but the air of richness imparted by the numberless hymeneal offerings of Walter's and

Muriel's friends and relations had given them a pleasant subject for conversation. Their opinion was that it was a mistake to have such valuable things lying about, but if "the doctor" collected them and took them up to put under his bed every night it would not so much matter.

"They all tell me that Dr. Pringle used this room as a dining-room," said Muriel. "It is the first thing they say, and it breaks the ice. We get on wonderfully well after that; but it is a pretty room, isn't it, Dick?"

She had her arm in Cicely's, and pressed it sometimes as she talked, but she did not talk to her.

"It's an uncommonly pretty room," said Dick. "Might be in Grosvenor Square. Where did you and Walter get your ideas of furnishing from, Muriel? We don't run to this sort of thing at Kencote and Mountfield. Content with what our forefathers have taught us, eh?"

"Oh, we know what's what, all right," said Muriel. "We have seen a few pretty rooms, between us. Now I'm going to take Cicely upstairs. You can wander about if you like, Dick, and there are cigarettes and things in Walter's room."

"I'll explore the gay parterre," said Dick. Then he turned to Cicely and took hold of her chin between his thumb and finger. "Look here, don't you worry any more, old lady," he said kindly. "You've been a little fool, and you've had a knock. Tell Muriel about it and I'll tell Walter. Nobody else need know."

She clung to him, crying. "O Dick," she said, "if you had only spoken to me like that at first!"

"Well, if I had," said Dick, "I should have been in a devil of a temper now. As it is I've worked it off. There, run along. You've nothing to cry for now." He kissed her, which was an unusual attention on his part, and went through the door into the garden. Muriel and Cicely went upstairs together.

Dick soon exhausted the possibilities of the garden and went into the house again and into Walter's room. It had red walls and a Turkey carpet. There was a big American desk, a sofa and easy-chairs and three Chippendale chairs, all confined in rather a small space. There was a low bookcase along one wall, and above it framed school and college photographs; on the other walls were prints from pictures at Kencote. They were the only things in the room, except the ornaments on the mantelpiece, and a table with a heavy silver cigarette box, and other smoking apparatus, that lightened its workmanlike air. But Dick was not apt to be affected by the air of a room. He sat down in the easy-chair and stretched his long legs in front of him, and thought over the occurrences of the morning.

He was rather surprised to find himself in so equable a frame of mind. His anger against Cicely had gradually worked up since the previous evening until, when he had seen her in the room with Mackenzie, he could have taken her by the shoulders and shaken her, with clenched teeth. She had done a disgraceful thing; she, a girl, had taken the sacred name of Clinton in her hands and thrown it to the mob to worry. That he had skilfully caught and saved it before it had reached them did not make her crime any the less.

But he could not now regain—he tested his capacity to regain, out of curiosity—his feeling of outraged anger against her. Curious that, in the train, he had felt no very great annoyance against Mackenzie. He asked himself if he hadn't gone rather near to admiring the decisive stroke he had played, which few men would have attempted on such an almost complete lack of opportunity. But face to face with him his dislike and resentment had flared up. His anger now came readily enough when he thought of Mackenzie, and he found himself wishing ardently for another chance of showing it effectively. It was this, no doubt, that had softened him towards his little sister, whom he loved in his patronising way. The fellow had got hold of her. She was a little fool, but it was the man who was to blame. And his own resource had averted the danger of scandal, which he dreaded like any woman. He could not but be rather pleased with himself for the way in which he had carried through his job, and Cicely gained the advantage of his self-commendation. There was one thing, though—

his father must never know. The fat would be in the fire then with a vengeance.

Turning over these things in his mind, Dick dropped off into a light doze, from which he was awakened by the entrance of Walter. Walter wore a tall hat and a morning coat. It was August and it was very hot, and in Bond Street he would have worn a flannel suit and a straw hat. But if he did that here his patients would think that *he* thought anything good enough for them. There were penalties attached to the publication of that list of wedding presents in the *Melbury Park Chronicle and North London Intelligencer*, and he had been warned of these and sundry other matters. He was not free of the tiresome side-issues of his profession even in Melbury Park. "Hullo, Dick, old chap!" he said as he came in with cheerful alacrity. "Is Cicely here, and what has happened?"

"Hullo, Walter!" said Dick. "Yes, Cicely is here and I have wired to the governor. She has led us a nice dance, that young woman. But it's all over now."

"What has she done? Run away with some fellow?"

"That's just what she did do. If I hadn't been pretty quick off the post she'd have been married to him by this time."

Walter sat down in the chair at his writing-table. His face had grown rather serious. He looked as if he were prepared to receive the confidences of a patient.

"Who did she go off with?" he asked.

Dick took a cigarette from the silver box, and lit it. "Mr. Ronald Mackenzie," he said, as he threw the match into the fireplace.

"Ronald Mackenzie! Where did she pick *him* up?"

"He picked her up. He was staying at Mountfield."

"I know, but he must have seen her before. He can't have persuaded her in five minutes."

"Just what I thought. But he did; damn him!" Then he told Walter everything that had happened, in his easy, leisurely way. "And the great thing now is to keep it from the governor," he ended up.

"Really, it's pretty strong," said Walter, after a short pause. "Fancy Cicely! I can't see her doing a thing like that."

"I could have boxed her ears with pleasure when I first heard of it," said Dick. "But somehow I don't feel so annoyed with her now. Poor little beggar! I suppose it's getting her away from that brute. He'd frightened her silly. He nearly got her, even when we were there fighting him."

"But what about poor old Jim?" asked Walter. "It's too bad of her, you know, Dick. She was engaged to Jim."

"Well, it was a sort of engagement. But I don't blame her much there. If Jim had gone off and married some other girl I don't know that any of us would have been very surprised."

"I should."

"Well, you know him better than I do, of course. I must say, when he told me in the train coming up that he was as much struck on Cicely as ever, it surprised me. He's a funny fellow."

"He's one of the best," said Walter. "But he keeps his feelings to himself. He has always talked to me about Cicely, but I know he hasn't talked to anybody else, because Muriel was just as surprised as you were when I told her how the land lay."

"He told Mackenzie—that's the odd thing," said Dick.

"Did he?"

"Yes. It makes the beast's action all the worse."

"Well, I don't understand that. Perhaps he had a suspicion and gave him a warning."

"I don't think so. He let him go off after her on Sunday afternoon, and didn't think anything of it. However, he's had a shaking up. He won't let her go now."

"Does he want to marry her still?"

"O Lord, yes, more than ever. That's something to be thankful for. It will keep the governor quiet if we can hurry it on a bit."

"But he's not to know."

"He knows she ran away here, without bringing any clothes. That's got to be explained. It's enough for the governor, isn't it?"

"I should think so. Enough to go on with. Didn't Jim want to throttle that fellow?"

"He did before we got there, but he knew he couldn't do anything. It would only have come back on Cicely. He behaved jolly well, Jim did. He didn't take the smallest notice of Mackenzie from first to last, but he talked to Cicely like a father. *She* says—I don't say it, mind you—that it was Jim who got her away from him; she wouldn't have come for me." Dick laughed. "I dare say we both had something to do with it," he said. "I got in a few home truths. I think Mr. Ronald Mackenzie will be rather sorry he came poaching on our land when he turns it over in his mind."

"Well," said Walter, rising, as the luncheon bell rang, "it's a funny business altogether. You must tell me more later. Like a wash, Dick? Is Cicely going to stay here for a bit?"

"Oh, yes," replied Dick, as they went out of the room. "Muriel says she'll keep her. We've wired for clothes." He lowered his voice as they went upstairs. "You must go easy with her a bit, you and Muriel," he said. "She's been touched on the raw. You'll find her in rather an excited state."

"Oh, I shan't worry her," said Walter. "But I think she's behaved badly to Jim all the same."

But Walter's manner towards his erring sister, when they met in the dining-room, showed no sign of his feelings, if they were resentful on behalf of his friend. She was there with Muriel when he and Dick came down. She was pale, and it was plain that she had been crying, but the parlour-maid was standing by the sideboard, and the two girls were talking by the window as if they had not just come from a long talk which had disturbed them both profoundly.

"Well, Cicely," said Walter. "Come to see us at last! You don't look very fit, but you've come to the right man to cure you." Cicely kissed him gratefully, and they sat down at the table.

The dining-room was Sheraton—good Sheraton. On the walls were a plain blue paper and some more prints. The silver and glass on the fresh cloth and on the sideboard were as bright as possible, for Muriel's parlour-maid was a treasure. She earned high wages, or she would not have demeaned herself by going into service at Melbury Park, where, however, she had a young man. The cook was also a treasure, and the luncheon she served up would not have disgraced Kencote, where what is called "a good table" was kept. It was all great fun—to Muriel, and would have been to Cicely too at any other time. The little house was beautifully appointed, and "run" more in the style of a little house in Mayfair than in Melbury Park. Muriel, at any rate, was completely happy in her surroundings.

They drank their coffee in the veranda outside the drawing-room window. They could hear the trains and the trams in the distance, and it seemed to be a favourite pursuit of the youths of Melbury Park to rattle sticks along the oak fencing of the garden, but otherwise they were shut in in a little oasis of green and could not be seen or overheard by anybody. There were certain things to be said, but no one seemed now to wish to refer to Cicely's escapade, the sharp effect of which had been over-laid by the ordinary intercourse of the luncheon table.

It was Cicely herself who broke the ice. She asked Dick nervously when he was going back to Kencote.

"Oh, to-morrow, I think," said Dick. "Nothing to stay up here for."

Muriel said, "Cicely would like Mrs. Clinton to come up. She doesn't want to ask her in her letter. Will you ask her, Dick?"

Dick hesitated. "Do you want to tell mother—about it?" he asked of Cicely.

"Yes," she said.

"Well, I think you had much better not. It'll only worry her, and she need never know."

"I am going to tell her," said Cicely doggedly.

"I wouldn't mind your telling her, if you want to," said Dick, after a pause, "but it's dangerous. If the governor suspected anything and got it out of her— —"

"Oh, she wouldn't tell Mr. Clinton," said Muriel. "I think Cicely is quite right to tell her. Don't you, Walter?"

"I suppose so," said Walter. "But I think it's a risk. I quite agree with Dick. It *must* be kept from the governor. It's for your own sake, you know, Cicely."

"None of you boys know mother in the least," said Cicely, in some excitement. "She's a woman, and so you think she doesn't count at all. She counts a great deal to me, and I want her."

"All right, my dear," said Walter kindly. "We only want to do what's best for you. Don't upset yourself. And you're all right with Muriel and me, you know."

"You're both awfully kind," said Cicely, more calmly, "and so is Dick now. But I do want mother to come, and I *know* she wouldn't tell father."

"I know it too," said Muriel. "I will write to her to-night and ask her; only we thought Mr. Clinton might make some objection, and you could get over that, Dick."

"Oh, I'll get over that all right," said Dick. "Very well, she shall come. Do you want me to tell her anything, Cicely, or leave it all to you?"

"You can tell her what I did," said Cicely in a low voice.

"All right. I'll break it gently. Now are we all going to Lord's, or are you two going to stay at home?"

"Cicely is going to lie down," said Muriel, "and I think I will stay at home and look after her." She threw rather a longing look at Walter. He didn't often allow himself a half holiday, and she liked to spend them with him.

"Don't stay for me, Muriel," Cicely besought her. "I shall be perfectly all right, and I'd really rather be alone."

"No," said Muriel, after another look at Walter. "I'm going to stay at home." And she wouldn't be moved.

Walter telephoned for his new motor-car and changed his clothes. "Do you know why Muriel wouldn't come with us?" he asked, when he and Dick were on their way. "It was because she thought you and I would rather sit in the pavilion."

"So we would," said Dick, with a laugh. "But she's a trump, that girl."

CHAPTER XIX

THE WHOLE HOUSE UPSET

The twins arose betimes on the morning after Cicely's flight, determined, as was their custom, to enjoy whatever excitement, legal, or within limits illegal, was to be wrested from a long new summer day, but quite unaware that the whole house around them was humming with excitement already.

For upon Dick's departure the night before the Squire had thrown caution to the winds, and be-stirred himself, as he said, to get to the bottom of things. Not content with Mrs. Clinton's report of Miles's statement, which was simply that she knew nothing, he had "had Miles up" and cross-examined her himself. He had then had Probin up, the head coachman, who would have known if Cicely had been driven to the station, which it was fairly obvious she had not been. He also had Porter the butler up, more because Porter was always had up if anything went wrong in the house than because he could be expected to throw any light on what had happened. And when the groom came back from Mountfield with Dick's note to Mrs. Clinton, late as it was, he had *him* up, and sent him down again to spread his news and his suspicions busily, although he had been threatened with instant dismissal if he said a word to anybody.

Having thus satisfied himself of what he knew already, that Cicely had walked to the station and had taken no luggage with her, and having opened up the necessary channels of information, so that outdoor and indoor servants alike now knew that Cicely had run away and that her father was prepared, as the phrase went, to raise Cain about it, the Squire went up to bed, and breaking his usual healthy custom of going to sleep immediately he laid his head on his pillow, rated Mrs. Clinton soundly for not noticing what was going on under her very nose. "I can't look after everything in the house and out of it too," he ended up. "I shall be expected to see that the twins change their stockings when they get their feet wet, next. Good-night, Nina. God bless you."

So, to return to the twins; when the schoolroom maid came to awaken them in the morning and found them, as was usual, nearly dressed, they learned, for the first time, what had been happening while they had slept, all unconscious.

"Why can't you call us in proper time, Hannah?" said Joan, as she came in. "We told you we wanted our hot water at half-past three, and it has just struck seven. You'll have to go if you can't get up in time."

Hannah deposited a tray containing two large cups of tea and some generous slices of bread and butter on a table and said importantly, "It's no time to joke now, Miss Joan. There's Miss Clinton missing, and most of us kep' awake half the night wondering what's come of her."

Hannah had not before succeeded in making an impression upon her young mistresses, but she succeeded now. Joan and Nancy stared at her with open eyes, and gave her time to heighten her effects as they redounded to her own importance.

"But I can't stop talking now, miss," she said. "I'll just get your 'ot water and then I must go and 'elp. Here I stop wasting me time, and don't know that something hadn't 'appened and I may be wanted."

"You're wanted here," said Joan. "What do you mean — Miss Clinton missing? Has she gone away?"

"I'll just tell you what I know, Miss Joan," said Hannah, "and then I must go downstairs and 'elp. I was going along the passage by the room last night, jest when they was ready to take in dinner, and Mr. Porter came along and says to me, 'What are *you* doing here?' Well, of course, I was struck all of a 'eap, because——"

"Oh, don't let's waste time with her," interrupted Nancy, "let's go and ask Miss Bird what it's all about."

"Wait a minute, Miss Nancy," cried Hannah. "I was telling you——"

But the twins were at the door. "Lock her in," said Joan. "We shall want her when we come back." And they locked her in, to the great damage of her dignity, and went along the passage to the room which had sheltered Miss Bird's virgin slumbers for nearly thirty years. They were at first refused admission, but upon Joan's saying in a clear voice outside the door, "We want to know about Cicely. If you won't tell us we must go and ask the servants," Miss Bird unlocked the door, and was discovered in a dressing-gown of pink flannel with her hair in curl papers. The twins were too eager for news to remark upon these phenomena, and allowed Miss Bird to get back into bed while they sat at the foot of it to hear her story.

"Well, you must know some time," said Miss Bird, "and to say that you will ask the servants is *not* the way to behave as you know very well and I am the proper person to come to."

"Well, we have come to you," said Joan, "only you wouldn't let us in. Now tell us. Has Cicely run away?"

"Really, Joan, that is a most foolish question," said Miss Bird, "to call it running away to visit Walter and Muriel her *own* brother and sister too as you might say and that is all and I suppose it is that Hannah who has been putting ideas into your head for I came in to see you last night and you knew nothing but were both in a *sweet* sleep and I often think that if you could see yourselves then you would be more careful how you behave and especially Nancy for it is innocence and goodness itself and a pity that it can't be so sleeping *and* waking."

"I've seen Joan asleep and she looked like a stuck pig," said Nancy. "But what *has* happened, starling darling? Do tell us. Has Cicely just gone up to stay with Muriel? Is that all?"

"It is very inconsiderate of Cicely," said Miss Bird, "nobody could *possibly* have objected to her going to stay with Muriel and Miles would have packed her clothes and gone up to London with her to look after her and to go by herself without a *word* and not take a *stitch* to put on her back and Mr. Clinton in the greatest anxiety and very naturally annoyed for with all the horses in the stable to walk to Bathgate in this heat for from Kencote she did *not* go one of the men was sent there to inquire I wonder at her doing such a thing."

"Keep the facts in your head as they come, Joan," said Nancy. "She didn't tell anybody she was going. She didn't take any clothes. She walked to Bathgate, I suppose, to put them off the scent."

"But whatever did she do it for?" asked Joan. "Something must have upset her. It is running away, you know. I wish she had told us about it."

"We'd have gone with her," said Nancy. "She must have done it for a lark."

"Oh, don't be a fool," said Joan. This was one of the twins' formulæ. It meant, "There *are* serious things in life," and was more often used by Joan than by Nancy.

"Joan how often am I to tell you not to use that expression?" said Miss Bird, "I may speak to the winds of Heaven for all the effect it has don't you know that it says he that calleth his brother thou fool shall be in danger of hell fire?"

"Nancy isn't my brother, and I'll take the risk," said Joan. "Didn't Cicely tell mother that she was going?"

"No she did not and for that I blame her," said Miss Bird. "Mrs. Clinton came to me in the schoolroom as I was finishing my dinner and although her calmness is a lesson to all of us she was upset as I could see and did my *very* best to persuade her not to worry."

"It's too bad of Cicely," said Joan. "What are they going to do now?"

"Your brother Dick went up to London by the late train and a telegram was to be sent the *first* thing this morning to relieve all anxiety though with Muriel no harm can come to Cicely if she got there safely which I hope and trust may be the case although to go about London by herself is a thing that she knows she would not be allowed to do, but there I'm saying a great deal too much to you Joan 'n Nancy you must not run away with ideas in your head Cicely no doubt has a *very* good reason for what she has done and she is *years* older than both of you and you must not ask troublesome questions when you go downstairs the only way you can help is by holding your tongues and being good girls."

"Oh, of course, that's the moral of it," said Nancy. "If the roof were to fall in all we should have to do would be to be good girls and it would get stuck on again. Joan, I'm hungry; I must go and finish my bread and butter."

"Thank you, starling darling, for telling us," said Joan, rising from her seat on the bed. "It seems very odd, but I dare say we shall get to the bottom of it somehow. Of course we shan't be able to do any lessons to-day."

"Oh, indeed Joan the very *best* thing we can do to show we——" began Miss Bird, but the twins were already out of the room.

They had to wait some little time before they could satisfy their curiosity any further, because, in spite of their threat to Miss Bird, and the excellent relations upon which they stood with all the servants in the house, they were not in the habit of discussing family affairs with them, and this was a family affair of somewhat portentous bearings. They kept Hannah busy about their persons and refused to let her open her mouth until they were quite dressed, and when they had let themselves loose on the house for the day paid a visit to Cicely's room.

Its emptiness and the untouched bed sobered them a little. "What *did* she do it for?" exclaimed Joan, as they stood before the dressing-table upon which all the pretty silver toilette articles lying just as usual seemed to give the last unaccountable touch of reality to the sudden flight. "Nancy, do you think it could have been because she didn't want to marry Jim?"

"Or because Jim didn't want to marry her," suggested Nancy.

But neither suggestion carried conviction. They looked about them and had nothing to say. Their sister, who in some ways was so near to them, had in this receded immeasurably from their standpoint. They were face to face with one of those mysterious happenings amongst grown ups of which the springs were outside the world as they knew it. And Cicely was grown up, and she and they, although there was so much that they had in common, were different, not only in the amount but in the quality of their experience of life.

They always went in to their mother at eight o'clock, but were not allowed to go before. They did not want to go out of doors while so much was happening within, nor to stay in their schoolroom, which was the last place to which news would be brought; so they perambulated the hall and the downstairs rooms and got in the way of the maids who were busy with them. And at a quarter to eight were surprised by their father's entrance into the library, where they happened to be sitting for the moment.

Their surprise was no greater than his, nor was it so effectively expressed. He saw at once, and said so, that they were up to some mischief, and he would not have it, did they understand that?

"We were only sitting talking, father," said Joan. "There was nowhere else to go."

"I won't have this room used as a common sitting-room," said the Squire. "Now go, and don't let me catch you in here again."

The twins went out into the big hall. "Why couldn't you cry a little at being spoke to like that?" said Nancy. "He would have told us everything."

"That's worn out," replied Joan. "The last time I did it he only said, 'For God's sake don't begin to snivel.' Besides I was rather frightened."

Just then the Squire opened his door suddenly. The twins both jumped. But he only said, "Oh, you're there. Come in here, and shut the door."

They went in. "Now look here," said the Squire, "you are old enough now to look at things in a sensible light. I suppose you have heard that your sister has taken it upon herself to take herself off without a with your leave or by your leave and has turned the whole house topsy-turvy—eh?"

"Yes, father," said the twins dutifully.

"Who told you—eh?"

"Miss Bird, father."

197

"I wish Miss Bird would mind her own business," said the Squire. "What did she tell you for?"

"Because she wanted us to be good girls, and not worry you with questions," replied Nancy.

"Oh! Well, that's all right," said the Squire, mollified.

"Now what I want to know is—did Cicely say anything to either of you about going away like this?"

"Oh no, father," replied the twins, with one voice.

"Well, I'm determined to get to the bottom of it. No daughter of mine shall behave in that way in this house. Here's everything a girl can want to make her happy—it's the ingratitude of it that I can't put up with, and so Miss Cicely shall find when she condescends to come home, as she shall do if I have to go to fetch her myself."

Neither of the twins saw her way to interpose a remark. They stood in front of their father as they stood in front of Miss Bird in the schoolroom when they "did repetition."

"Do either of you know if Cicely wasn't contented or anything of that sort?" inquired the Squire.

"She has been rather off her oats since Muriel was married," said Joan.

"Eh! What's that!" exclaimed the Squire, bending his heavy brows on her with a terrific frown. "Do you think this is a time to play the fool—with me? Off her oats! How dare you speak like that? We shall have you running away next."

Joan's face began to pucker up. "I didn't mean anything, father," she said in a tremulous voice. "I heard you say it the other day."

"There, there, child, don't cry," said the Squire. "What I may say and what you may say are two very different things. Off her oats, eh? Well, she'd better get *on* her oats again as quick as possible. Now, I won't have you children talking about this, do you understand?—or Miss Bird either. It's a most disagreeable thing to have happened, and if it gets out I shall be very much annoyed. I don't want the servants to know, and I trust you two not to go about wagging your tongues, do you hear?"

"O father, we shouldn't think of saying anything about it to anybody," exclaimed Nancy.

"Eh? What? There's nothing to make a mystery about, you know. Cicely has gone up to London to visit Walter and Muriel. No reason why anybody should know more than that. There *isn't* any more to know, except what concerns me—and I won't have it. Now don't interrupt me any more. Go off and behave yourselves and don't get in the way. You've got the whole house to yourselves and I don't want you here. Ring the bell, Joan, I want Porter to send a telegram."

The twins departed. They could now go up to their mother. "Don't want the servants to know!" said Nancy as they went upstairs. "Is it the camel or the dromedary that sticks its head in the sand?"

"The ostrich," said Joan. "It seems to me there's a great deal of fuss about nothing. Cicely wanted to see her dear Muriel, so she went and *saw* her. I call it a touching instance of friendship."

"And fidelity," added Nancy.

Their view of the matter was not contradicted by anything that Mrs. Clinton did or said when they went in to her. She was already dressed and moving about the room, putting things to rights. It was a very big room, so big that even with the bed not yet made nor the washstand set in order, it did not look like a room that had just been slept in. It was over the dining-room and had three windows, before one of which was a table with books and writing materials on it. There were big, old-fashioned, cane-seated and backed easy-chairs, with hard cushions covered with chintz, other tables, a chintz-covered couch, a bookcase with diamond-paned glass doors. On the broad marble mantelpiece were an Empire clock and some old china, and over it a long gilt mirror with a moulded device of lions drawing chariots and cupids flying above them. On the walls, hung with a faded paper of roses, were water-colour drawings, crayon portraits, some fine line engravings of well-known pictures, a few photographs in Oxford frames. The bedroom furniture proper was of heavy mahogany, a four-post bed hung with white dimity, a wardrobe as big as a closet. Nothing was modern except the articles on the dressing-table, nothing was very old.

Never later than eight o'clock the Squire would rise and go into his dressing-room, and when Mrs. Clinton had dressed and in her orderly fashion tidied her room she would sit at her table and read until it was time to go down to breakfast. Whenever he got up earlier she got up earlier too, and had longer to spend by the window open to the summer morning, or in the winter with her books on the table lit by candles. They were for the most part devotional books. But once the Squire had come in to her very early one October morning when he was going cub-hunting and found her reading *The Divine Comedy* with a translation and an Italian dictionary and grammar. He had talked of it downstairs as a good joke: "Mother reading Dante — what?" and she had put away those books.

She was a little paler than usual this morning, but the twins noticed no difference in her manner. She kissed them and said, "You have heard that Cicely went to London yesterday to stay with Muriel. Father is anxious about her, and I am rather anxious too, but there is nothing really to worry about. We must all behave as usual, and two of us at least mustn't give any cause of complaint to-day."

She said this with a smile. It was nothing but a repetition of Miss Bird's exhortation to hold their tongues and be good girls, but they embraced her, and made fervent promises of good behaviour, which they fully intended to keep. Then they read something for a few minutes with their mother and left her to her own reading and her own thoughts.

The morning post brought no letter from Cicely, and again the Squire remained standing while he read prayers. Immediately after breakfast he went down to the Rectory, ostensibly to warn Tom and Grace not to talk, actually to have an opportunity of talking himself to a fresh relay of listeners. He expressed his surprise in the same terms as he had already used, and said repeatedly that he wouldn't have it. Then, as it was plain that, whether he would or no, he already had had it, he rather weakly asked the Rector what he would do if he were in his place.

"Well, Edward," said the Rector thoughtfully, "of course it is very tiresome and all that, and Cicely ought not to have gone off in that way without any warning. Still, we don't know what is going on in girls' minds, do we? Cicely is a sensible girl enough, and I think when she comes back if you were to leave it to Nina to find out what there was to make her go off suddenly like that—well, how would that be, eh?"

"I can't understand it," said the Squire for the twentieth time. "Nina knows no more about it all than I do. I can't help blaming her for that, because——"

"O Edward," said Mrs. Beach, "whoever is to blame, it is not Nina. Cicely is devoted to her, and so are the dear twins, for all their general harum-scarumness."

"Well, I was going to say," said the Squire, who had been going to say something quite different, "that Nina is very much upset about this. She takes everything calmly enough, as you know, but she's a good mother to her children—I will say that for her—and it's enough to upset any woman when her daughter behaves to her in this monstrous fashion."

"How do you think it would be," asked the Rector, "if Nina were to go up to London and have a talk with Cicely there?"

The Squire hummed and ha'd. "I don't see the sense of making more fuss about it than has been made already," he said. "I told Nina this morning, 'If you go posting off to London,' I said, 'everybody will think that something dreadful has happened. Much better stop where you are.'"

"If she wants to go," said Mrs. Beach, "I think it would be the very best thing. She would bring Cicely to a right frame of mind—nobody could do it better; and you would be at home, Edward, to see that nothing was done here to complicate matters. I think that would be very important, and nobody could do that but you."

"So you think it would be a good idea if I let Nina go up to her?" said the Squire.

The Rector and Mrs. Beach both thought it would be a very good idea.

"Well," said the Squire, "I thought perhaps it would, but I hadn't quite made up my mind about it. I thought we'd better wait, at any rate, till we got an answer to my wire to Walter. And that reminds me—I'd better be getting back. Well, good-bye, Tom, good-bye, my dear Grace. Of course I needn't ask either of *you* not to let this go any further."

The non-arrival of an answer to his message had a cumulative effect upon the Squire's temper during the morning. At half-past eleven o'clock he gained some temporary relief to his discomfort by despatching another one, and did not entirely recover his balance until Dick's telegram arrived about luncheon time. Then he calmed down suddenly, joked with the twins over the table and told Miss Bird that she was getting younger every day. He also gave Mrs. Clinton her marching orders. "I think you had better go up, Nina," he said, "and see what the young monkey has been after. I'm excessively annoyed with her, and you can tell her so; but if she really *is* with Walter and Muriel I don't suppose any harm has come to her. I must say it's a relief. Still, I'm very angry about it, and so she'll find out when she comes home."

So another telegram was despatched, and Mrs. Clinton went up to London by the afternoon train accompanied by the discreet and faithful Miles.

CHAPTER XX

MRS. CLINTON

That night Cicely and her mother sat late together in Mrs. Clinton's bedroom. Mrs. Clinton was in a low easy-chair and Cicely on a stool at her feet. Outside was the continuous and restless echo of London pushing up to the very feet of its encircling hills, but they were as far removed from it in spirit as if they had been at home in still and spacious Kencote.

Mrs. Clinton had arrived at Muriel's house in time for dinner. Walter had come home from Lord's soon enough to meet her at the station and bring her out in his motor-car. He had made Miles sit in front with his servant and he had told his mother what Dick would have told her if she had waited to come to Cicely until after he had returned to Kencote. She had listened to him in silence as he unfolded his story, making no comment even when he told her of Dick's opening her daughter's letter to her; but when he told her that Cicely had asked that she should be sent for she had clasped her hands and said, "Oh, I am so glad."

Muriel had met her at the door, but Cicely had stayed in the drawing-room, pale and downcast. She had gone in to her alone and kissed her and said, "I am glad you wanted your mother, my darling. You shall tell me everything to-night when we go upstairs, and we won't think about it any more until then."

So the evening had passed almost pleasantly. At times even Cicely must have forgotten what lay behind and before her, for she had laughed and talked with a sort of feverish gaiety; only after such outbursts she had grown suddenly silent and trembled on the verge of tears. Walter had watched her and sent her upstairs before ten o'clock, and her mother had gone up with her and helped her to undress as if she had been a child again. Then she had put on her dressing-gown and gone to Mrs. Clinton's room, and resting her head on her mother's knee had told her everything with frequent tears and many exclamations at her own madness and folly.

It was more difficult to tell even than she had thought. When all was said about her discontent and the suddenness with which she had been urged towards a way of escape from surroundings that now seemed inexpressibly dear to her, there remained that inexcusable fault of leaving her mother without a word, for a man whom she couldn't even plead that she loved. With her mother's hand caressing her hair it seemed to her incredible that she could have done such a thing. She begged her forgiveness again and again, but each time that she received loving words in answer she felt that it must be impossible that they could ever be to one another again what they had been.

At last Mrs. Clinton said, "You must not think too much of that, my darling. You were carried away; you hardly knew what you were doing. It is all wiped out in my mind by your wanting me directly you came to yourself. We won't talk of it any more. But what we ought to talk of, Cicely dear, and try to see our way through, is the state of mind you had got into, which made what happened to you possible, and gave this man his opportunity. I think that six months ago, although he might have tried to behave in the same way, you would only have been frightened; you would have come straight to me and told me."

"Oh yes, I should, mother," she cried.

"Then what was it that has come between us? You have told me that you were discontented at home, but couldn't you have told me that before?"

Cicely was silent. Why hadn't she told her mother, to whom she had been used to tell everything, of her discontent? A sudden blush ran down from her cheeks to her neck. It was because she had judged her mother, as well as her father and brothers, her mother who had accepted the life that she had kicked against and had bent a meek head to the whims of her master. She couldn't tell her that.

"The thing that decided me," she began hesitatingly, "when I was sitting in my room that night not knowing what I was going to do, I heard father and Dick talking as they came up, and they had decided to turn Aunt Ellen and Aunt Laura out of the house they had lived in nearly all their lives and let it to those MacLeod people. It seemed to me so—so selfish and—and horrible."

"You cannot have heard properly," said Mrs. Clinton. "It was what they had decided not to do. Father woke me up to tell me so. But even if——I don't understand, Cicely dear."

"O mother, can't you see?" cried Cicely. "If I was wrong about that, and I'm very glad I was, it is just what they *might* have done. They had talked it all over again and again, and they couldn't make up their minds—and before us!"

"Before us?"

"Yes. We are nobodies. If father were to die Dick would turn us out of the house as a matter of course. He would have everything; we should have nothing."

Mrs. Clinton was clearly bewildered. "Dick would not turn us out of the house unless he were married," she said, "and we should not have nothing. We should be very well off. But surely, Cicely, it is impossible that you can have been thinking of money matters in that way! You cannot be giving me a right impression of what has been in your mind."

"No, it isn't that," said Cicely. "I don't know anything about money matters, and I haven't thought about them—not in that way. But father and the boys do talk about money; a lot seems to depend upon it, and I can't help seeing that they spend a great deal of money on whatever they want to-do, and we have to take what's left."

"Still I don't understand, dear," said Mrs. Clinton. "Certainly it costs a great deal to keep up a house like Kencote; but it is our home; we are all happy there together."

"Are you quite happy there, mother?" asked Cicely.

Mrs. Clinton put by the question. "You know, of course," she went on, "that we are well off, a good deal better off than most families who have big properties to keep up. For people in our position we live simply, and if—if I were to outlive father, and you and the children were still unmarried, we should live together—not in such a big house as Kencote—but with everything we could desire, or that would be good for us."

"And if we lived like that," said Cicely, "wouldn't you think some things good for us that we don't have, mother? If we had horses, wouldn't you let me have one to ride? Wouldn't you take me to London sometimes, not to go to smart parties, but to see something of interesting people as Angela and Beatrice do at Aunt Emmeline's, and see plays and pictures and hear music? Wouldn't you take us abroad sometimes? Should we have to live the whole year round in the country, doing nothing and knowing nothing?"

Mrs. Clinton's hand stopped its gentle, caressing movement, and then went on again. During the moment of pause she faced a crisis as vital as that which Cicely had gone through. She had had just those desires in her youth and she had stifled them. Could they be stifled—would it be right to stifle them—in the daughter who had, perhaps, inherited them from her?

"You asked me just now," she said, "whether I was happy. Yes, I am happy. I have my dear ones around me, I have my religion, I have my place in the world to fill. I should be very ungrateful if I were not happy. But if you ask me whether the life I lead is exactly what it would be if it rested only with me to order it—I think you know that it isn't?"

"But why shouldn't it be, mother? Other women do the things they like, and father and the boys do exactly what they like. If you have wanted the same things that I want now, I say you ought to have had them."

"If I had had them, Cicely, I should not have found out one very great thing—that happiness does not come from these things; it does not come from doing what you like, even if what you like is good in itself. I might almost say that it comes from not doing what you like. That is the lesson that I have learned of life, and I am thankful that it has been taught me."

Cicely was silent for a time. She seemed to see her mother, dear as she had been to her, in a new light, with a halo of uncomplaining self-sacrifice round her. Her face burned as she remembered how that morning in church, and since, she had thought of her as one who had bartered her independence for a life of dull luxury and stagnation. It came upon her with a flash of insight that her mother was a woman of strong intelligence, who had, consciously, laid her intellectual gifts on the altar of duty, and found her reward in doing so. The thought found ineffective utterance.

"Of course it is from you that Walter gets his brains," she said.

Mrs. Clinton did not reply to this. "You are very young to learn the lesson," she said. "I am not sure—I don't think it is a lesson that every one need learn—that every woman need learn. I should like you to make use of your brains—if that is really what you have been unhappy about, Cicely. But is it so, my dear?"

"Oh, I don't know," said Cicely. "I suppose not. If I had wanted to learn things, there are plenty of books at Kencote and I had plenty of time. It was in London—it was just one of the things. First I was jealous—I suppose it was that—because Dick and Humphrey had always had such a good time and seemed to belong to everything, and I was so out of it all. I still think that very unfair. Then when I went to Aunt Emmeline's and saw what a good time Angela and Beatrice had in a different sort of way—I wanted that too. And I think *that* is unfair. When I talked to them—I like them very much, but I suppose they wanted to show how much better off they were than I am—the only thing they seemed to think I was lucky in was my allowance, and even then they said they didn't see how I could spend it, as I never went anywhere. I felt so *ignorant* beside them. Once Angela said something to me in French—the maid was in the room—and I didn't understand her. I was ashamed. Mother, I think I ought to have had the chances that Angela and Beatrice have had."

Mrs. Clinton listened with a grave face. How could she not have believed most of it to be true? She knew that, in marrying her, her husband had been considered to be marrying rather beneath him. And yet, her brother's daughters were—there was no doubt of it— better fitted to take a place, even a high place, in the world than her own daughter. Her husband could never have seen it, but she knew that it was true. Her younger niece was already engaged to be married to a man of some mark in the world, and she would be an intellectual companion to him. If Cicely had caught the fancy of such a man she would have had everything to learn. Even in this deplorable danger through which she had just passed, it was her ignorance that had laid her open to it. Perhaps her very ignorance had attracted the man to her, but he certainly would not have been able so to bend her to his will if she had lived more in the world.

"There is one thing, darling," said Mrs. Clinton, "that we have not spoken of. I don't want to complicate the troubles you are passing through, but it has a bearing on what you have been saying."

"You mean about Jim," said Cicely courageously.

"Yes. Father and I have both been very glad of what we have always looked upon as an engagement, although it could not be a recognised one when—when it was first mooted. You must remember, dear, that we are country people. It seems to us natural that our daughters should marry country gentlemen—should marry into the circle of our friends and neighbours. And the prospect of your living near us has always given us great pleasure. You seemed to me quite happy at home, and I thought you would have the best chance of happiness in your married life in another home not unlike ours. I thought you were well fitted to fill that place. I did not think of you—I don't think it ever crossed my mind to think of you—as wanting a different life, the sort of life that your cousins lead, for instance."

"Jim was very good to me, this morning," Cicely said, in a low voice. "I love him for it. Of course I do love him, in a way, just as I love Dick or Walter. I was very much ashamed at having left *him* like that, for somebody who—who isn't as good as he is. Jim *is* good, in a way a man ought to be. But, mother—I can't marry Jim now, after this."

"It is too soon to talk of it, or perhaps even to think of it. And you have no right to marry anybody unless you love him as a woman should love her husband, not as you love your brothers. We need not talk of marriage now at all. But, my dearest, I want you to be happy when you come home again. If you come back to think that you are badly used, that — —"

"Oh, but, mother," Cicely interrupted her, "that is all over. I have only been trying to tell you what I did feel. I never thought of the other side at all. Last night I lay awake and simply longed for home. I have been very ungrateful. I love Kencote, and the country and everything I do there, really. I never knew before how much I loved it. It was a sort of madness that came over me."

"I am glad you feel like that. You have a very beautiful home, and you are surrounded by those who love you. You *ought* to be able to make yourself happy at home, even if you have not got everything that you might like to have. Can you do so?"

"Yes, mother, I can. I was happy enough before."

"Before you went to London."

"Oh, yes, I suppose it was that. I must be very foolish to let a visit to London upset me. I don't want to see London again now for a long time. O mother, I have been very wicked. You won't be different to me, will you?"

She buried her face in her mother's lap. She was overwrought and desperately tired. Mrs. Clinton felt that except for having done something towards healing the wound made by her late experience she had accomplished little. Cicely's eyes had been partially opened, and it was not in her mother's power to close them again. It was only natural that she should now turn for a time eagerly towards the quiet life she had been so eager to run away from. But when her thoughts had settled down again, when weeks and months had divided her from her painful awakening, and its memory had worn thin, would she then be content, or would these desires, which no one could say were unreasonable, gain strength again to unsettle and dispirit her? It was only too likely. And if they did, what chance was there of satisfying them?

Mrs. Clinton thought over these things when she had tucked Cicely up in her bed and sat by her side until she was asleep. Cicely had begged her to do this, Cicely, her mother's child again, who, the night before had lain awake hour after hour, alone, trembling at the unknown and longing for the dear familiar. There was deep thankfulness in the mother's heart as she watched over her child restored to her love and protection, but there was sadness too, and some fear of the future, which was not entirely in her hands.

Cicely was soon asleep. Mrs. Clinton gently disengaged the hand she had been holding, stood for a time looking down upon her, fondly but rather sadly, and crept out of the room. It was nearly one o'clock, so long had their confidences lasted, but as she came downstairs, for Cicely's room was on the second floor, Walter came out of his bedroom dressed to go out.

"Hullo, mother!" he said. "Not in bed yet! I've been called up. Child with croup. I don't suppose I shall be long, and Muriel is going down to make me some soup. If you'd like a yarn with her ——"

Muriel came out in her dressing-gown. "I said I would always make him soup when he was called out at night," she said, "and this is the first time. I'm a good doctor's wife, don't you think so, Mrs. Clinton? Is Cicely asleep?"

"Yes, I have just left her. I will come down with you, dear, and help you make Walter's soup."

So they went down together and when they had done their work, bending together over a gas stove in the kitchen, which was the home of more black beetles than was altogether desirable, although it was otherwise clean and bright and well-furnished, they sat by the dining-room table awaiting Walter's return.

There was sympathy between Mrs. Clinton and her daughter-in-law, who recognised her fine qualities and loved her for them, privately thinking that she was a woman ill-used by fate and her husband. Mrs. Graham thought so too, but she and Mrs. Clinton had little in common, and in spite of mutual esteem, could hardly be called friends. But the tie which had bound Muriel to Kencote all her life had depended almost as much upon Mrs. Clinton as upon Cicely, and until the last few months more than it had upon Walter. They could talk together knowing that each would understand the other, and Muriel's downrightness did not offend Mrs. Clinton.

She plunged now into the middle of things. "You know it is Jim I am thinking of, Mrs. Clinton," she said, "now that this extraordinary business is over. I want to know where Jim comes in."

"I am afraid, my dear," said Mrs. Clinton, with a smile, "that poor Jim has come in very little."

"Did you know," asked Muriel, "that Jim was head over ears in love with Cicely, or did you think, like everybody else, that he was slack about it?"

Mrs. Clinton thought for a moment. "I have never thought of him as head over ears in love with Cicely," she said.

"And I didn't either, till Walter told me. But he is. He behaved like a brick to-day. Dick told Walter. And Cicely told me too. It was Jim who got her away from that man—the horrible creature! How can a man be such a brute, Mrs. Clinton?"

"I don't want to talk about him, Muriel," said Mrs. Clinton quietly. "He has come into our life and he has gone out again. I hope we shall never see him again."

"If I ever see him," said Muriel, "nothing shall prevent my telling him what I think of him. How Cicely could! Poor darling, she doesn't know how she could herself, now. She told me that she saw him as he was beside Jim and Dick. He isn't a gentleman, for all the great things he has done, and somehow that little fact seemed to have escaped her until then. Don't you think it is rather odd that it matters so tremendously to women like us whether the men we live with are gentlemen or not, and yet we are so liable at first to make mistakes about them?"

Mrs. Clinton was not quite equal to the discussion of a general question. "It would matter to any one brought up as Cicely has been," she said, "or you. Can you tell me exactly what you mean when you say that Jim is head over ears in love with Cicely? I don't think he has shown it to her."

"Nobody quite knows Jim, except Walter," replied Muriel. "I don't, and mother doesn't; and dear father never did. I suppose there is not much doubt about his being rather slow. Slow and sure is just the phrase to fit him. He is sure of himself when he makes up his mind about a thing, and I suppose he was sure of Cicely. He was just content to wait. You know, I'm afraid Walter thinks that Cicely has behaved very badly to him."

"Do you think so?" asked Mrs. Clinton.

Muriel hesitated. "I think what Walter does," she said, rather doggedly. "But I don't feel it so much. I love Cicely, and I am very sorry for her."

"Why are you sorry for her?"

"Oh, well, one could hardly help being after what she has gone through."

"Only that, Muriel?"

Muriel hesitated again. "I don't think she has had quite a fair chance," she said.

"She has had the same chances that you have had."

"Not quite, I think," said Muriel. She spoke with her head down and a face rather flushed, as if she was determined to go through with something unpleasant. "I'm not as clever as she is, but if I had been—if I had wanted the sort of things that she wants—I should have had them."

"I think she could have had them, if she had really wanted them," said Mrs. Clinton quietly. "I think I should have seen that she did have them."

"Oh, dear Mrs. Clinton, don't think I'm taking it on myself to blame you. You know I wouldn't do that. But I must say what I think. Life is desperately dull for a girl at houses like Kencote or Mountfield."

"Kencote and Mountfield?"

"Well, don't be angry with me if I say it is much more dull at Kencote than at Mountfield. Cicely isn't even allowed to hunt. I was, and yet I was glad enough to get away from it, although I love country life, and so does Walter. We never see anybody, we never go anywhere. I am heaps and heaps happier in this little house of my own than I was at Mountfield."

"Muriel," said Mrs. Clinton "what is it that Cicely wants? You and she talk of the same things. First it is one thing and then it is another. First it is that she has had no chances of learning. What has she ever shown that she wants to learn? Then it is that she does not go away, and does not see new faces. Is that a thing of such importance that the want of it should lead to what has happened? Then it is that she is not allowed to hunt! I will not add to Cicely's trouble now by rebuking these desires. Only the first of them could have any weight with me, and I do not think that has ever been a strong desire, or is now, for any reason that is worth taking into consideration. But the plain truth of the whole trouble is that Cicely had her mind upset by her visit to London two months ago. *You* should not encourage her in her discontent. Her only chance of happiness is to see where her duty lies and to gauge the amusements that she cannot have at their true value."

"I haven't encouraged her," said Muriel, "I said much the same as you have when she first talked to me. I told her she had had her head turned. But, all the same, I think there is something in what she says, and at any rate, she has felt it so strongly as nearly to spoil her life in trying to get away from it all. She'll be pleased enough to get home now, if—if—well, excuse my saying it, but—if Mr. Clinton will let her alone—and yet, it will all come back on her when she has got used to being at home. Do you know what I think, Mrs. Clinton? I think the only thing that will give her back to herself now is for her to marry Jim as quickly as possible."

"But Kencote and Mountfield both are desperately dull for a girl!"

Muriel laughed, "She wouldn't find Mountfield so if she really loved Jim. I don't know whether she does or not. She won't hear of him now."

Mrs. Clinton was silent for a time. Then she said slowly, "It was Jim who rescued her to-day from a great danger. I think it is only Jim who can rescue her from herself."

CHAPTER XXI

CICELY'S RETURN

"When Cicely comes, send her in to me at once," said the Squire, with the air of a man who was going to take a matter in hand.

Cicely, convoyed by the reliable Miles, was returning to Kencote after having stayed with Muriel for a fortnight. Mrs. Clinton had left her at Melbury Park after a three days' visit.

"And I won't have the children meeting her, or anything of that sort," added the Squire. "She is not coming home in triumph. You can go to the door, Nina, and send her straight in to me. We'll get this business put right once for all."

Mrs. Clinton said nothing, but went out of the room. She could have small hopes that her husband would succeed when she had failed in putting the business right. She told herself now that she had failed. During her many talks with Cicely, although she had been able, with her love and wisdom, to soothe the raw shame that had come upon her daughter when she had looked back in cold blood to her flight with Mackenzie, she had not been able to do away with the feeling of resentment with which Cicely had come to view her home life. Her weapons had turned back upon herself. Neither of them had been able to say to each other exactly what was in their mind, and because Cicely had to stay herself with some reason for her action, which with her father, at any rate, must be defended somehow, she had fallen back upon the causes of her discontent and held to them even against her mother. And there was enough truth in them to make it difficult for Mrs. Clinton to combat her attitude, without saying, what she could not say, that it was the duty of every wife and every daughter to do as she had done, and rigidly sink her own personality where it might clash with the smallest wish or action of her husband. She claimed to have gained her own happiness in doing so, but the doctrine of happiness through such self-sacrifice was too hard a one for a young girl to receive. She had gained Cicely's admiration and a more understanding love from the self-revelation which in some sort she had made, but she had not availed to make her follow her example, and could not have done so without holding it up as the one right course. Cicely must fight her own battle with her father, and whichever of them proved the victor no good could be expected to come of it. She was firm in her conviction now that in Jim Graham's hands lay the only immediate chance of happiness for her daughter. But Jim had held quite aloof. No word had been heard from him, and no one had seen him since he had parted with Dick on the evening after their journey to London, when they had dined together and Jim had said he would bide his chance. If he were to sink back now into what had seemed his old apathy, he would lose Cicely again and she would lose her present chance of happiness.

The twins, informed by their mother that they must not go to the station to meet Cicely, or even come down into the hall, but that she would come up to them when she had seen her father, of course gathered, if they had not gathered it before, that their elder sister was coming home in disgrace, and spent their leisure time in devising methods to show that they did not share in the disapprobation; in which they were alternately encouraged and thwarted by Miss Bird, whose tender affection for Cicely warred with her fear of the Squire's displeasure.

Mrs. Clinton was in the hall when the carriage drove up. Cicely came in, on her face an expression of mixed determination and timidity, and her mother drew her into the morning-room. "Father wants to see you at once, darling," she said. "You must be good. If you can make him understand ever so little you know he will be kind."

It was doubtful if this hurried speech would help matters at all, and there was no time for more, for the Squire was at his door asking the servants where Miss Clinton was, for he wanted to see her at once.

"I am here, father," said Cicely, going out into the hall again.

"I want you in here," said the Squire. They went into his room and the door was shut, leaving Mrs. Clinton alone outside.

The Squire marched up to the empty fireplace and took his stand with his back to it. Cicely sat down in one of the big chairs, which seemed to disconcert him for a moment.

"I don't know whether you have come home expecting to be welcomed as if nothing had happened," he began.

"No, I don't expect that, father," said Cicely.

"Oh! Well now, what is the meaning of it? That's what I want to know. I have been pretty patient, I think. You have had your fling for over a fortnight, the whole house has been upset and I've said nothing. Now I want to get to the bottom of it. Because if you think that you can behave in that way"—here followed a vivid summary of the way in which Cicely had behaved—"you are very much mistaken." The Squire was now fairly launched. It only rested with Cicely to keep him going with a word every now and then, for she knew that until he had wrought himself into a due state of indignation and then given satisfactory vent to it, nothing she could say would have any effect at all.

"I am very sorry, father," she said. "I know it was wrong of me, and I won't do it again."

This was all that was wanted. "Won't do it again?" echoed the Squire. "No, you won't do it again. I'll take good care of that." He then went on to bring home to her the enormity of her offence, which seemed to have consisted chiefly in upsetting the whole house, which he wouldn't have, and so on. But when he had repeated all he had to say twice, and most of it three or four times, he suddenly took his seat in the chair opposite to her and said in quite a different tone, "What on earth made you do it, Cicely?" and her time had come.

"I was not happy at home, father," she said quietly.

This set the Squire off on another oration, tending to show that it was positively wicked to talk like that. There wasn't a girl in England who had more done for her. He himself spent his days and nights chiefly in thinking what he could do for the happiness of his children, and the same might be said of their mother. He enumerated the blessings Cicely enjoyed, amongst which the amount of money spent upon keeping up a place like Kencote bulked largely. When he had gone over the field a second time, and picked up the gleanings left over from his sheaves of oratory, he asked her, apparently as a matter of kindly curiosity, what she had to grumble about.

She told him dispiritedly, leaving him time after each item of her discontent to put her in the wrong.

Item: She had nothing to do at home.

He said amongst other things that he had in that very room a manuscript volume compiled by her great-great-grandmother full of receipts and so forth, which he intended to get published some day to show what women could do in a house if they really did what they ought.

Item: She hadn't been properly educated.

That was wicked nonsense, and he wondered at a daughter of his talking such trash. In the course of further remarks he said that when all the girls in the board schools could play the piano and none of them could cook, he supposed the Radicals would be satisfied.

Item: There were a great many horses in the stable and she was not allowed to ride one of them.

Did she think she had gone the right way to work to have horses given her, bolting out of the house without a with your leave or a by your leave, etc.? Had her six great-aunts ever wanted horses to ride? Hunting he would not have. He might be old-fashioned, he dared say he was, but to see a woman tearing about the country, etc. — —! But if she had come to him properly, and it had been otherwise convenient, he gave her to understand that a horse might have been found for her at any time. He did not say that one would be found for her *now*.

Item: She never went anywhere.

A treatise on gadding about, with sub-sections devoted to the state of drains in foreign cities, the game of Bridge, as played in country houses, and the overcrowded state of the Probate and Divorce Court.

Item: She never saw anybody interesting.

A flat denial, and in the course of its expansion a sentence that brought the blood to Cicely's face and left her pale and terrified. "Why, only the other day," said the Squire, "one of the most talked of men in England dined here. I suppose you would call Ronald Mackenzie an interesting man, eh? Why, what's the matter? Aren't you well?"

"Oh yes, father dear. Please go on."

The Squire went on. Fortunately he had not noticed the sudden blush, but only the paleness that had followed it. Supposing he had seen, and her secret had been dragged out of her! She gave him no more material on which to exercise his gift of oratory, but sat silent and frightened while he dealt further with the subject in hand and showed her that she was fortunate in living amongst the most interesting set of people in England. Her uncle Tom knew as much as anybody about butterflies, her Aunt Grace played the piano remarkably well for an amateur, Sir Ralph Perry, who lived at Warnton Court, four miles away, had written a book on fly-fishing, the Rector of Bathgate had published a volume of sermons, the Vicar of Blagden rubbed brasses, Mrs. Kingston of Axtol was the daughter of a Cambridge professor, and the Squire supposed he was not entirely destitute of intelligence himself. At any rate, he had corresponded with a good many learned gentlemen in his time, and they seemed anxious enough to come to Kencote, and didn't treat him exactly as if he were a fool when they did come.

"The upshot of it all is, Cicely," concluded the Squire, "that you want a great many things that you can't have and are not going to have, and the sooner you see that and settle down sensibly to do your duty the better."

"Yes, father," said Cicely, longing to get away.

The Squire bethought himself. He had nothing more to say, although as he was considering what to do next he said over again a few of the more salient things that he had said before. He hoped he had made an impression, but he would have liked to end up on a note rather less tame than this. With Cicely so meek and quiet, however, and his indignation against her, already weakened by having been spread over a fortnight, having now entirely evaporated by being expressed, as his indignation generally did evaporate, he had arrived somehow at a loose end. He looked at his daughter for the first time with some affection, and noticed that she was pale, and, he thought, thinner.

"Come here and give me a kiss," he said, and she went to him and put her head on his big shoulder. "Now you're going to be a good girl and not give us any more trouble, aren't you?" he said, patting her on the sleeve; and she promised that she would be a good girl and not give any more trouble, with mental reservations mercifully hidden from him.

"There, don't cry," said the Squire. "We won't say any more about it; and if you want a horse to ride, we'll see if we can't find you a horse to ride. I dare say you think your old father a terrible martinet, but it's all for your good, you know. You must say to yourself when you feel dissatisfied about some little twopenny-halfpenny disappointment that he knows best."

Cicely gave him a hug. He was a dear old thing really, and if one could only always bear in mind the relative qualities of his bark and his bite there would be no need at all to go in awe of him. "Dear old daddy," she said. "I am sorry I ran away, and I'm very glad to get home again."

Then she went upstairs quite lightheartedly, and along the corridor to the schoolroom. The twins, arrayed in long blue overalls, were tidying up, after lessons, and Miss Bird was urging them to more conscientious endeavour, avowing that it was no more trouble to put a book on a shelf the right way than the wrong way, and that if there were fifty servants in the house it would be wrong to throw waste paper in the fireplace, since waste paper baskets existed to have waste paper thrown into them and fireplaces did not.

After a minute pause of observation, the twins threw themselves upon Cicely with one accord and welcomed her vociferously, and Miss Bird followed suit.

"My own darling," she said warmly, "we have missed you dreadfully and how are Muriel and Walter I suppose as happy as anything now Joan 'n Nancy there is no occasion to pull Cicely to pieces you can be glad to see her without roughness and go *at once* and take off your overalls and wash your hands for tea I dare say Cicely will go with you."

"Have you been to your room yet, darling?" asked Joan.

"Not yet," said Cicely.

"Now *straight* to your own room first," said Miss Bird, clapping her hands together to add weight to her command. "You can go with Cicely afterwards."

"All right, starling darling, we'll be ready in time for tea," said Nancy. "You finish clearing up" and one on each side of Cicely, they led her to her own bedroom, and threw open the door. The room was garlanded with pink and white paper roses. They formed festoons above the bed and were carried in loops round the walls, upon which had also been hung placards printed in large letters and coloured by hand. "Welcome to our Sister," ran one inscription, and others were, "There is No Place like Home," "Cicely for Ever," and "No Popery."

The twins watched eagerly for signs of surprised rapture and were abundantly rewarded. "But that's not all," said Joan, and led her up to the dressing-table, upon which was an illuminated address running as follows:

"We, the undersigned, present this token of our continued esteem to Cecilia Mary Clinton, on the occasion of her home-coming to Kencote House, Meadshire. Do unto others as you would be done by.

"*Signed*, JOAN ELLEN CLINTON NANCY CAROLINE CLINTON."

"I think it's rather well done," said Nancy, "though our vermilions had both run out and we didn't like to borrow yours without asking. Starling bought us the gold paint on condition that we put in the Golden Rule. It doesn't look bad, does it, Cicely?"

"I think it's lovely," said Cicely. "I shall always keep it. Thanks so much, darlings."

After the subsequent embraces, Nancy eyed her with some curiosity. "I say, there *was* a dust-up," she said. "Have you made it up with father, Cis?"

"Don't be a fool," said Joan. "She doesn't want you bothering her. It is quite enough that we're jolly glad to have her back."

"I was rather dull," said Cicely, with a nervous little laugh, "so I went away for a bit."

"Quite right too," said Joan. "I should have done the same, and so would Nancy. We thought of putting up 'Don't be Downtrodden,' but we were afraid mother wouldn't like it, so we put up 'No Popery' instead. It comes to the same thing."

"We're doing the Gordon Riots in history," Nancy explained further. "Father was awful at first, Cis, but he has calmed down a lot since. I think Dick poured oil on the troubled waters. Dick is a brick. He gave us half a sovereign each before he went up to Scotland."

"We didn't ask him for it," said Nancy.

"No," said Joan, "we only told him we were saving up for a camera, and it took a long time out of a bob a week each pocket-money."

"Flushed with our success," said Nancy, "we tried father; but the moment was not propitious."

"It was your fault," said Joan. "You would hurry it. Directly I said, 'When we get our camera we shall be able to take photographs of the shorthorns,' you heaved a silly great sigh and said, 'It takes *such* a long time to save up with only a shilling a week pocket-money,' and of course what *could* he say but that when he was our age he only had sixpence?"

"I don't believe it for a moment," said Nancy.

"It doesn't matter. He had to say it. I was going to lead up much more slowly. How often has starling told you that if a thing's worth doing at all it's worth doing well?"

Here Miss Bird herself appeared at the door and said it was just as she had expected, and had they heard her tell them to do a thing or had they not, because if they had and had then gone and done something else she should go straight to Mrs. Clinton, for she was tired of having her words set at nought, and it was time to take serious measures, although nobody would be more sorry to have to do so than herself, Joan and Nancy being perfectly capable of behaving themselves as they should if they would only set their minds to it and do exactly as she told them.

Cicely heard the latter part of the address fading away down the corridor, shut the door with a smile and began to take off her hat with a sigh. The chief ordeal was over, but there was a good deal to go through still before she could live in this room again as she had lived in it before. If, indeed, she ever could. She looked round her, and its familiarity touched her strangely. It spoke not of the years she had occupied it, the five years since she had left the nursery wing, but of the one night when she had prepared to leave it for ever. It would be part of her ordeal to have that painful and confusing memory brought before her whenever she entered it. She hated now to think of that night and of the day and night that had followed it. She flushed hotly as she turned again to her glass, and called herself a fool. Then she resolutely turned pictures to the wall of her mind and made herself think of something else, casting her thoughts loose to hit upon any subject they pleased. They struck against her aunts at the dower-house, and she grappled the idea and made up her mind to go and see them after tea, and get that over.

She found them in their morning-room, engaged as before, except that their tea-table had been cleared away. "Well, dear Aunt Ellen and Aunt Laura, I have come back," she said, kissing them in turn. "Muriel's house *is* so pretty. You would love to see it."

But Aunt Ellen was not to be put off in this way. The Squire had come down to them on the afternoon of the day after Cicely had disappeared, and had gained more solid satisfaction from the attitude taken up by Aunt Ellen and Aunt Laura when he had unfolded his news than from any reception it had before or after. Cicely was still in their black books.

"Oh, so you have returned at last," said Aunt Ellen, receiving her kiss, but not returning it. Aunt Laura was not so unforgiving. She kissed her and said, "O Cicely, if you had known what unhappiness your action would cause, I am sure you would have thought twice about it."

Cicely sat down. "I have made it all right with father now," she said. "I would rather not talk about it if you don't mind, Aunt Laura. Muriel sent her love to you. I said I should come and see you directly I came back."

"When I was a girl," said Aunt Ellen—"I am speaking now of nearly eighty years ago—I upset a glass of table ale at the commencement of luncheon, and your great-grandfather was very angry. But that was nothing to this."

"I have seldom seen your dear father so moved," said Aunt Laura. "I cannot see very well without my glasses, and I had mislaid them; they were on the sideboard in the dining-room where I had gone to get out a decanter of sherry; but I believe there were tears in his eyes. If it was so it should make you all the more sorry, Cicely."

"I am very sorry," said Cicely, "but father has forgiven me. Mayn't we talk about something else?"

"Your father was very high-spirited as a child," said Aunt Ellen, "and I and your aunts had some difficulty in managing him; not that he was a naughty child, far from it, but he was full of life. And you must always remember that he was a boy. But I feel quite sure that he would never in his wildest moments have thought of going away from home and leaving no word of his address."

"I sent a telegram," pleaded Cicely.

"Ah, but telegrams were not invented in the days I am speaking of," said Aunt Ellen.

"Pardon me, sister," said Aunt Laura. "The electric telegraph was invented when Edward was a boy, but not when we were girls."

"That may be so, sister," said Aunt Ellen. "It is many years since we were girls, but I say that Edward would not have run away."

"Certainly not," said Aunt Laura. "You should never forget, Cicely, what a good father you have. I am sure when I heard the other day from Mr. Hayles that your dear father had instructed him to refuse Lady Alistair MacLeod's most advantageous offer to rent this house, solely on account of your Aunt Ellen and myself, I felt that we were, indeed, in good hands, and fortunate to be so."

"It is quite true," said Aunt Ellen, "that this house is larger than your Aunt Laura and I require, I told your father that with my own lips. But at the same time it is unlikely that at my age I have many more years to live, and I said that if it could be so arranged, I should wish to die in this house as I have lived in it for the greater part of my life."

"He saw that at once," said Aunt Laura. "There is nobody that is quicker at seeing a thing than your dear father, Cicely. He spoke very kindly about it. He said we must all die some time or other, which is perfectly true, but that if your Aunt Ellen did not live to be a hundred he should never forgive her. He is like your dear Aunt Caroline in that; he is always one to look at the bright side of things."

"But didn't he tell you at once that he didn't want to let the house?" asked Cicely. "Did he leave it to Mr. Hayles to tell you afterwards?"

"There was a delicacy in that," replied Aunt Laura. "If there is one thing that your dear father dislikes, it is being thanked. And we could not have helped thanking him. We had gone through a week of considerable anxiety."

"Which he might have saved you," Cicely thought, but did not say.

"When we lived at Kencote House with our father," said Aunt Ellen, "it was never thought that the dower-house possessed any advantages to speak of. I do not say that we have made it what it is, for that would be boasting, but I do say that it would not be what it is if we had not made it so; and now that the danger is past, it causes both your Aunt Laura and myself much gratification, and would cause gratification to your other dear aunts if they could know what had happened, as no doubt they do, that it should now be sought after."

The topic proved interesting enough to occupy the conversation for the rest of Cicely's visit. She kept them to it diligently and got through nearly an hour's talk without further recurrence to her misdoings. Then she took her leave rather hurriedly, congratulating herself that she had got safely over another fence.

CHAPTER XXII

THE LIFE

Mrs. Graham, in spite of her good points, was not overburdened with the maternal spirit. She had little love for children as children, and when her own were small she had lavished no great amount of affection on them. In the case of other people's children she frankly averred that she didn't understand them and preferred dogs. But she was equable by nature and had companionable gifts, and as Jim and Muriel had grown up they had found their mother pleasant to live with, never anxious to assert authority, and always interested in such of their pursuits as chimed in with her own inclinations; also quite ready with sensible advice and some sympathy when either was required of her, and showing no annoyance at all if the advice was not followed.

It was not altogether surprising then that Jim, when he had been back at Mountfield for three or four days, should have taken her into his confidence. She had heard what, thanks to the Squire, every one in that part of the county had heard, that Cicely had run off to London without taking any clothes with her—this point always emerged—and that Dick, and, for some as yet unexplained reason, Jim, had gone up after her. But when Jim returned, and told her simply that Cicely was staying with Muriel and that everything was all right, she had asked no further questions, although she saw that there was something that she had not been told. She had her reward when Jim, sitting in her drawing-room after dinner, told her that he would like to talk over something with her.

The drawing-room at Mountfield was a long, rather low room, hung with an old French paper of nondescript grey, upon which were some water-colours which were supposed to be valuable. The carpet was of faded green, with ferns and roses. The curtains were of thick crimson brocade under a gilt canopy. There was a large Chippendale mirror, undoubtedly valuable, over the white marble mantelpiece, upon which were three great vases of blue Worcester and some Dresden china figures. The furniture was upholstered in crimson to match the curtains. There was an old grand piano, there were one or two china cabinets against the walls, a white skin rug before the fire, palms in pots, a rosewood table or two, and a low glass bookcase with more china on the top of it. There was nothing modern, and the chairs and sofas were not particularly comfortable. The room had always been like that ever since Jim could remember, and his mother, sitting upright in her low chair knitting stocking tops, also belonged to the room and gave it a comforting air of home. She had on a black gown and her face and neck were much redder than the skin beneath them, but, like many women to whom rough tweeds and thick boots seem to be the normal wear, she looked well in the more feminine attire of the evening.

"Talk away, my dear boy," she said, without raising her head. "Two heads are better than one. I suppose it is something about Cicely."

"When Cicely went away the other day she didn't go to see Muriel; she went to marry Mackenzie."

She did raise her head then to throw an astonished look at her son, who did not meet it, but she lowered it again and made one or two stitches before she replied, "She didn't marry him, of course?"

"No. Dick and I found them, and got her away just in time. That is all over now, and I can't think about that fellow."

"Well, I won't ask you to. But I suppose you won't mind telling me why she did such an extraordinary thing."

"Because she is bored to death at Kencote, and I don't wonder at it."

"And do you still intend to bring her to be bored to death at Mountfield?"

"Yes, I do, if she will come. And I'll see that she's not bored. At least that is what I want to talk to you about. Muriel could tell me what she wants to make her happy, but I can't go to Muriel as long as Cicely is there, and I can't write; I've tried. You've been happy enough here, mother. You ought to be able to tell me."

Mrs. Graham kept silence for a considerable time. Then she said, "Well, Jim, I'm glad you have come to me. I think I can help you. In the first place, you mustn't play the martinet as Mr. Clinton does."

"It isn't likely I should treat her as he does Mrs. Clinton, if that is what you mean."

"I mean a good deal more than that. If Mr. Clinton knew how disagreeable it was to other people to hear him talk to her as he does, he probably wouldn't do it. But even if he didn't he might still make her life a burden to her, by taking away every ounce of independence she had. I don't know whether her life is a burden to her or not; I don't pretend to understand her; but I do know that you couldn't treat Cicely like that, and I suppose this escapade of hers proves it."

"The poor old governor was a bit of a martinet," said Jim, after a pause.

"He thought he was," said Mrs. Graham drily.

Jim looked at her, but did not speak.

"I know what it all means," his mother went on. "I think things over more than you would give me credit for, Jim, and I've seen it before. This quiet country life happens to suit me down to the ground, but I don't believe it satisfies the majority of women. And that is what men don't understand. It suits *them*, of course, and if it doesn't they can always get away from it for a bit. But to shut women up in a country house all the year round, and give them no interests in life outside it—you won't give one woman in ten what she wants in that way."

"What *do* they want then?"

"It is more what Cicely wants, isn't it? I don't know exactly, but I can give a pretty shrewd guess. If you want to find out something about a person, it isn't a bad thing to look at their parentage on both sides. On one side she comes of a race of yokels."

"Oh, come, mother. The Birkets are——"

"I'm not talking about the Birkets, I'm talking about the Clintons. Poor dear Mr. Clinton *is* a yokel, for all his ancestry. If he had been changed at birth and brought up a farm labourer, he wouldn't have had an idea in his head above the average of them; he would only have had a little more pluck. Any Birket's brains are worth six of any Clinton's in the open market. Mrs. Clinton is a clever woman, although she doesn't show it, and her dear, stupid old husband would smother the brains of Minerva if he lived with her. You've only got to look at their children to see where the Birket comes in. Dick is exactly like his father, except that he is not a fool; Humphrey *is* a fool to my thinking, but not the same sort of fool; Walter—there's no need to speak of him; Frank I don't know much about, but he isn't a yokel; Cicely simply hasn't had a chance, but she'll take it fast enough when she gets it; and as for the twins, they're as sharp as monkeys, for all their blue eyes and sweet innocence."

"Well, what does it all lead to, mother?"

"It leads to this, Jim: I believe Cicely will be as happy living in the country as most girls, but at Kencote she doesn't even get the pleasures that a woman *can* get out of the country; those are all kept for the men. You *must* take her about a bit. Take her to other houses and get people to come here. Don't shut her up. Take her to London every now and then, and try and let her see some of the sort of people that go to her Uncle Herbert Birket's house. I believe she could hold her own with any of them, and you'll be proud of her. Let her stir her mind up; she doesn't know what's in it yet. Take her abroad. That always helps; even I should have liked it, only your father didn't, and I wasn't keen enough to let it make a disturbance. Give her her head; that's what it comes to. She won't lose it again."

Jim thought for a long time while Mrs. Graham went on knitting.

"A woman wants some brightness in her life, especially before the babies begin to come," she said, before he spoke.

"Thanks, mother," he said simply. "I'll think it all over."

"I have thought it over," she answered, "and it's all sound sense."

Jim's next speech was some time coming, but when it did come it was rather a startling one.

"I've given Weatherley notice to leave the Grange at Christmas."

Mrs. Graham's needles stopped, and then went on again rather more quickly. Her voice shook a little as she said in a matter-of-fact tone, "I suppose you won't mind altering the stables for me. There is only one loose-box."

"I thought it would be best to add on a couple under another roof," said Jim, and they went on to discuss other alterations that would be necessary when Mrs. Graham should leave Mountfield to go to live at the Grange, but without any approach to sentiment, and no expressions of regret on either side.

When they had done, and there had followed another of those pauses with which their conversations were punctuated, Mrs. Graham said, "You are making very certain of Cicely, Jim."

"I'm going to claim her," said Jim quietly. "I was a fool not to do it before. I've wanted her badly enough."

Perhaps this news was as fresh to Mrs. Graham as it had been to all those others who had heard it lately. Perhaps it was no news at all. She was an observant woman and was accustomed to keep silence on many subjects, except when she was asked to speak, and then she spoke volubly.

"I have often wondered," she said, "why you left it so long."

Jim did not reply to this, but made another surprising statement. "I'm going to stand for Parliament," he said.

Mrs. Graham's observation had not covered this possibility. "Good gracious!" she exclaimed. "Not as a Liberal, I hope!"

"No, as a Free Trade Unionist."

"I should think you might as well save your time and your money."

"I don't expect to get in. But if I can find a seat to fight for, I'll fight."

"Well, I'll help you, Jim. I believe the others are right, but if you will give me something to read I dare say I can persuade myself that they're wrong. I like a good fight, and that is one thing you don't get the chance of when you live with your pigs and your poultry. Excuse me asking, but what about the money?"

"I've settled all that, and I'm going to let this place for two years at least."

Mrs. Graham dropped her knitting once more. "Well, really, Jim!" she said. "Have you got anything else startling to break to me, because I wish you would bring it out all at once now. I can bear it."

"That's all," said Jim, with a grin. "I shall save a lot of money. I shall take a flat or a little house in London and do some work. There are lots of things besides Free Trade; things I'm keener about, really. I don't think Cicely will mind. I think she will go in with me."

Mrs. Graham took up her knitting again and put on another row of stitches. Then she said, "I don't know why you asked my advice as to what Cicely wanted. It seems to me you have thought it out pretty well for yourself."

Jim rode over to Kencote two days after Cicely's return. It was a lovely morning, and harvesting was in full swing as he trotted along between the familiar fields. He felt rather sad at being about to leave it all; he was a countryman at heart, although he had interests that were not bucolic. But there was not much room for sadness in his mind. He was sure of himself, and had set out to grasp a great happiness.

He met the Squire on his stout cob about a mile from Kencote, and pulled up to speak to him.

"How are you, Jim?" he said heartily. "Birds doing all right? Ours are first-class this year."

"I was coming to see you," he said. "I've got something to say."

"Well, say it here, my boy," said the Squire, "I'm not going to turn back."

So they sat on their horses in the middle of the road and Jim said, "I want to marry Cicely as soon as possible."

The Squire's jaw dropped as he stared at the suitor. Then he threw back his head and produced his loud, hearty laugh. "Well, that's a funny thing," he said. "I was only saying to my wife this morning that Cicely would die an old maid if she looked to you to come and take her."

Jim's red face became a little redder, but the Squire did not give him time to reply. "I was only joking, you know, Jim, my boy," he said kindly. "I knew *you* were all right, and I tell you frankly there's nobody I'd sooner give my girl to. But why do you want to rush it now? What about those rascally death duties?"

"It's only a question of income," said Jim shortly. "And I'm going to let Mountfield for a year or two."

The Squire's jaw fell again. "Let Mountfield!" he cried. "O my dear fellow, don't do that, for God's sake. Wait a bit longer. Cicely won't run away. Ha! ha! Why she did run away—what? Look here, Jim, you're surely not worrying yourself about that. She won't do it again, I'll promise you that. I've talked to her."

"I think it is time I took her," said Jim, "if she'll have me."

"Have you? Of course she'll have you. But you mustn't let Mountfield. Don't think of that, my boy. We'll square it somehow, between us. My girl won't come to you empty-handed, you know, and as long as the settlements are all right you can keep her a bit short for a year or two; tell her to go easy in the house. She's a good girl, and she'll do her best. No occasion to let down the stables, and you must keep a good head of game. We'll make that all right, and it won't do you any harm to economise a bit in other ways. In fact it's a good thing for young people. You might put down your carriage for a year, and perhaps a few maids—I should keep the men except

233

perhaps a gardener or two. Oh, there are lots of ways; but don't let the place, Jim."

"Well, I'll think about it," said Jim, who had no intention of prematurely disclosing his intentions to the Squire, "but you'll let me have her, Mr. Clinton? I thought of going over to see her now."

"Go by all means, my boy," said the Squire heartily. "You'll find her about somewhere, only don't make her late for lunch. You'll stay, of course. You haven't seen Hayles about anywhere, have you? He's not in the office."

Jim had not, and the Squire trotted off to find his agent, with a last word of dissuasion on letting Mountfield.

The ubiquitous twins were in the stableyard when he rode in, raiding the corn bin for sustenance for their fantails. "Hullo, Jim, my boy," said Joan. "You're quite a stranger."

"You'll stay to lunch, of course," said Nancy. "How are the birds at Mountfield? I think we ought to do very well here this year."

"Where is Cicely?" asked Jim, ignoring these pleasantries.

"She's out of doors somewhere," said Joan. "We'll help you find her. We ought to be going in to lessons again, but starling won't mind."

"I can find her myself, thanks," said Jim. "Is she in the garden?"

"We'll show you," said Nancy. "You can't shake us off. We're like the limpets of the rock."

But here Miss Bird appeared at the schoolroom window, adjuring the twins to come in *at once*. "Oh, how do you do, Jim?" she cried, nodding her head in friendly welcome. "Do you want to find Cicely she has gone down to the lake to sketch."

"Bother!" exclaimed Joan. "Starling is so officious."

"You will find our sister in the Temple of Melancholy," said Nancy. "It will be your part to smooth the lines of trouble from her brow."

"Oh, coming, coming, Miss Bird!" called out Joan. "We've only got an hour more, Jim—spelling and dictation; then we will come and look you up."

Jim strode off across the park and entered the rhododendron dell by an iron gate. He followed a broad green path between great banks of shrubs and under the shade of trees for nearly a quarter of a mile. Every now and then an open grassy space led to the water, which lay very still, ringed with dark green. He turned down one of these and peeped round the edge of a bush from whence he could see the white pillared temple at the head of the lake. Cicely was sitting in front of it, drawing, and his heart gave a little leap as he saw her. Then he walked more quickly, and as he neared the temple began to whistle, for he knew that, thinking herself quite alone. Cicely would be disagreeably startled if he came upon her suddenly.

Perhaps she thought it was a gardener who was coming, for she did not move until he spoke her name, coming out from behind the building on to the stained marble platform in front of it. Then she looked up with a hot blush. "O Jim!" she said nervously. "I was just trying to paint a picture."

"It's jolly good," said Jim, looking at it with his head on one side, although she had not as yet gone further than light pencil lines.

"It won't be when I've finished," she said hurriedly. "How is Mrs. Graham? I am coming over to see her as soon as I can, to tell her about Muriel."

"She's all right, thanks," said Jim. "She sent her love. Do you mind my watching you?"

"I'd much rather you didn't," she said, with a deprecating laugh. "I shall make an awful hash of it. Do you want to see father? I'll go and find him with you if you like."

"No, I've seen him," said Jim, going into the temple to get himself a chair. "I've come to see you, to tell you something I thought you'd be interested in. I want to stand for Parliament, and I'm going to let Mountfield."

She looked up at him with a shade of relief in her face. "O Jim," she said, "I do hope you will get in."

"Well, to tell you the truth, I don't expect to get in," said Jim. "They won't have fellows who think as I do in the party now if they can help it. But there's a good deal to do outside that. I kept my eyes open when I was travelling, and I do know a bit about the Colonies, and about land too. There are societies I can make myself useful in, even if I don't get into Parliament. Anyway I'm going to try."

"I am so glad, Jim," said Cicely. "But won't you miss Mountfield awfully? And where are you going to live?"

"In London for a year or two. Must be in the thick of things."

"I suppose you won't go before the spring."

"I want to. It depends on you, Cicely."

She had nothing to say. The flush that coloured her delicate skin so frequently, flooded it new.

"I want you to come and help me," said Jim. "I can't do it without you, my dear. You're much cleverer than I am. I want to get to know people, and I'm not much good at that. And I don't know that I could put up with London, living there by myself. If you were with me I shouldn't care where I lived. I would rather live all my life at Melbury Park with you, than at Mountfield without you."

"O Jim," she said in a low voice, bending over her drawing board, "you are good and generous. But you can't want me now."

"Look here, Cicely dear," he said, "let's get over that business now, and leave it alone for ever. I blame myself for it, I blame—that man, but I haven't got the smallest little piece of blame for you, and I shouldn't have even if I didn't love you. Why, even Dick is the same. He was angry at first, but not after he had seen you. And Walter thinks as I do. I saw him one day and we had it all out; you didn't know. There's not a soul who knows who blames you, and nobody ever will."

"I know," she said, "that every one has been most extraordinarily kind. I love Dick and Walter more than ever for it, because I know how it must have struck them when they first knew. And you too, Jim. It makes me feel such a beast to think how sweet you were to me, and how I've treated you."

Jim took her hand. "Cicely, darling," he said. "I'm a slow fellow, and, I'm afraid, rather stupid. If I hadn't been this would never have happened. But I believe I'm the only person in the world that can make you forget it. You'll let me try, won't you?"

She tried to draw away her hand, but he held it.

"Oh, I don't know what to say," she cried. "It is all such a frightful muddle. I don't even know whether I love you or not. I do; you know that, Jim. But I don't know whether I love you in the right way. I thought before that I didn't. And how can I when I did a thing like that? I'm a girl who goes to any man who calls her."

She was weeping bitterly. All the shame in her heart surged up. She pulled her hand away and covered her face.

"You never loved that man—not for a moment," said Jim firmly.

"No, I didn't," she cried. "I *hate* him now, and I believe I hated him all the time. If I were to meet him I should die of shame. Oh, why did I do it? And I feel ashamed before you, Jim. I can't marry you. I can't see you any more. I am glad you are going away."

"I am not going unless you come with me, Cicely," he said. "I want you. I want you more than ever; I understand you better. If this hadn't happened I shouldn't have known what you wanted; I don't think I should have been able to make you happy. Good heavens! do you think I believe that you wanted that man? I *know* you didn't, or I shouldn't be here now. You wanted life, and I had never offered you that. I do offer it you now. Come and help me to do what I'm going to do. I can't do any of it without you."

She smiled at him forlornly. "You *are* good," she said. "And you have comforted me a little. But you can't forget what has happened. It isn't possible."

"Look here, my dear," said Jim simply. "Will you believe me when I say that I have forgotten it already? That is to say it doesn't come into my mind. I don't have to keep it out; it doesn't come. I've got other things to think of. There's all the future, and what I'm going to do, and you are going to help me to do. Really, if I thought of it, I ought to be glad you did what you did, in a way, for all I've thought of since comes from that. I saw what you were worth and what you could make of a man if he loved you as I do, and you loved him. We won't play at it, Cicely. I'm in earnest. I shall be a better fellow all round if I'm trying to do something and not only sitting at home and amusing myself. We shall have to make some sacrifices. We shall only be able to afford a flat or a little house in London. I must keep things going here and put by a bit for an election, perhaps. But I know you won't mind not having much money for a time. We shall be together, and there won't be a thing in my life that you won't share."

She had kept her eyes fixed upon him as he spoke. "Do you really mean it, Jim?" she asked quietly. "Do you really want *me*, out of all the people in the world?"

"I don't want anybody but you," he said, "and I don't want anything without you."

"Then I will come with you, dearest Jim," she said. "And I will never want anything except what you want all my life."

He took her in his arms, and she nestled there, laughing and crying by turns, but happier than she had ever thought she could be. They talked of a great many things, but not again of Cicely's flight. Jim had banished that spectre, which, if it returned to haunt her thoughts again, would not affright them. They came no nearer to it than a speech of Cicely's, "I do love you, dear Jim. I love you so much that I must have loved you all the time without knowing it. I feel as if there was something in you that I could rest on and know that it will never give way."

"And that's exactly how I feel about you," said Jim.

Two swans sailed out into the middle of the lake, creasing the still water into tiny ripples. The air was hot and calm, and the heavy leaves of trees and shrubs hung motionless. The singing-birds were silent. Only in the green shade were the hearts of the two lovers in tumult—a tumult of gratitude and confident happiness.

The peace, but not the happiness, was brought to an end when the twins, relaxed from bondage, heralded their approach by a vociferous rendering of "The Campbells are coming." They came round the temple arm-in-arm. Cicely was drawing, and Jim looking on.

"Yes, that's all very well," said Joan, "but it doesn't take two hours to make three pencil scratches."

"Girls without the nice feeling that we possess," said Nancy, "would have burst upon you without warning."

"Without giving you time to set to partners," said Joan.

Cicely looked up at them; her face was full of light. "Shall I tell them, Jim?" she said.

"Got to, I suppose," said Jim.

"My child," said Joan, "you need tell us nothing."

"Your happy faces tell us all," said Nancy.

Then, with a simultaneous relapse into humanity, they threw themselves upon her affectionately, and afterwards attacked Jim in the same way. He bore it with equanimity.

"You don't deserve her, Jim," said Joan, "but we trust you to be kind to her."

"From this day onwards," said Nancy, "you will begin a new life."

CHRONICLES OF THE CLINTONS

BY ARCHIBALD MARSHALL

To be read in the following order

THE SQUIRE'S DAUGHTER
THE ELDEST SON
THE HONOUR OF THE CLINTONS
THE OLD ORDER CHANGETH
THE CLINTONS, AND OTHERS

Lightning Source UK Ltd.
Milton Keynes UK
UKHW041241120223
416857UK00030B/35